Praise for *New York Times* bestselling author
Kay Hooper

"A dark thriller that plunges readers into the disturbing side of the paranormal." —*Fresh Fiction*

"Kay Hooper . . . provide[s] a welcome chill on a hot summer's day." —*Orlando Sentinel*

"Filled with page-turning suspense." —*The Sunday Oklahoman*

"Readers will be mesmerized." —*Publishers Weekly*

"Thought-provoking entertainment." —*Calgary Herald*

"When it comes to delivering the creepy and supernatural, Hooper is on a roll." —RT Book Reviews

"Hooper's unerring story sense and ability to keep the pages flying can't be denied." —*Ellery Queen Mystery Magazine*

"Kay Hooper has given you a darn good ride, and there are far too few of those these days." —*Dayton Daily News*

"Keep[s] readers enthralled until the last page is turned." —*Booklist*

"A stirring and evocative thriller." —*Palo Alto Daily News*

"It passed the 'stay up late to finish it in one night' test." —*The Denver Post*

Titles by Kay Hooper

Bishop / Special Crimes Unit Novels

HAVEN

HOSTAGE

HAUNTED

FEAR THE DARK

WAIT FOR DARK

HOLD BACK THE DARK

The Bishop Files

THE FIRST PROPHET

A DEADLY WEB

FINAL SHADOWS

HOLD BACK THE DARK

KAY HOOPER

JOVE
New York

A JOVE BOOK
An imprint of Penguin Random House LLC
1745 Broadway, New York, NY 10019

ISBN: 9780515156058

Berkley hardcover edition / April 2018
Berkley premium edition / March 2019

Printed in the United States of America
1   3   5   7   9   10   8   6   4   2

Cover photo by Valentino Sani
Cover design by Rita Frangie

HOLD BACK
THE DARK

THE SUMMONS

In the middle of the journey of our life I came to myself within a dark wood where the straight way was lost.

—DANTE ALIGHIERI

ONE

Olivia Castle had experienced some monster headaches in her time, but this one, she felt sure, was about to make her head quite literally explode. It had come out of nowhere, as if something had just yanked her head into an invisible, tightening vise without warning. A vise with teeth. In pain, queasy, and shaking, she managed to lever herself up from the couch, holding one hand against the head she was sure was about to fall off, and hardly spared a moment to wonder why she'd been on the couch.

Work. She should have been at work.

Shouldn't she be at work?

Had she come home for lunch? She didn't remember.

Her head hurt too much to keep thinking about that.

She made it to the kitchen by holding on to various pieces of furniture as she passed, fighting nausea and accidentally grabbing Rex's tail when she gripped the edge of the sink.

"Waaaurr!"

"Sorry, sorry," she muttered, the headache so bad by then that her cat's cry sounded like a dozen angry crows, her own quiet voice sounded like booming thunder in her head, and even her vision was affected in some way she didn't understand; she couldn't see the pleasant Vermont view normally visible from this window. She couldn't see any real view at all.

She was seeing colors she was reasonably sure didn't exist in nature. Or anywhere else, for that matter. Moving, swirling, like colorful smoke driven by a capricious breeze, opaque and translucent by turn. And everything was so damned *bright*. "Shouldn't sit on the counter. How many times have I told you? Didn't see you, pal. Oh, *damn*, what is going on?"

There was a large economy-sized bottle of an OTC painkiller near the sink (just as there was one in almost every room of her small house, and in her purse, with a box of extra bottles in the storage closet, in case the zombie apocalypse came without warning and all the pharmacies got looted before she could get to them). Olivia closed her eyes against the unnatural brightness, fumbling the bottle open while bitterly cursing childproof caps foisted upon people who had no children, fumbled just as blindly for a glass and the faucet, and managed, finally, to swallow about eight pills, hoping she could keep them down long enough to do some good.

"Prrupp," Rex said.

"I know it's too many, you don't have to tell me that." She stood there, eyes still closed, still hanging on to the edge of the sink with one hand and her head with the other, trying to breathe normally despite the pain keeping all her muscles rigid and snatching at her ability to breathe at all, her stomach churning, the weird colors still swirling even though her eyes were closed, wishing pain meds took effect faster. Like immediately. It would have been nice, she thought, to just take a shot of morphine and become unconscious for the duration. But she'd discovered the hard way that both the law and doctors frowned on patients self-medicating, far less walking out the door of any hospital, clinic, or pharmacy with their own supply of morphine or any other industrial-strength painkiller. And besides, they said it was only migraines.

Only migraines. *Only migraines. Jesus.* Even though no migraine remedy known to medical science and quite a few exotic possibilities Olivia had experimented with herself had so much as touched her periodic killer headaches.

She fumbled blindly for the bottle again.

"Waauurr!"

"All right, all right. I know there hasn't been enough time. But if the pain doesn't stop soon, I'm gonna take more. *Shit.*"

A moment later, Rex hissed.

Olivia managed to pry her eyes open no matter how much the ungodly brightness all around her hurt, and squinted at her cat in surprise. Because Rex didn't hiss, or at least never had. But as she focused on her rather odd-looking cat, his brindle-tortie coat at odds with the brilliant blue eyes of a Siamese, she realized even through the bright, swirling colors she was still seeing that Rex was scared.

Really scared.

And Rex didn't scare easily. Or . . . at all.

He was staring past her into the space behind her, the kitchen and den, and his pupils were so narrow that his eyes looked incredibly creepy, like the unnaturally blue eyes of a snake. The fur along his back was standing straight up, and his tail was about three times its natural size.

At the same time, Olivia began hearing a strange rustling sound. At first it sounded like dry leaves skittering along pavement, which was weird enough to hear inside her house with no pavement around. But then she realized it was . . . whispering. Lots of voices. Lots and lots of voices. Whispering.

It was coming from behind her.

Olivia did *not* want to turn around. Her mouth was dry despite the nausea, her skin was crawling unpleasantly, the pain in her head was getting impossibly worse rather than better, and she was afraid if she turned to confront an axe murderer, she'd beg him to just cut off her head and be quick about it.

Axe murderer. Idiot.

Not an axe murderer, of course. Not anyone.

Not any one . . . thing. Because she heard more than one whisper, many whispers, countless whispers. And she didn't know what they were saying, but she had the eerie feeling they were all whispering the same thing. The same words.

Still holding the edge of the sink with one hand, Olivia turned slowly to see what so frightened her cat and was making her own skin crawl in a sensation she'd never felt before.

"Oh, shit," she whispered.

The headache that was still hellishly painful didn't seem such a big deal now. Because despite all the swirling colors nearly blinding her, she could see, very clearly, why Rex was afraid. Every sharp object in her kitchen and den—every single one from every kitchen knife and fork she owned to three letter openers, two pairs of scissors, two box cutters with razor blades visible, the iron fireplace poker, and half a dozen pens and twice that many sharpened pencils—floated in midair. Different levels, some low, some as high as eye level.

With their pointy ends aimed right at her.

And they were all whispering.

"Waaurr," Rex muttered, his voice unusually quiet, questioning.

"I'm not doing it. I'd know if I were doing it, right? I always know. I have to concentrate to do it. I mean, unless I'm mad. Angry, not crazy. Though maybe crazy too. Because this has never . . . And, anyway, even if I'm mad, I don't . . . know how . . . to make anything . . . whisper."

Or how to stop it when she instinctively tried, an effort that was definitely not rewarded.

Unconsciously, both her hands lifted to her head, pressing as if to hold something in, because the headache suddenly grew horribly worse, impossibly worse, dragging a guttural groan from somewhere deep inside her, and through the bright swirl of colors that was beginning to truly blind her, she could still see all the scary-sharp weapons floating inexorably toward her.

Whispering.

What was whispering? Inanimate objects couldn't communicate, right? Not like this, at least.

The pain edged into agony, but even so she heard as if from a great distance her own shaking, pleading question.

"What? What are you saying? What do you want of me?"

And from the same great distance, she heard the whispered demand that made no sense to her.

Prosperity. Go to Prosperity.

They were still floating eerily toward her, all the pointy things that promised even more pain if they came much closer, and hard as she tried, Olivia couldn't do anything about it, couldn't stop it, couldn't see anything but them or hear anything except for that whispered demand.

Go to Prosperity.

Go to Prosperity.

Olivia heard one last thing: A moan of agony escaped her, and then everything went black.

TUESDAY, OCTOBER 7

Logan Alexander considered himself a man of hard-headed practicality, which to his way of thinking was ironclad proof that the universe had a twisted sense of humor. Because he was also a medium.

A medium.

And he hated *being* a medium. He hated being called a medium, being dragged from peaceful obscurity into an unwelcome spotlight of sorts, what he was and what he could do named if not understood, word spreading among those who scorned with suspicion and those who believed or desperately wanted to. Both always, always finding him eventually and making his life hell so that he'd have to pull up stakes again, usually in the middle of the night, and find another place to live, in another town or city or state where he could be anonymous again, just another stranger and left in peace. Until the next time he was found, and the lost ones began to seek him out again.

Not the "Can you contact my uncle George and ask him where he hid all the family money?" sort of questions that only made him impatient. Those were relatively easy to either avoid or else respond to with some bullshit answer that would satisfy the sort of people who would even ask that kind of silly question.

It was the truly lost ones that got to him, the religious who had lost their faith and needed proof of some kind of an existence after death. The parents hollow-eyed and haunted in a very human sense by the inexplicable and heartbreaking disappearance of a child. The widows and widowers bereft by the loss of the other half of themselves. And others, so many others, lost people who were desperately hopeful that he could help them.

He hated it.

But what he hated most about an ability way too many people with no understanding of what they were talking about called a gift or a curse (as if it could be anything so simple as either) was that he had absolutely no control over it. And he had been told by someone who *did* understand and should certainly know all about it that the "door" most mediums opened in order to communicate with the dead was, in him, always open.

Always. Or, hell, just missing entirely.

And also that mediums naturally attracted spirits. Whether they wanted to or not.

He didn't talk to the dead, certainly not willingly. They talked to him. Anywhere. Everywhere. No matter how hard he tried to ignore them. Persistent, insistent, often desperate. Dogging his steps. Showing up in different places. Making it impossible for him to go out to dinner, or to a theater and enjoy a play or movie.

Impossible to attend a party, or even to date—or at least date the same woman more than once.

He'd learned that lesson the hard way, with too many first dates ending with a woman eyeing him uneasily because he'd spent too much time sending brief, fierce glares at nothing she could see past her shoulder or over her head, or at the empty chair at their table. Most were either too kind or too wary to say it aloud, but at least one date had told him frankly that she didn't see the sense in a second date since it was obvious he had more baggage than she did and she wasn't getting any younger.

And the last time an instant physical attraction had cut an evening short for energetic (if not desperate) sex in his bed, the lady had left before dawn after waking to find him sitting up in bed having a whispered but clearly angry argument with someone named Josephine.

His bedmate's name wasn't Josephine, he was wide-awake—and as far as the lady could see, nobody else was in the room. So she snatched up her clothing and ran.

Logan had not blamed her one bit. He was just grateful that she hadn't called the police to report an escaped lunatic.

At least a few before her had done something of the sort over the years, reporting him as potentially danger-ous, or mentally ill, or just a man who had frightened them in an age when police were finally paying more attention to that sort of thing, leaving him to spend time in this jail or that "detention room" or in some clinic or other while the police and sometimes doctors got things sorted out to their satisfaction in the quest to determine whether he was actually a danger—to himself or others. Sometimes there were fines, sometimes an order for a psychiatric evaluation.

All because he could see and talk to the dead.

They stole any chance he had of living a normal life, these spirits, and while his sympathy was sometimes roused by a particularly sad or frightened spirit killed in some brutally unfair manner and desperate for his help, he seldom could do anything *to* help them, and that only added to his resentment.

At least most of them had had a shot at a normal life, before whatever unfair act or illness or accident had put them in the ground. Logan, on the other hand, could hardly get a normal *day* to himself. Impossible to do everyday things. Wherever he went, whatever he was doing, there was at least one dead person anxious to talk to him.

Like now. He was just blamelessly walking in the park near his current home in San Francisco, needing some morning air before he returned to the freelance IT work he did from his home office, because *of course* he couldn't work in a normal office setting with people all around him.

Besides, even the living had begun to wear on his nerves after a while.

Maybe especially the living.

He'd just wanted some air, that was all. And there was a dead guy walking beside him. Talking to him.

"She didn't *mean* to poison me, I'm sure," the older gentleman of about sixty was saying earnestly, for about the third time.

Logan paused on an arched footbridge and leaned his elbows on the wooden railing, gazing down at the happily burbling, man-made creek. A quick glance had shown him no one else was near, but he still kept his voice low; bitter experience had taught him that, as with dates, office jobs, and lovers, speaking aloud in public to people only he could see whenever normal people were within earshot too often meant a quick trip to the nearest loony bin, or at least a night in a cell.

Adding insult to injury, the cells too were always filled with dead people. Usually far more hostile than his living cellmates.

"Listen, buddy—"

"My name is Oscar."

Logan didn't bother telling him names didn't really matter. "Oscar, I don't know if your wife poisoned you—"

"My girlfriend."

Logan sent him a glance, mildly surprised, but shrugged. "Whatever. I don't know if she poisoned you, but if you're looking for justice, I can tell you from experience that cops take a dim view of dead witnesses communicating through mediums, and judges take an even dimmer view. *And* I've had more than my fair share of time on a shrink's couch, thank you very much."

"But—"

"Were you buried or cremated?"

"Cremated."

"Then you're really out of luck."

"The medical examiner took samples. Of . . . of everything. I saw him." He sounded, suddenly, a bit queasy.

Logan felt the first flicker of sympathy, even though he didn't want to. This wasn't the first spirit who had shared details of his own autopsy. That had to be unnerving, to say the least, watching your own body being opened up on a slab.

"Must not have been anything conclusive enough to interest the cops," he said.

"But that's the thing." Oscar sounded near tears. "They were convinced. They arrested her. They're going to put her on trial for murder. And I *know* she didn't poison me. But my wife hired a PI and he's come up with a theory of how and why she could have done it, and I know he planted evidence and other stuff the police believe, or maybe they just slipped me the poison and made it look like she did. I think they're both in on it, my wife and her PI, because I've seen them together, and I just—"

"Oscar, what do you want from me?" Logan tried his best to keep impatience out of his voice.

"My girlfriend doesn't deserve to go to prison. She didn't do anything wrong. She *didn't* poison me."

"And how do you think *I* can prove that?" A glance showed him that Oscar was looking even more miserable.

"I don't know. All I know is that it isn't fair—"

"Life isn't fair, buddy. Why should death be?" But then the way Oscar's voice had broken off tugged at Logan's attention, and he looked at the spirit again.

The spirit named Oscar seemed to be enveloped in a strange, multicolored aura, all the intensely bright colors swirling and dancing around him.

Logan didn't see auras.

"What the hell?"

Oscar shook his head slightly, as though trying to throw off an unwelcome distraction, while at the same time his expression was straining as though trying to hear something. And then he looked frightened. "I . . . I don't . . . I don't . . . Oh, damn, there won't be time. Promise me, Logan. Promise me you'll come back here and help me prove Lucy's innocent."

"Come back from where? Oscar—"

"Prosperity. When you come back from Prosperity."

A weird sensation of unease was beginning to crawl over Logan's skin, unfamiliar and distinctly unpleasant. And his head had begun to pound. "What are you talking about, Oscar? I'm not going anywhere. My job—"

"You have to take a leave or quit or something. You have to go to Prosperity, Logan. You have to help them." Now he looked terrified. "We'll all be in danger if you can't help them stop it. The living and the dead."

Logan wondered abstractedly what sort of danger could or would trouble a spirit. Before he could even form the words to ask, Oscar and his rainbow aura vanished like a soap bubble.

Decision out of my hands, Logan told himself with relief, ignoring the stab of guilt.

"Nothing I could've done anyway," he muttered, straightening and turning to head back home.

After only two steps, he jerked to a stop and stood very, very still, only his eyes moving as he scanned the park in front of him.

There were people moving around, just as there had been before. Couples holding hands, dog walkers, a couple of guys tossing a football and another two throwing a Frisbee. There were a few people on benches or just leaning up against a tree here and there with a book or tablet or laptop. Normal, even on a slightly chilly but sunny October day.

What wasn't normal were the others.

The spirits.

They looked as real as the living, not transparent. But as his gaze rested on them one by one, he saw them shimmer almost like heat off the pavement or a jittery image on a computer or special effects in a movie before becoming solid again. And every single one of them was just standing there, utterly still.

Turned toward him.

Staring at him.

That was new. That was . . . different.

Logan turned in a slow circle, scanning as much of the park as he could see from his position.

They were everywhere. Dozens. Scores. More.

A lot more. More than he'd ever seen in one place. Ever.

As he completed the slow circle, he started in surprise to find one of the spirits standing only about three feet away. A woman. Too young to be dead, though people did die young and, anyway, he had learned that he didn't always see spirits as they had appeared at death, but at some earlier stage of their lives. And he almost never saw what had killed them, spared at least that horror of nightmares of the living dead haunting him.

He had no idea why.

He didn't care.

All he knew was that he was far colder than the October day, cold down to his bones, that the unpleasant crawly sensation roving over his entire body was getting stronger and more unsettling, his head was *really* hurting now, and a very strong sense of foreboding gripped him.

"No," he said softly.

"You have to go to Prosperity," she said, her voice a bit hollow and distant, as they were sometimes. Her face was without expression, which was something else that was occasionally true of the spirits he encountered.

This time, the total lack of expression on her face and in her voice was creepy as hell.

Trying to hold his voice low and not betray to the living around him that he was a madman who saw what they didn't, that they were moving blithely about among spirits, too many spirits, nothing normal about that even out on the *para*normal fringes of his reality, he said, "I don't have to go anywhere. Leave me alone."

"They need you. We need you, Logan."

They always knew his name. It had always bugged him.

"Tap another medium," he advised her. "It's got to be somebody else's turn."

"You have to go. Please, Logan. It's so important."

"What—" But the half-formed question was never finished, because the spirit faded away quickly and with an eeriness he'd never seen before, like she just became smoke dispersed by the slight, chill breeze.

It was a long moment before Logan could force himself to scan the park as he had before. But when he did, he saw no spirits. Only the living, going about their business as they probably did every ordinary day of their nice normal lives.

"Goddammit," he whispered.

The day felt colder than he knew it was.

TUESDAY, OCTOBER 7

Reno Bellman was congratulating herself for what had so far been a successful brunch date. She had not, after all, absently told her date, Jake Harper, any of the bits of information that had floated through her mind like flotsam on a calm sea since they'd met at this sidewalk café more than an hour earlier. She hadn't reminded him not to forget his mother's birthday next week, or told him his treasured high school football championship ring was not gone forever but had instead rolled under his nightstand, or even that he was going to get that promotion he was anxious about.

She didn't mention any of those things. Instead, she had chatted casually just as Jake had, on the safe topics generally reserved for a first date. Likes and dislikes, the undoubtedly miserable winter looming ahead for Chicago, and how the Cubs had done during the season. They both tacitly avoided politics and religion, those trickier subjects more suited to later—if there was a later—when disagreements would either be handled amicably or else judged to be insurmountable differences.

Everything was *fine*, just fine, so when she became conscious of a rustling sound like dead leaves skittering over pavement, she glanced around in surprise. This sidewalk café was moderately crowded for a Tuesday morning in October, but nobody else seemed to see or hear anything unusual, and she couldn't see any leaves or anything else skittering past.

Reno was about to just chalk it up to her generally heightened senses when the rustle of dry leaves became instead whispering. Whispering by many voices. Or by . . . something else. Something tugging at her with increasing insistence, causing the fine hairs on the back of her neck to stir and the skin all over her body to go unpleasantly pins-and-needles. Her head began to hurt. Badly.

"Reno?"

At first, it was only whispering, just sounds that seemed normal and ordinary, the background hum of a busy city neighborhood. But then, slowly, she believed she detected a sort of pattern to what she was hearing. And then words. Words whispered by many voices, all saying the same thing.

"Reno—"

"Hush," she said absently, all but forgetting her date in the need to concentrate on listening. What *was* it? What were they saying? She wasn't sure at first, but slowly some of the static faded, and she was just able to make out words.

Words that gradually became clearer.

Come . . . come to . . . come to Prosperity. They . . . need you. We all need you. You have to come to Prosperity—

"Reno?"

She never found out if she might have heard something more, an explanation, a reason, something she could glean safely and peacefully, in warm daylight and without fear, without being touched by violence, because in that moment Jake reached across the small table and laid his hand over hers.

Before she could warn him.

So he was yanked with her into the hellish maelstrom of a vision.

And this one was bad.

Anyone could have been forgiven for believing that where they were was, literally, hell. Or, at the very least, some acid trip or horror movie version of hell. All the worst bits of Revelation and Dante's *Inferno*, with even scarier stuff added in for horror fun.

The air was full of a horrible smell and choking ash,

and as Reno stood there looking around, trying to tell herself that this was no worse than other visions had been, it became worse.

It became a lot worse.

The ash in the air thinned out enough to allow her to see more of her surroundings. Unfortunately.

The heat was searing, the rotten-egg smell of brimstone acrid, and the ash from unseen but roaring fires drifted down—and drifted up—and drifted sideways. The alien landscape, as far as the eye could see, was a sickly reddish brown, with jagged rocks that looked razor-sharp and thick, muddy streams slopping between the rocks, and here and there a stunted, twisted tree, bare limbs charred and bent downward in defeated submission.

And . . . the creatures. Dozens of them, more, dotting the raw landscape as far as she could see. Crouched and standing, still or swaying back and forth, with a few curled up on the rocky ground making pitiful soft noises that were awful to hear and impossible to ever forget.

They might once have been human but looked deformed now, bodies twisted, limbs partially missing, their faces skewed, almost melted, the features blunted or open or missing. Some of them looked skeletal but with burned flesh clinging to bones, crackling sounds audible as they shifted and turned.

To stare at Reno and her forgotten companion, or to listen if they had no eyes, or maybe just obeying the blind and deaf but primitive sense of an unusual presence and possible threat in their horrific reality.

"What is this place?" she demanded of the nearest . . . creature.

It did not answer, but cringed away as a shadow detached itself from a towering, jagged rock and stepped forward, toward Reno. She recognized it only because she had heard of Shadow People, beings from the spirit realm, or even deeper and much farther away, that might have once been human in some distant past.

But now, from everything she had heard whispered on what some wryly or mockingly called the psychic grapevine, the current thinking was that they were simply the human-shaped utter blackness of everything wrong, twisted, sick, perverted, and evil—the psychic spillover of horrors poured into a creepily recognizable shape. Pure negative energy. As if they had been feeding for eons on the evil emotions and evil acts committed by humans.

And maybe they had.

Some people had called them demons.

This one made itself taller, elongated, towering over Reno and the stunned, terrified date she had completely forgotten about.

"Neat trick," she said to the Shadow creature, tilting her head slightly to look up, but not otherwise moving. "Now answer my question. What is this place?"

"Hell," it answered in a croak.

"No, this isn't hell," she countered immediately. "Been there."

A laugh like dry kindling scraping together came

from the Shadow. "This is your earth, Reno," it said in that scratchy, unused voice.

She had been holding fear at bay, most of a lifetime of practice allowing her to keep it out of her voice and expression, because she knew that whatever and wherever this place *was*, she was here only in spirit. It was a vision. And in her visions, she had discovered, the bad ones at least, any fear from her gave the various . . . beings . . . she confronted power over her. And sometimes made it more difficult for her to escape the vision if things got dicey. But when the towering Shadow said this was earth, she felt a genuine jolt of horror.

"What are you talking about? Some kind of war is going to do this?" The ugly landscape all around her certainly could have been the seared devastation of some insane nuclear conflict.

Without the creatures, at least.

Or maybe with them too.

"Not that kind of war. Not soldiers in uniform fighting for flag and country, dying on battlefields." The Shadow creature's voice was still inhuman, yet managed to be mocking as well. "A different struggle. Too much evil building unchecked for too long. Darkness. Hunger. Need. Gathering. Growing stronger. Upsetting the natural balance."

Trying to think clearly, Reno said, "I would have thought you . . . creatures . . . would love that. Why show me? I'm shown things I can change, always."

The Shadow laughed again, weirdly both scornful

and anxious. "This is something you need to change. Need to stop . . . if you can. To prevent if you can. Hold the line. Better for all if the boundaries between our worlds, our realities, are . . . maintained. An occasional portal or door opened here and there is one thing, releasing pressure, easing the strain. Natural. Normal. The way things are supposed to be.

"This . . . is something else. A dead and burning earth is no more use to us than it is to you. And if you die, if you are destroyed, so are we. We need the chaos of humanity, the destructive fear and evil you create. The negative energy. We need to . . . feed. To exist. We balance you. The universe demands balance. Go to Prosperity, Reno. The very earth there is ready to heave itself open. To spill out evil even we can't absorb. Can't control. You must stop it."

"What, alone?"

"There will be others. Those who need to be there with you are being called. Some already on their way. Balance, Reno. We all need balance if we're to survive."

Reno had more questions than she could count, but as quickly as the vision had begun, it was over. And she was sitting at a small table at a sidewalk café on a cool Chicago morning, breathing in fresh air, the weak October sunshine making her blink.

She felt the death grip on her hand abruptly released, and looked up to see her date lurching to his feet. His face was pasty white, and though he tried several times, he was clearly unable to say a word.

Dammit, there goes another potential boyfriend.

"It's okay, Jake," she said wryly. "I don't expect to hear from you again. As for this little . . . adventure . . . I'm sure you'll be able to explain it away somehow."

"You're crazy!" he finally yelped.

"I expect that'll do," she murmured.

And, as he hurried away without a backward look, almost running, she called after him, "No, really, I'll take care of the check." And then her worser self reared its head, and she shouted, "And don't forget your mother's birthday next week!"

By then, he was definitely running.

The shout made the pain in her head worse, but she decided it had been worth it.

She was being stared at by others at the café. She could feel it. But Reno ignored them all. After most of a lifetime, she'd gotten pretty good at that. No use trying to control what she couldn't.

She summoned a waiter with a glance, asked for the check, then asked, "Can you give me the time?" She wasn't wearing a watch.

The young waiter looked at the large watch on his own wrist and replied, "It's eleven forty-five, ma'am."

"Exactly?"

"Yes, ma'am. Your check, ma'am." He looked after her hastily departed date, clearly somewhat indignant on her behalf.

Reno didn't notice. She glanced at the total printed on the check and placed several bills in the folder, covering the meal and adding a generous tip, then closed it and returned it to him. "Keep the change."

"Thank you, ma'am. More coffee?"

She looked up at him, saw him, and blinked. "No. No, thank you. I'll just sit here a bit if that's okay." Fewer than half a dozen of the sidewalk tables were occupied by now, in the lull between the departure of early brunch customers and the next wave of people wanting actual lunch. An exodus that had apparently happened during her vision. Which had, she estimated, lasted little more than five minutes. Time was always different in a vision.

"Of course, ma'am." He silently retrieved her date's cup, saucer, water glass, and napkin, flicked a few invisible crumbs off the table with the napkin, and just as silently went away again.

Reno reached up to rub one temple briefly, then dug in her casual purse, produced a small bottle of OTC painkillers, and swallowed several capsules with a sip of water.

"Prosperity," she murmured.

After a thoughtful moment, she reached again into her bag, this time for her cell phone, grateful not for the first time that she was one of the few psychics they knew of who was able to depend on having a charged phone for a reasonable amount of time, just like a normal person. She could even wear a watch when she wanted to, something else many psychics couldn't do because of how they used energy.

Someone had told her once it was because she was wholly a receiver, her own energy not the sort that would blast outward and interfere with electronics of any kind.

Whatever. As long as it gave her an edge.

She keyed in the single preprogrammed number and leaned back in her chair, staring at nothing as she waited for him to answer.

"Bishop."

"Hey, there, it's Reno. Funny thing happened at brunch today," Reno said. "Thought you might be interested."

TWO

"Oh, God." Special Agent Tony Harte groaned, holding his head with both hands. "What the *hell* was that?"

His boss, Special Crimes Unit Chief Noah Bishop, shook his own head slightly, then grimaced and lifted a hand to rub his left temple, where a rather exotic white streak stood out starkly in his thick black hair. He was far paler than normal, and his sentry-sharp pale gray eyes were darker than Tony had ever seen them, like tarnished silver.

"Vision?" Tony demanded. "Because I'll swear I saw colors I've never seen before. I didn't pick up all that from you, surely?" He was a clairvoyant, though not a particularly strong one; even so, he had been known to easily pick up information, experiences, and even emotions from other SCU agents, especially if they were "broadcasting" for some reason.

Bishop looked down at the legal pad lying before him on the conference table in the room at Quantico where the SCU teams usually met to discuss cases, and where he and Tony had been, in fact, going over several cold cases, as they regularly did, as evidenced by a dozen or so folders scattered on the table.

"Not a normal vision," Bishop said finally, characteristically answering only one of the questions asked. He looked at the pen in his right hand with a brief frown before dropping it into a cup of pencils and pens nearby on the table.

"That's an oxymoron," Tony said, scrabbling in the first-aid case he had located in a cabinet. "Normal vision. Our kind, I mean. If we're out of aspirin, I'm gonna kill somebody."

Special Agent Miranda Bishop, walking rather carefully, came into the room just then, a legal pad beneath one arm, holding something in that closed hand and a large bottle of OTC painkillers in the other hand. She caught Tony's eye and tossed him the bottle.

"Try these."

"Thanks."

Miranda sat down beside her husband at the conference table and held out her closed hand, opening it to reveal several capsules. "Here, take these." And before Bishop, notoriously unwilling to take anything that might blunt any of his senses, could shape a refusal, she added, "I know *exactly* what your head feels like. Take them. We both need to be able to think clearly."

Bishop looked at his wife's startlingly lovely face,

now unusually pale, her electric blue eyes dark with pain, and he swallowed the capsules.

Beloved?

I'm all right. Getting there, anyway. Was worried about our connection since I couldn't . . . feel you there for a while. But as long as that's all right, then we're all right.

Yes, love. We're all right.

You couldn't feel me either, though, could you? While it was happening?

No. But we're fine now. Whatever that was . . . I don't believe it intended to damage us.

Noah . . . What's coming . . . Can it be stopped?

If it can be stopped, we'll do all we can to stop it. We've been warned, and a heads-up from the universe is . . . rare.

We weren't summoned. Not us, not directly.

No. But we were shown enough that I can't help believing we're meant to help those summoned. We have resources. Experience. Knowledge most of those summoned can't possibly have.

But we can't interfere.

Not once it really starts. Once they're in place and it all begins to evolve. But I think we have a little time before that—otherwise, why the warning? Time to gather, to plan. Which means what we do in the next twenty-four to forty-eight hours is critical.

Yes. Darling . . . if we fail, if they fail . . .

Then the world will see evil in forms only we've seen until now. Forms none of their armies can fight, none of their weapons can destroy.

It should have sounded melodramatic. It did not.

Her hand found his, beneath the table, their fingers twining together on his upper thigh. Because sometimes the physical connection of flesh to flesh was more comforting even than the very deep and very intimate psychic one.

Tony, a handful of painkillers in him now and oblivious of the mind talk that Bishop and Miranda tended to limit with others around so as to avoid confusion, looked at the other two. "What *was* that?" he asked again. "I've never felt anything like it in my life."

Miranda looked at him. "What did you feel? Besides the pain, I mean."

"Dizzy and sick, and like the skin was trying to crawl off my bones," he replied succinctly. Then, going even more pale, he pushed himself away from the table as he had before, rolling his chair rather than standing, and reached for a landline phone on a nearby shelf. "Shit. Kendra."

While he checked in with his very pregnant wife, who had only just gone on maternity leave, Miranda looked at her husband. "If that affected the whole unit . . ."

"They'll start calling in." One of the few ironclad rules in the SCU was that if any agent experienced *anything* out of the ordinary that could even loosely be connected to their psychic abilities, they were to report in to base—meaning Bishop—ASAP. It was always his cell number, though most agents knew that wherever he happened to be, which could be literally anywhere in the world, he made sure he had close access to a land-line or satellite phone, and that was where the call would be forwarded.

Most powerful psychics could seldom carry a working cell phone for any normal length of time; with few excep-tions, the more powerful the psychic, the quicker cell phones went dead, despite all the attempts by various brilliant scientists both in the FBI and elsewhere to fig-ure out a way to fix that sometimes dangerous problem.

Bishop leaned forward and reached out his free hand to the multi-lined conference phone on the table, key-ing in the preprogrammed command that would for-ward any call made to his cell number to any of the six separate lines shared by the conference phone and three other landline phones set up permanently in the room. The phone Tony was using was one of them; two more phones sat on small desks on either side of the door leading out to the hallway. The spacious room's other door led out to the SCU bullpen, visible through three large glass panes along that wall.

The bullpen was currently occupied only by admin-istrative staff, since all other SCU agents save those in the conference room were either away on leave, inactive for whatever reason, or else working cases scattered across the country.

"We'll need a fourth agent to help man the phones in here," he said almost absently. "At least. Preferably SCU, and not administrative."

"Galen's here today," Miranda said.

Bishop looked at her.

She nodded. "He's been in and out the last couple of weeks, while you were on the St. Louis case. Still closed down tight as a drum, but I think he's getting restless. I heard he's run the trainee course several times, and he's been at the shooting range half a dozen times. So, though he hasn't gone anywhere near his desk, he's been . . . around. Just about every day. Making small talk, which we both know is hardly his way. This thing could be what it takes to bring him off official leave and back to the unit. Because if this is . . . as bad as we saw, then we may need a Guardian in the worst way, an experienced Watcher. Especially given who's been . . . summoned. And always assuming they answer the summons."

She had placed her legal pad on the table before them when she'd joined him, and now she pushed it toward him a few inches. On the pad were written—rather shakily, with her normally clear handwriting showing severe stress—three names: Olivia Castle, Logan Alexander, and Reno Bellman.

Bishop barely glanced at the names, for the moment far more concerned about his wife.

It hit you harder than it did me, beloved.

I wonder why.

My guess would be your connection with Bonnie. Your instinct is always to reach out and protect her, especially when something unusual and potentially threatening happens. It's instinct, deeper than thought. That moment of reaching out left you vulnerable to the sheer power of . . . whatever this is.

Bonnie was Miranda's younger sister, currently on track to graduate early from the University of Virginia, where she lived on campus with her longtime boyfriend, Seth, who was in medical school there. And though both Miranda and Bishop did everything they could to provide a normal life for her and keep her far from the difficult and dangerous life's work they had chosen, Bonnie was a born medium-healer, exceptionally powerful, and she possessed a very strong psychic connection to her sister, something not uncommon among blood siblings, especially in a family that had produced psychics for generations.

And most especially when they had only had each other for too many years after their family had been devastated.

She's safe, I feel that. Not among the summoned, thank God.

And I believe I know why. We'll find out soon enough about our own people, but my guess is that psychics with specific individual abilities were summoned with, perhaps, some others with similar abilities not summoned because they're intended to be held in reserve.

In case the first line of defense fails?

If this warning is due to some kind of attack or something we've never before dealt with, yes. We won't know until everyone checks in or is located, but . . .

"I think most of them will at least call in," he said out loud. "Especially if they experienced some version of what we saw and felt." Bishop pushed the legal pad on the table in front of him toward her until it touched hers. On his legal pad were written the names Sully Maitland, Victoria Stark, and Dalton Davenport.

Leaning an elbow on the table as she absently rubbed the back of her neck, Miranda studied the names on his legal pad. "Not the same names I got, but all of them are high on the 'maybe one day' list, some for years. People you've kept a close eye on. And the abilities of these six run the gamut and then some. But why untrained people, lacking experience as well as unwilling, or unable, for one reason or another, to be feds, cops, or other kinds of investigators?"

"There's always a reason," Bishop noted.

"If we can only figure it out. Or if they can." Her gaze was still on the legal pads. "Medium, telekinetic, seer and clairvoyant, empath— Did we ever come up with a definition for Victoria's ability?"

"No," Bishop replied, adding rather cryptically, "and I'm still not convinced she has only the one."

"I remember she refused to be tested."

"Repeatedly. And since she has exceptionally strong shields, none of us could read her. Those shields could help protect her. But we can have no idea of her control, or how her ability could change in the field."

"That's true of all of them, really."

Bishop nodded slowly. "We always gain the best and most useful information on most psychics involved during multiple investigations over time. But these psychics haven't been tested in the field; they've been tested in trying to live ordinary lives, which was all most of them could cope with, and even that gave most of them problems. With the possible exceptions of Reno and Sully, I wouldn't say any of them live normal lives. But . . . in the field on this, it could all be so much worse for them . . . The situation is already radically different from anything we've encountered, and we barely know anything about it at this point, nothing about what's going on or could be starting in Prosperity. How to fight it, what the cost could be. We can't predict anything unless there's another vision, can't extrapolate from data because we don't really have any."

Miranda knew her husband too well not to know that he was deeply troubled by this unprecedented situation and the extreme, if undefined, threat they both knew it represented, but she also knew that only time and a successful resolution to . . . whatever this was . . . could really ease his mind.

Assuming a successful resolution could be achieved.

Calm, she said, "I have a hunch we'll have a lot more data once our people and the others begin checking in." She kept her eyes on the legal pad, adding, "And rounding out the list is a telepath. When was the last time you talked to Dalton?"

"Six months ago."

"How was he holding up?"

Bishop made a sound that wasn't quite a laugh. "Not at all happy to hear from me. He was still living in Alaska. About as far away from people as he could get without going out into the wilderness and totally off the grid. And wary as he is, he doesn't want to be *that* alone."

"So not quite ready to sacrifice civilization," she noted.

"No. He has ties whether he's willing to admit it, ties he isn't able to completely sever, and he's holding on to the phone when he could have tossed it, so not willing to disappear."

"But you're sure he was summoned? Like these others?"

"I'm sure he got the call, just like you're sure the people on your list got the call. Just not entirely sure if he'll answer it with anything but a grim no, at least initially. He spent most of the twenty-five years since he was a kid medicated to the gills, institutionalized, thinking, if he was able to think clearly at all, that he was crazy, and listening to doctors telling him almost daily that he was delusional. It really is amazing that he emerged from that sane."

"I know you hoped Diana could reach him, since she's the only one in the unit with a past similar to his."

"Similar," Bishop said, "but not the same. Diana's mediumistic instincts kept themselves alive and functional at a subconscious level from her childhood on in spite of all the meds and so-called therapy, and her father's determination to *fix* her—or just control her. And she wasn't institutionalized."

Miranda said, "You're right. It's almost impossible to imagine how Dalton came through that sane."

"I'm not at all sure he believes he's sane."

"Well . . . neither did Diana. For a long time."

"Yes. And she wasn't locked away completely from

anything like a normal life, or surrounded by people with real, serious mental illnesses for years on end. At least her father never subjected her to that."

"True. And her abilities *were* exceptionally strong at the subconscious level."

"Yeah. But Dalton's a telepath; in him, the meds dulled and blunted all his senses, including the basic five, so none of them could function properly, and he never got the opportunity to build a shield. With all the drugs out of his system now and all his senses really awake and functional for the first time, he's like one giant exposed nerve. Even after nearly three years with no meds. They're out of his system, but . . . he still has so much baggage to drag along behind him. No wonder he wants to stay put."

"I know you took Diana with you to see him about a year ago, when he'd been off the meds. For a while."

Bishop nodded. "Yeah, but she couldn't help him, bad as she wanted to, except to tell him she'd found her way through it and he could too. That he wasn't alone, not that the knowledge seemed to cheer him any. I couldn't help him except to offer the meditation and biofeedback techniques we've developed, and given the state he was in, I doubt he was even capable at the time of being able to concentrate and focus."

He shook his head, rather carefully since the painkillers hadn't completely kicked in. "He didn't want anybody close enough to touch him, but even though I couldn't read him, I got the distinct impression he thought we were all freaks, himself included. And he was pretty definite about not seeing anyone else, most especially an empath. Probably because of his extreme emotional strain. I don't think I've ever seen a man that close to the edge. It all takes time and practice to learn how to cope, and it's an individual thing, we know that. What works for one psychic is no help at all to another. He still didn't have a handle on it six months ago; I have no idea if things are any better for him now."

Miranda half nodded and looked across the table as Tony hung up the phone. "Kendra's okay?"

"She didn't feel a thing," Tony replied. "Matter of fact, I woke her up from a nap. She asked if she should come in, but I persuaded her to go back to bed. Figure if she didn't feel anything, she's not meant to be a part of this. Whatever this is."

Miranda nodded again, unsurprised. "Probably left untouched by this because of her pregnancy, and since I've never thought of the universe as particularly benevolent, I'm guessing it's purely a matter of those called or otherwise affected being able to concentrate fully on this . . . situation without fluctuations in hormones or other nonpsychic distractions."

"Makes sense," Bishop agreed.

"I'm also guessing there may be a few more of our people as well as Haven's who weren't affected, for one reason or another. Many if not most of them likely felt . . . something . . . but not a summons. Something that powerful clearly directed out in numerous directions had to produce a spillover of energy, and it likely affected most psychics to some degree. And probably latents and nonpsychics as well, even though they won't have a clue what happened."

"A summons?" Tony rubbed his head, frowning. "Am I the only one who doesn't know what's going on? I have a hell of a headache that came out of nowhere, but I didn't hear anyone—or anything—calling me, if that's what you meant by a summons. I didn't get anything like that."

Miranda lightly touched the two legal pads. "These six people did. A definite summons, probably geared to each in some way unique to their abilities. None of them are in the unit. None are cops, or even investigators. Something they all have in common."

"But psychics," Tony said, leaning forward and peering at the legal pads. He possessed the quite-often-useful knack of reading upside down. "I don't recognize most of those names, but I remember Bishop talking once about Dalton Davenport. Said he could have blown the top off our scale as a telepath if he'd had training and support, especially early on."

Bishop nodded. "That's the second thing every person on these two lists has in common. All are exceptionally powerful, or have the potential to be, even though most lack even nominal control."

Tony grappled with that for a moment in frowning silence, then asked, "Is there a third thing they have in common?"

It was Miranda who answered. "Yeah. They've all met each other, spent some time together. For a while, they lived in a sort of group home. Some have known each other for years. And some of them were, at least at one time, close."

"To each other? I take it you mean emotionally close? Or psychically close?" Tony lifted a brow.

"In some cases, both." She nodded. "There have been a few . . . let's call them informal support groups . . . and group homes . . . formed over the years in different parts of the country, usually whenever there were a number of psychics in the same city or area. Noah encouraged that from the beginning, set up the logistics along with John Garett's help, and by now it's official SCU and Haven policy. The homes are privately owned and run, inspected regularly by any . . . interested state or federal parties. There's at least one doctor and nurse on staff, as well as visiting psychiatrists trained by our own people specializing in psychic as well as emotional trauma. And, of course, with no drain on the taxpayers, the FBI didn't have much to complain about."

"Though they did try," Bishop murmured.

Miranda sent him a quick smile. "Not even they could argue with success, especially given the amount of knowledge we've learned about psychic ability."

"Lab rats?" Tony asked, a bit troubled.

"No, nothing like that," Bishop answered. These were and are people who . . . need to know they aren't alone. Need to feel safe. Need to know there are others they can talk to openly about what they can do, and how they feel about that. No meds, no forced therapy, no medical procedures whatsoever. Just a safe place

where they can live for a few months or as many years
as they like."

"Indefinitely?" Tony asked.

"If they need a safe place that long, then of course.
John and I set up the group homes very carefully, and
we have a list of very trustworthy caretakers as well as a
healthy endowment to make certain the homes exist
long after we do."

Tony didn't much like to think about a time "after"
Bishop, which surprised him a little. Not that it had ever
bothered him, because he'd never considered the matter
before. But now he had a strong hunch that Bishop had
"set up" a great many things so that the SCU as well as
his "rogue" psychics would remain protected and enjoy
useful lives long after he was gone.

Miranda continued, "We know that psychics are
drawn to one another, and even if they're reluctant to
join us or Haven, they still need whatever knowledge we
can provide, plus emotional support that mainstream
medicine doesn't offer. Just the relief of being able to talk
to someone else who understands what it is to be psychic
can break down a lot of walls." She paused, adding wryly,
"And build a few."

The phone rang just then, and Bishop reached out to
take the call, automatically hitting the speaker button.
Before he could even say his name, a strong voice that
sounded somewhere between highly irritated and intensely curious erupted from the speaker.

"What the *hell* was that?" Agent Hollis Templeton

demanded. "I thought my head was going to split open, and even Reese got a nosebleed."

NEITHER BISHOP NOR Miranda was surprised that Hollis was the first to call in; she was, arguably, the most powerful individual psychic in the unit.

Miranda asked, "Are you okay?"

"Yeah, now. Hurt like hell for a few minutes there, but we finally managed to stop the pain. And Reese's nosebleed."

In the background, clearly on speaker, her partner, Reese DeMarco, could be heard to say with his usual calm that he appreciated that.

"It was a mutual effort and you know it," Hollis told her partner, adding to those on the other end of the connection. "Neither of us was shielding at all, so we really got slammed."

"What else did you both experience?" Bishop asked.

"You mean aside from pain, nausea, a dandy color light show, and the unpleasant sensation of our skin wanting to depart our bodies?"

"Yeah. Aside from all that."

"Prosperity," she said distinctly. "Reese got it via a voice in his head. I got it from a very upset spirit who popped out of nowhere—well, you know what I mean— insisting we had to go to Prosperity, that something awful is going to happen unless we stop it. She was crying, and by the time she popped away again, I was too." The last few words held a slight quaver as well as irritation, and she added, "Oh, damn, this empath thing is hard. *Why* do I have to feel what spirits feel as well as the living? What have I done to piss off the universe?"

Rightly judging those to be rhetorical questions, Bishop said, "I gather you and Reese both felt a sense of urgency?"

"Well . . . yes and no. The urge to start packing, but not the urge to take off right this instant."

"Where are you?" he asked. They had been taking accumulated annual leave time and hadn't checked in for more than six weeks.

"You mean you don't know? I thought this sat phone had a GPS locator in it. As a matter of fact, I'm sure it does."

"Yes. But I took Reese at his word when he said you didn't want to be disturbed and that you two would go looking for a deserted island or cave where I couldn't find you even if I retasked a satellite."

"I'm not entirely sure I believe you," she told him with characteristic frankness. "But thanks for not bothering us these last weeks."

"You're welcome. Where are you?"

Reese replied to that one, his voice still calm. "The Bahamas. One of the virtually uninhabited islands. We would have aimed for an entirely deserted one, but Hollis doesn't camp."

"You can say that again. My idea of roughing it is no room service. Which we don't have here, but it turns

out Reese can cook, so he's been my room service."
There was a brief silence, and then she laughed and
added, "I didn't mean that the way it sounded."

Bishop looked at Miranda and Tony, both of whom
were smiling, and said dryly, "Okay. Are you two planning to answer that summons?"

"Summons?" Hollis's voice was interested now. "Is
that what it was? Who's calling?"

"We aren't sure yet," Bishop replied. "We're expecting most of the unit and some psychics on our watch list
to begin checking in. We should know more after that."

"You and Miranda had a vision?"

"Yeah. And got six names of psychics who were summoned, none of them current SCU members. We also
got that whatever is going to happen—or not happen
or is already happening—will be in Prosperity."

Clearly unsurprised that Bishop didn't offer more
details of the vision, Hollis merely said, "It's another
seemingly peaceful little mountain town, isn't it?"

"In North Carolina," he confirmed.

"Huh. They seem to get more than their fair share
of monsters, don't they?" There was a brief silence, during which she undoubtedly consulted with her partner,
and then she said, "Okay, we're in. You want us to go
straight to Prosperity?"

Bishop exchanged a glance with his wife, and said,
"No, the mountain house. It's large enough and near
enough to Prosperity to serve as our command center.
And since we don't yet know what, if anything, has

happened in Prosperity, or which psychics will answer the summons, it's as good a place as any to meet up, put our heads together, and figure out a plan."

"A *plan*?" Hollis was politely incredulous. "You think we're actually going to have a plan this time, Yoda?" She was the only agent who had ever been heard to assign him a rather mocking—if amused—nickname.

Being Bishop, he ignored that, as well as her question. "I gather Reese flew you two to your island on a chopper?"

A brief laugh escaped her, but she didn't push. "Yeah. So we can be at the mountain house in a few hours."

"Wait until tomorrow morning to start," Bishop said. "Assuming most if not all of the psychics on our list decide to come, it's going to take some time just for them to get to the mountain house. One of them is in Alaska."

"Must have taken a hell of a lot of power to reach that far," Hollis said slowly. "Unless we're talking individual power sources all around us. Which I don't much like the idea of, just so you know."

"Neither do I," Bishop said.

Reese spoke up then to ask, "Anybody you need us to pick up along the way?"

"I'll let you know by tomorrow morning. Call in before you take off."

"Copy that."

Hollis said, "See you guys tomorrow." And hung up.

Bishop reached over to tap the conference phone to cut the connection on his end, and said almost absently,

"Depending on who calls in and when, it may take a tight scheduling of both jets to get everybody to the airstrip near the mountain house within a reasonable amount of time."

Tony eyed him. "You seem to be very sure that most of those summoned are going to come," he said.

"Yes," Bishop said. "I am. One way or another, I believe they'll all come."

Before Tony could question that, the multi-lined phones in the conference room began ringing all at once. Every line showed a blinking light.

"Here we go," Bishop said. "We need to take notes on every call. Who, where they are, what they felt and what the local time was—exactly, if possible—and what they feel now."

"And if they ask what they're supposed to do now?" Tony lifted a brow at the unit chief. "What do we tell them?"

"For now, we tell them to stand by their phones," Bishop answered immediately. "What we tell them when we call them back will depend on all the calls."

THREE

Chief Deputy Katie Cole had lived in Prosperity for less than a year but had settled in to the town and her job quickly and without fuss. She had an easy manner and the knack of both talking to people and listening when they needed to talk, so even though she wasn't a native, she had been accepted completely.

As far as she could tell, anyway.

Even though it was a smallish town, and fairly isolated, Prosperity was not entirely off the beaten path; no major highway was close, but the town was located in a section of the Appalachian Mountains considered particularly scenic, so it was the rule rather than the exception that plenty of sightseers and other tourists drove through pretty steadily from spring right up to winter.

Some of them even stopped for a few days or at least a long weekend, enjoying one of the two very nice hotels in the main part of town, good food, the scenery, and local crafts sold for reasonable prices in small shops staffed by smiling, friendly people.

Crime was practically nonexistent, in part because Sheriff Jackson Archer was a good cop and a highly respected, homegrown citizen of the town, and in part because Prosperity was . . . well, a prosperous small town. So there were enough jobs to go around and good schools that not only educated the kids but also offered plenty of after-school and summer activities. On the whole the citizens were happy.

Which was maybe, Katie thought, why it struck her as so odd to feel a very unusual tension as she strolled along Main Street, stretching her legs and having a look around. She'd been vaguely conscious of an uneasiness she couldn't pinpoint for more than a week, but now there was nothing vague about what she felt.

Except a good reason for it.

Because she didn't *see* any reason for tension; it looked to her like a perfectly normal Tuesday morning in early October. There were quite a few tourists about, she noted, wearing the slightly harried but pleased look of people who were not at home but were bent on enjoyment of their surroundings.

This far south the leaves hadn't turned yet, so that wave of visitors was still some weeks away, but the season so far had been nicely busy since spring. And now that the kids had gone back to school, Katie hadn't had to tell even one teenager that the downtown sidewalks weren't to be used for skateboarding, they *knew* that, and what was wrong with the half pipe and surrounding skateboarding area in the very nice park on the west end of town?

A normal Tuesday.

Katie said hi to a few people she knew, nodded politely to visitors she didn't, and tried to hide her own increasing tension behind a pleasant smile as she strolled along the sidewalk.

What was bugging her? It was an uneasiness inside her, but even more it was something outside her, something she . . . sensed. She caught herself looking back over her shoulder more than once, for some reason always surprised that there was nobody following her, even watching her as far as she could see, and the part of Main Street behind her looked just as normal as what lay ahead. But the feeling had been with her too long to ignore, and it was growing stronger.

It felt like something was about to happen.

Something bad.

And what was going on with her skin? Something else that had begun days ago and had intensified. It was tingling, an unpleasant sort of pins-and-needles sensation as if she had a pinched nerve somewhere. Somewhere that it would affect her whole body. Was that even possible? What—

Get off the street.

The commanding voice in her head was something she had experienced enough times in her life to obey without question. She glanced around quickly, knowing she was too far from the station and her office, too far from her Jeep, her apartment.

And there were people everywhere.

Without many options, Katie slipped through one of the few narrow alleyways to be found downtown, this one far too narrow to do anything creative with; it was just a musty-smelling passage between brick buildings, out of the sunlight and so growing mold or algae or something on the walls and the concrete floor. At the back, behind each of the buildings on either side, tall wooden fences enclosed small areas where the trash was discreetly hidden from the businesses and homes behind Main Street.

Quickly, Katie stepped inside one of the areas, knowing she wouldn't be visible unless someone on a rooftop was peering down at her. She wrinkled her nose at the faint rancid smell of garbage even though it was further hidden from sight by the big rolling trash containers, their lids closed.

She barely had time to sort of brace herself in one corner, the tall wooden fence support on two sides, before she was hit with something so powerful it literally stole her breath.

She dimly felt herself sliding down the wood, trying to do that rather than fall over the garbage cans.

Then everything went black.

TWO WEEKS PREVIOUSLY

Sam Bowers found a bottle of OTC pain relievers in his desk drawer and swallowed several with a sip of cold coffee, grimacing. He hadn't noticed that the coffee had grown cold while he'd sat there staring at the computer screen without really seeing the information it offered.

He also hadn't noticed that the bottle of pills was more than half empty.

The headache was getting worse, dammit.

It had started just a few days before, mild enough in the beginning to be no more than a minor irritant. He'd taken a few pills, and it had gone away, or so he had thought. But by the time he'd driven home after work it was back, stronger, a throbbing behind his eyes that was unusual for him.

"Maybe a migraine?" his wife, Stacey, had suggested, her expression and tone worried.

"I don't get migraines," he said, smiling at her.

"Just because you never have before doesn't mean you're immune," she reminded him. "People often develop them later in life. Sam—"

"Probably a storm system up in the mountains or something," he'd said dismissively, soothing her worry. "You know how the weather affects me."

"We usually don't get storms in October," she reminded him.

"Well, tension, then. I've been staring at a computer screen all day. Probably just eye strain. It's nothing to worry about."

She might have said something else, but he kissed her then, effectively distracting her.

"The kids," she murmured. "Supper—"

He reached to turn off two burners without even

noticing what was in the pots, then took her hand and led her out of the kitchen and toward the stairs. "The kids are next door; I saw them when I pulled into the driveway. They're very, very occupied. And, besides, the bedroom door has a lock."

"Sam!" But she was laughing, and stopped protesting.

His headache had gone away that evening, only to reappear late the next morning. And it had remained with him during the following days, held at bay usually by pain meds, but never quite gone. It sort of surged and ebbed, pushing as though against some barrier in his own head, and the surges were more painful every time.

He was still convinced it wasn't a migraine, because none of the other symptoms he'd read about (having finally broken down and Googled migraines) accompanied the pain. It was just pain, that's all. Just a sort of throbbing pain that made him feel irritable.

Except that day by day the pain grew stronger. Day by day the pain meds were less effective. Barely taking the edge off and not even that for very long. And by Monday he was waking several times in the night, trying not to disturb Stacey as he fumbled in his nightstand for the pain meds he'd stashed there.

By Tuesday afternoon, he was beginning to get worried about it. Because the pain was worse, because his irriration was edging into an uncharacteristic anger, and because sometimes when he looked around, there seemed to be a faint, red mist just at the periphery of his vision. And there was a whispery sound in his head. Not words, not that. Just a whispery sound.

Not words. He couldn't hear words.

But he swallowed the pills and waited for them to take effect, promising himself that if his headache wasn't really better by tomorrow, he'd go see the doctor. Just to put Stacey's mind at rest that nothing bad was wrong.

That was what Sam Bowers told himself.

TUESDAY, OCTOBER 7

Galen hung up the phone and leaned back in his chair to look at the others in the conference room. Along with Bishop, Miranda, and Tony, he'd been taking calls from SCU agents all over the country as well as a few currently working in other countries, and the legal pad on the desk in front of him was filled with his neat printing.

He noted the lull in what had been a very busy afternoon, with Bishop and Tony looking over notes they'd made on the calls they had taken (and, in Bishop's case, at least a few calls he'd placed), and Miranda seated across from Galen at the other desk working intently on a laptop.

"So," he said, "does anybody know what the hell's going on?" He was a big man, dark, extremely powerful, with a hard but curiously impassive expression that rarely changed. "I've talked to a dozen agents with pounding headaches who also experienced a skin-crawling sensation and saw some kind of color effect they mostly described as 'not normal.' So far, none I've talked to has felt any compulsion to leave their current assignments or vacations, and nobody mentioned Prosperity."

Absently, Tony said, "Maggie reported in from Haven that, so far, none of their operatives has been summoned. But most felt what the majority of our agents did, all the physical . . . symptoms."

Haven was the unofficial civilian counterpart to the SCU, a private organization that had originally been the brainchild of Agent Quentin Hayes, one of the first group of psychics Bishop had recruited, after an incredible case in Seattle that had involved Quentin's longtime billionaire friend John Garrett. Not a psychic himself, Garrett had married a rather amazing empath-healer involved in the same case, Maggie Barnes.

Haven had officially been co-founded by Bishop and the Garretts, the organization meant both to comple-ment the SCU and to serve as a place where psychics unable or unwilling to cope with the rigors of being full-time FBI agents trained and functioned as private investigators. It was, by design, a calmer, more peace-ful, and more laid-back organization than the FBI could ever be, offering highly flexible hours and jobs, to say nothing of a warm and welcoming home where many psychics, for the first time in their lives, didn't feel like freaks.

Sited on more than five hundred acres of fairly remote

land outside Santa Fe, New Mexico, the sprawling compound that was Haven boasted a huge central home and command center where both the Garretts and dozens of operatives could live in comfort, temporarily or for years, as some had. There were also numerous neat homes built near the main house, also for operatives and sometimes their families, plus for some of the technical and maintenance people necessary to keep such a large compound clean and operating at peak efficiency.

On the same acreage but not near the compound was a private airstrip, fully staffed, with a hangar large enough to house the three company jets plus two helicopters.

Haven had grown just as the SCU had, now boasting dozens of operatives trained and working cases all over the country, and dozens more learning about their own abilities as well as how to be effective investigators. Some made their home base in different cities across the map, while others lived or spent most of their off-duty time at the Haven compound.

John Garrett's wealth and brilliant business mind kept Haven running, practically speaking, but it was Maggie Garrett, with her deep empathy and compassion, and her unique ability to heal wounds of the mind and soul as well as those of the body, who was without question the heart of Haven.

"Did she say any of their people experienced nothing?" Bishop asked, looking up from his notes.

Tony nodded. "Yeah, five so far. One operative is, like Kendra, pregnant. The other four are brand-new, not yet trained, and tested low on our scale in terms of how strong their abilities are."

Slowly, Bishop said, "So far, with the exception of Hollis and Reese, all of those summoned are not members of the SCU."

"And that means?" There was a frown in Galen's voice, if not on his impassive face. He had experienced all the symptoms of something extraordinary, as most of the unit had, but had not felt anything beyond those, and certainly not anyone or anything calling him to go to Prosperity.

And he hadn't needed to tell anyone in the room that being contacted in such a way, with all his walls up and likely stronger than they had ever been in his life, had disturbed him more than it had most of the other agents. He was a guarded man by nature, and after a fairly recent case in which his mind had been touched and even used without his awareness, he was extremely wary of anything similar happening again.

"At a guess, it could mean that whatever happens in Prosperity won't be the sort of situation that drives law enforcement to invite us in officially," Bishop replied.

"So no actual crime?"

"Could be. Or crimes that seem normal, crimes the locals believe they should be able to solve."

"You and Miranda didn't see anything that could answer at least that question?" Despite the rather impatient words, his tone could best be described as deceptively mild. Not that anyone in the room was deceived.

Bishop shook his head. "No, we saw nothing specific as far as actual events are concerned."

"Then what did you see?" An edge had crept in.

Tony looked at Galen in faint surprise but didn't comment or question the other agent's uncharacteristic insistence. He just looked at Bishop and waited, curious.

"Nothing specific," Bishop repeated, calm. "Except . . . evil. A doorway we have to keep closed. And seal."

"A door someone or something is trying to open?" Galen asked.

"So it seems."

"But not an enemy we know."

"Not one we can put a name to. But likely a negative force we've encountered before."

"Want to explain that?" Galen invited.

"At this point, all I know is what I feel, what Miranda and I felt during that vision. We've destroyed countless evil killers over the years. But only a handful were truly destroyed in a real sense, their negative energy transformed and dispersed."

"So they exist. Their evil still exists."

"As I said, it's nothing we can point to specifically. More an emotional . . . certainty."

"That somebody's out to get even? Maybe a lot of somebodys?"

"It's what we feel, Galen. That we . . . received . . . emotions is rare enough. The power of these . . . Whatever this enemy is, it's something very old and very dark. And very determined. It's pressing against the other side of that door. Trying to force it open."

"To get at us?"

Bishop glanced at his wife. "That's the way it feels."

"But?

It was Miranda who answered that, her voice very steady. "What we felt was something gleeful. Playful. Destroying us may be the endgame, but this . . . thing . . . intends to have fun. To manipulate people. To hurt people in ways most sane minds can't even imagine."

Tony muttered, "No wonder you both looked so shook."

Galen said, "But not a crime? Not a killer?"

"It's not what we saw, Galen." Bishop remained calm—and was uncharacteristically willing to talk about that vision; normally he and Miranda said as little as possible, wary of doing anything that could make a bad situation worse. "No specifics, just emotions. But that doesn't mean it won't happen. In fact, it's very likely to happen. If something dark, maybe negative energy, begins to exert an influence over the people in Prosperity, anything could happen."

"Hell," Tony murmured, "*everything* could happen."

Bishop didn't appear to find that statement overly dramatic. "Yeah, everything could. Including horrific crimes. We've seen monsters shaped like human beings. We've seen negative energy affect people and events, causing death and chaos. We've seen men able to manipulate negative energy who thought they were gods." That last seemed to be very deliberate, and Bishop kept his gaze steadily on Galen.

After a moment, without looking away, Galen said, "I have to be there."

"You weren't summoned."

"Doesn't matter. I have to be there."

"Why?" Bishop asked simply.

Entirely unwilling and not trying to hide it, Galen said, "It's something I feel."

Almost immediately, Bishop nodded. "Okay. Hope you brought your go bag."

"I did."

Bishop exchanged glances with his wife, who had looked up from her laptop to silently observe. She had been right; Galen was ready to come off official leave and rejoin the unit.

Do you think he's really ready?

He obviously believes he is. We have to respect that, beloved.

Yes . . .

Out loud, Miranda merely said, "So far, I'm not finding anything on Prosperity except chamber of commerce stuff. Pretty little town with much to recommend it to passing tourists. No crime to speak of, so far, at least. Popular sheriff, well-trained deputies, well-funded police, fire, and other emergency services. They have a very good small hospital with quite a lot of state-of-the-art equipment and first-class doctors. A weekly newspaper still in print, with the online version updated daily. A radio station, but no local TV station."

Galen asked, "Is anything unusual happening yet?"

"If it is, it's being kept quiet. No law enforcement alerts, nothing unusual from the radio station, and the closest TV stations are all wrapped up in politics and their own local stories, including the usual sort of local crimes."

Tony said, "We probably should have someone monitor social media."

"We already have someone doing that at the mountain house," Bishop said.

Though he hadn't been there very many times, Tony was fairly certain that Bishop kept either permanent or semipermanent technical and maintenance people onsite at the mountain house, which was a remote but huge complex, dug into the mountain so that it was even more vast than it appeared, with an impressive command center that nonetheless was also a home that could probably house more than a couple dozen people indefinitely and in comfort. And though he'd never heard anyone say, he was also fairly certain that the house was privately owned by Bishop and Miranda, and that whatever went on there was not an official part of FBI functions.

He hadn't asked before and didn't ask now.

"What else are they doing?" Galen asked.

With a faint smile, Bishop said, "Working on official identity credentials for the six non-SCU people summoned."

"Credentials?"

"They'll officially be private investigators with Haven. On the books if anybody wants to check."

Tony murmured, "All six? Add in Hollis, Reese, and Galen, and that's nine investigators descending on a town that hasn't asked for help. Yet."

But Galen was clearly thinking along different lines. "I guess not even you could make them FBI agents with a wave of your hand." It wasn't a disrespectful tone, exactly, just a Galen tone.

Bishop's faint smile remained. "No?"

Galen eyed him, a slight frown pulling his brows together.

Miranda intervened to say calmly, "We've set most everything in motion, pretty much all we can do from here. I say we get to the jet, fly up to Vermont to pick up Olivia Castle, then head for the mountain house tonight."

Tony asked, "Do we pick up anyone else along the way?"

Bishop looked at him, clearly undisturbed by Galen's continued frowning stare. "No. Reno Bellman has already headed west in the other jet to pick up Dalton Davenport, Logan Alexander, and Sully Maitland. I doubt they'll reach the mountain house before late tomorrow.

"I spoke to Victoria Stark; she was already heading north, on the road leaving New Orleans. She'll probably be at the airstrip near the mountain house by the time we land."

Tony lifted an eyebrow. "Determined, stubborn, independent, or all of the above?"

"All of the above." Before Tony could ask anything else, Bishop said, "We need you to stay here at Quantico, Tony. Quentin and Diana are on their way in. Isabel and Rafe. Possibly others as they wind up their investigations. Depending on how long this takes."

"And what're we supposed to do here?" Tony asked.

Bishop's reply sobered him a lot more than he cared to admit.

"You'll coordinate with us at the mountain house to begin forming a second line of defense. In case those summoned aren't able to . . . hold the line."

TUESDAY, OCTOBER 7

It was still fall even in Kodiak, Alaska, but a chilly one, and the temperature had been dropping all day. Still, when Dalton Davenport wrenched open the front door of his small cottage in response to an imperative fist pounding on the wood, his breath was only slightly visible in the low light of the front porch fixture. It was dark, it was getting late, and Dalton was very clearly in no mood for visitors.

Even a visitor he knew. Maybe especially a visitor he knew.

"What the fuck are you doing here?" he snapped.

"Hello to you too, Dalton." Serenely undisturbed by the greeting, Reno Bellman strolled in, pretty much forcing him to give way or be touched. And he hated to be touched. He all but slammed the door behind her and followed her into the small but comfortable den, whose best feature was a large picture window that overlooked the beautiful harbor far below, not much of which was visible currently except a number of twinkling lights.

Reno was a tall, willowy woman with shoulder-length black hair and exotic green eyes. Not conventionally beautiful, but completely unforgettable.

Dalton hadn't seen her in two years.

"Well, if you're going to get away from people, at least you found a nice view," she commented, standing with her hands in the pockets of her light jacket as she faced the picture window. "At least, I assume the view would be nice if we could see it. The harbor, I think."

"How did you find me?" he asked roughly.

"I found you two months after you bolted from Chicago."

"I didn't—"

"It wasn't long after that last conversation in person with Bishop, as I recall. It apparently occurred to you that he was not about to give up on you. Maybe it even occurred to you that I wasn't going to give up on you. So you bolted without a word. Or even a note left on the pillow." Her voice remained serene. "For future reference, Dalton, should you ever need it, going to bed with a man and waking up without even a note is rough on a woman with even the strongest ego, especially when her bedmate flees the city."

He couldn't see her face. "Reno—"

"You bolted. To Alaska, of all places. You do realize he knows exactly where you are, I hope? Those sat phones he gave us contain nice FBI-strength GPS trackers. And no matter how much you might want him to butt out of your life, you hang on to that phone like we all do. Just in case."

"Never mind Bishop. Reno, what are you doing here?"

No expletives, she noted. Maybe he was mellowing. "Oh, just visiting."

"Fuck that. You're here for a reason and I damned well want to know what it is."

Or maybe not.

She swung around to face him, a challenge in the tilt of her head. "Tell me you didn't experience something very strange earlier today, and I'll get back on that damned floatplane and be on my way back to the mainland and the far more comfortable jet waiting there for me."

He scowled at her.

Reno decided he hadn't changed much in two years, at least not physically. He was still too thin for his height of just under six feet, though his wide shoulders and strong bones made that fact less obvious than it might have been. His thick brown hair needed cutting as usual, and his hazel eyes, which still changed color according to his mood, were dark and angry under slash-straight, frowning eyebrows.

"Well?" she prompted.

"I'm not going anywhere," he snapped.

She nodded. "Ah. So you did get the summons. Just guessing, but I'd say you got slammed by the worst headache of your life, saw some very weird and very bright colors, and heard voices or whispers, a whole lot of them, telling you that you have to go to Prosperity."

"I," he repeated grimly, "am not going anywhere."

Pulling one hand from her pocket, Reno gestured with a thumb over one shoulder to a small desk in a corner of the den. "And that's not a map of the south-eastern US of A spread out on your desk. I take it you found Prosperity? A hitherto peaceful little mountain town in North Carolina?"

If an already murderous glare could get worse, his did.

Reno wondered idly why she'd never been afraid of him. He was a very dangerous man, after all, far more so than even Bishop knew. Or, at least, she thought so. "Come on, Dalton, if you were curious enough to look for Prosperity, then you're curious enough to at least wonder what it's all about."

For several moments it appeared he was too angry and determined not to care to give in, but then he winced and reached up to rub his left temple briefly, and some of the rage drained away, leaving his eyes lighter but his face weary. "I don't want to go," he muttered.

"Still no luck with the shield, huh?" Reno didn't have much of one herself, but she knew both that she was in the rather amazingly small percentage of people he couldn't read, and that her own abilities made her a pure receiver, so she didn't broadcast to telepaths anyway.

They were likely the only reasons she had been able to get closer to him than anyone else had. Once upon a time.

She wondered, as she had wondered silently more than once, if he even realized that the sheer raw power of his abilities, unshielded, made any sensitive person anywhere near him completely aware of the hot fury of his constant wordless rage. She doubted it, even though he had spent time with empaths and telepaths who could certainly have explained it to him.

Being a pure receiver herself, she could most certainly have explained it to him. Which might have been another reason he had bolted from Chicago.

"No," he said finally. "No luck building a shield." He stepped past her, automatically keeping an obvious distance between them that might have discouraged most women, and sank down in what looked like a comfortable leather chair at right angles to a long leather sofa.

She moved far enough to sit down on the end of the sofa nearest his chair, respecting his personal space and knowing better than to wait for an invitation. "Bishop says it's the sort of thing that tends to happen in the field," she reminded him.

"I know what Bishop says," he snapped, but more quietly.

"Then why not try it," she said practically. "Trying to do the thing on your own hasn't worked. Obviously. Being a hermit hasn't done anything except make you more angry and, if possible, more ill-mannered. What've you got to lose?"

"My mind," he said grimly. "What's left of it, anyway."

Reno considered briefly, then said, "Well, if my

vision was accurate, and they mostly are, you may not have to worry about that much longer." She stopped there and waited. Patiently.

Dalton glared at her again, clearly unwilling to ask. But she merely smiled and waited. Patiently. And finally he swore at her and added, "You are the most maddening woman I've ever known."

"Yeah, I'd be flattered by that except I know most of the women you've known have been doctors and nurses and therapists."

He stiffened.

Reno held his angry gaze, smiling faintly now. "It is what it is, Dalton. We've all done time on shrinks' couches, in clinics, even in jail and locked up in other . . . facilities . . . occasionally. Most of us have been on too many meds and forced into way too many *programs* of one kind or another designed to fix what mainstream doctors insist is broken. You had it rougher than most on that score, and for longer than most, but a lot of psychics went through a dozen different kinds of hell that make yours look like a party. Stop being so touchy. Get over it."

Dalton smiled, though few would have recognized the expression. "You were always the psychic in the center, weren't you, Reno? You and your collection of freaks."

With a chuckle, she said, "As a general rule, I like psychics better than the so-called normal people. So, yeah, I keep in touch with a few other freaks like us."

"I'm surprised you didn't join that FBI unit of Bishop's."

"Somebody had to stay out here in the world and keep an eye on the freaks who wouldn't or couldn't be cops."

Dalton shifted slightly in his chair and frowned. "All right, you can stop using that word."

"What, *freaks*? Thought it was your preferred label for us." Her faint smile remained.

"I don't like labels," he snapped.

"Doesn't matter what you like. The world's full of them. Something else that is what it is." Changing subjects smoothly, she said, "I don't see any little womanly touches about the place. Still determined to go it solo?"

An indefinable emotion passed over his angry face and was gone. "Some people should be alone. You know that."

"I know you believe that. I should think you've scared away most women you've encountered here without much effort whether you could read them or not," she said in an agreeable tone. "Just the way you did in Chicago. But I don't scare so easily."

"No?"

"No. Enough apocalyptic visions tend to put all kinds of other things into their proper perspective."

His frown deepened. "That's twice you've hinted something bad is coming. Either explain it or cut it out."

"I doubt I have to explain much. You were never a

stupid man, Dalton—about anything except people, at least—so I'm sure you've figured out for yourself that the threat we were warned about is something way, way beyond bad."

His mouth tightened. "So what if it is. I plan to stay here and mind my own business, and if you're as smart as you think you are you'll do the same thing."

"Stay here?"

Dalton glared at her.

With a soft laugh, Reno shook her head. "Such an angry man. That hasn't changed. Well, to be honest, neither have I. Much. Except that I've decided I sort of like this world the way it is, flaws and all. Not really ready for an apocalypse of any kind, not if there's a chance we can stop it."

"We?"

"Mmm. We weren't the only ones summoned. I understand there are six of us outside Bishop's unit plus two SCU agents who were called and one more coming along for reasons of his own. We should make up a highly unusual team, to say the least. I left Chicago earlier today on the jet. Stopped briefly in Montana to pick up Sully Maitland. I'm sure you remember him. He and the jet are here waiting on the mainland. After we leave Alaska, we fly down to San Francisco to pick up Logan Alexander, who you also remember, and then head cross-country to North Carolina to meet up with the rest."

He was still frowning. "Long trip."

"Yeah, even if I manage a nap on the leg back, jet lag

doesn't begin to describe the way I'll feel by the time we finally get to North Carolina."

"To Prosperity?"

"Eventually. First, the plan is to gather at what Bishop describes as our command center not very far from Prosperity."

"That place of his in the mountains?"

"I believe so. I'm told there'll be technical people staying there for the duration, plus Bishop and Miranda, standing ready to support our efforts in any and every way they can. So we can basically call on FBI resources plus just about anything else in order to do whatever we have to do."

"Reno—"

"And at Quantico, they're already forming up a second line of defense. In case we fail." She got to her feet. "Not that I mean to fail, and I doubt anyone else does. But you never know, after all. It'll be the first team effort for us, so we'll have to wait and see. Go pack a bag, Dalton. We need to get going."

"I'm not coming."

"Of course you're coming."

"No."

"No?"

"You heard me. No."

Reno was not Bishop's "perfect psychic," which meant she could not control her abilities a hundred percent of the time. But like all psychics she had at least one quality unique to her: Pulling someone else into a vision with her was one of those unique qualities.

Another was that she could, at least for a relatively short while afterward, remain connected to one of her visions.

And experience it a second time.

Without warning, she leaned over and grasped Dalton's wrist. And pulled him into that seared and blasted hell with her.

FOUR

Victoria Stark leaned back against the front of her white Chevy Cruze and watched as excellent artificial lighting held back the night and allowed her to see the sleek private jet touch down on the single long runway of this small private airstrip. She wondered idly who the airstrip belonged to. There was, as far as she could tell, no name posted anywhere; Bishop had given her turn-by-turn directions from the nearest main highway but hadn't referred to her destination as anything other than "the airstrip."

It was a remote place in a small and otherwise apparently deserted valley in the Appalachians, but very well kept, with a staffed office; a control tower that, though small, was clearly adequate and well staffed as well; and a small group of quiet but efficient people who took care of whatever traffic landed here.

Two somewhat unusual-looking large green helicopters had only a half hour before been towed from the big hangar, gleaming and obviously ready to go . . . wherever. And several people stood ready to guide the jet to its place near the hangar and the choppers, should it need guidance.

Since she'd arrived just before dark some hours ago, Victoria had gotten the chance to explore and to observe, an opportunity she hadn't had on her single prior visit here years before.

She had already eyed with faint interest the simultaneous arrival of a big black SUV that practically screamed *federal vehicle*, a more nondescript Jeep, a Bronco, and a very nice but not new light-colored BMW X5 SUV. All were parked out to the side of the small office that adjoined the hangar, not far from where she waited with her own car. The drivers had parked the vehicles, apparently leaving the keys inside, and then had all gotten into another black SUV and driven away, without saying anything to anyone as far as Victoria had been able to see.

Curiouser and curiouser.

Coffee had been offered when she'd arrived, and it was gratefully accepted; the temperature at this altitude had already been dropping, promising a bracingly chilly October evening. Especially to someone who had come from the far warmer city of New Orleans.

She had also been invited to wait inside the small office section, where there was a warm, comfortable if small lounge area with newspapers, magazines, and a flat-screen offering, a woman named Karen had told her pleasantly, satellite channels, and a recliner comfortable enough for a nap.

Instead, refusing the offer with polite thanks, Victoria had wandered around on foot for a while, drinking her coffee and stretching her legs after the long trip north. Not thinking about why she was here, but distracting her mind with far more trivial things. About the airstrip. The people who had delivered vehicles so silently and efficiently, and those who clearly worked here in other capacities in what appeared to be a 24/7, year-round operation. All were pleasant, smiling—and not disposed to talk overmuch. Were they feds? She didn't know. Maybe only technical support? Private security? She hadn't seen a sign of anyone being armed, and nobody had objected to her wandering, either before or after darkness had fallen.

She found that interesting.

Victoria had entered the office area only once more, for a second cardboard cup of coffee that she carried back outside. That plus the jacket she'd gotten from her car left her warm enough to remain outside. And allowed her to witness the arrival of at least part of the group gathering here, probably for no more than a few minutes before they'd be choppered up to the mountain house.

The jet taxied to within about twenty yards from the hangar, closer to her at this end of the structure, and its roar quieted and then dropped off even more to a low rumble as men carrying blocks hurried to place them in front of and behind the wheels.

Victoria watched as the jet's door opened, the stairs that were part of the door let down with it. She wasn't very surprised when Bishop was first off the plane, heading immediately toward her. His lithe, almost feline grace and deceptively easy stride marked him as an athletic man very comfortable in his own skin, and Victoria thought every time she saw him that he was physically more powerful than he looked and that he wielded a great deal more of other kinds of power than even the massive government organization to which he belonged could boast.

He could, she believed, be a very dangerous man.

He was most certainly the first man she would turn to in times of trouble. Any kind of trouble.

Beating him to the punch, she said as he reached her, "I knew you'd get us eventually. I made a bet with Sully. He owes me a hundred bucks."

"He didn't think I'd get you?"

"Not in less than five years. I guessed within three. So I win."

Bishop smiled faintly. "How have you been, Victoria?"

"Fine," she said mildly. "Until this morning. Still wondering if you had anything to do with that, by the way."

"Not one of my abilities," he said, equally mild. "If I could summon psychics from thousands of miles away, I think I would have known about it before now."

"Then who—or what—did?"

"That is the question, isn't it? One of them, at least. Are you ready to go up to the house?"

"Yeah. Bag's in the backseat. Do I lock up the car?"

"Not unless you want to. Excuse me for a minute." He headed toward the office end of the building, apparently to make or finalize arrangements, and Victoria remained where she was, watching others disembark from the jet, only two carrying bags like her duffel.

She knew them, to varying degrees. Except the one bringing up the rear, carrying three bags in his large hands. He was very large all over, an obviously powerful man who looked like he worked out hard for a living and then tossed around granite boulders for fun. Big granite boulders.

Miranda reached her first; she was carrying a single bag. "Hey, Victoria."

"Miranda. Who's the big guy?"

"I forgot you hadn't met Galen. He's SCU."

Victoria glanced past her to look at the big man again. "He doesn't look much like a healer," she said. She had always been interested in names and their meanings and origins.

"You'd be surprised," Miranda murmured. "If we're leaving as quickly as I believe we are, I'll introduce you up at the house."

"Yeah, I thought Bishop wasn't wasting any time, at least not getting us to Base." Then she looked past Miranda again, this time at the other woman she definitely recognized. "Hey, Olivia."

"Hey, Tory." The only person Victoria allowed to get away with the diminutive of her name, Olivia was, at twenty-eight, two years older than Victoria, but at five-foot-nothing and petite, with copper hair that framed her heart-shaped face in a simple shoulder-length cut, large blue eyes holding a faintly startled expression, plus a childlike voice, Olivia had always seemed the younger of the two.

An indignant feline howl from the carrier she held in one hand drew Victoria's attention, and her smile widened. "I can tell Rex still hates to travel."

"He made a horrible fuss on the jet until Bishop talked to him," Olivia confessed. "Then he settled down for the rest of the flight, I think. But he wants out, and I think he saw the choppers. He hates them even worse than planes." She brushed a strand of copper hair away from her face with a small, fragile hand, an unconscious sigh escaping her.

"Still the headaches?" Victoria asked with genuine sympathy, noting that the other woman's pretty face was unusually pale even for her, and that the big eyes were darkened.

"Yeah. And since this morning worse than usual. Miranda gave me a couple of pills when the jet picked me up in Vermont, and they knocked me out for most of the flight so I got some rest, but the pain was back when I woke up." There was nothing of complaint in her childlike voice, merely a matter-of-fact acceptance of something she lived with virtually every day of her life.

Victoria looked at Miranda. "Are we getting an actual healer to go along with us on this jaunt? I'm thinking we'll need one, and not just to help Olivia and Sully with their headaches."

"We're getting the best in the unit, but Hollis and Reese won't get here until sometime tomorrow."

"Hollis Templeton?"

Miranda nodded.

Victoria let out a low whistle. "Heard of her. A lot. And some pretty wild stuff even for us. According to the psychic grapevine, there isn't much she *can't* do."

"There are always limits, but it's fair to say Hollis is still exploring hers, so we aren't yet sure of which abilities she'll end up with, or how strong they'll ultimately become. In the meantime, we're certainly hoping she can help with Olivia's and Sully's headaches—and any other painful problems that might come along."

Olivia set Rex's carrier down on the ground, ignoring the profane feline muttering from inside it, and said, "How come everybody else hears stuff on the psychic grapevine? And how do you, Tory? Telepathy's still not your thing, right?"

"Right. No more than it's yours." Victoria smiled. "But this grapevine is the real sort with people— psychics—talking out loud and otherwise communicating via traditional channels. Usually on the phone. And there's e-mail, at least for those of us who don't short out electronics. Reno keeps in touch."

Olivia nodded. "Oh, *that* grapevine. She keeps in touch with me too. But I don't remember her mentioning anybody named Hollis."

Victoria wasn't surprised. Olivia was very nearly as fragile as she looked, in more ways than one, and no doubt Reno's checking in with her had been more about making sure Olivia was all right than it was about passing on information.

Victoria had always believed that Reno was a born

caretaker, though she didn't look it and seldom sounded it. It was also interesting that her first name, more commonly given to a Latin-American male child, meant "to rise again." *Like a phoenix.* Except that a phoenix rose from the ashes of its own destruction, and as far as Victoria knew, Reno had never come close to being destroyed.

Yet, at least.

She hunched her shoulders against the chill she told herself was only the October night.

Miranda was saying easily, "Things tend to happen quickly with Hollis, especially during investigations, so it's sometimes hard to keep score. But you'll be meeting her and Reese tomorrow."

Victoria nodded, then said curiously, "I was wondering about Dalton. Did he call in?"

"No."

"But he was summoned?"

Miranda nodded, smiling faintly.

Victoria looked at her for a moment, and then laughed. "Don't tell me. You sent Reno to fetch him?"

"Do you know anybody else who could take Dalton somewhere he doesn't want to be?"

"No," Victoria said, and laughed again. "Not even Bishop."

TUESDAY EVENING, OCTOBER 7

Leslie Gardner slipped from the bed, not trying to be particularly quiet since Ed was snoring and always slept like the dead anyway. His was a curiously gentle, rhythmic snore, and she had teased him their entire married life about it. Her own personal sound machine, lulling her to sleep.

At least, it always had.

They'd been in bed by a bit after eleven, as usual after a busy weekday, and as usual he fell asleep right away.

But not Leslie. Not even her own personal sound machine helped much lately.

Her head was pounding so hard she had to feel her way to the bathroom, and when she got there and eased the door closed, she turned on only the light in the shower, dim behind its curtain.

Even that hurt her eyes.

She didn't know what time it was except that it was late—and she had to be up early to fix the kids' lunches and make breakfast. She needed her sleep. The supposed painkillers she'd taken hardly two hours before had not even taken the edge off the pain. She wanted to take more, but the bottle was empty.

Her head had been hurting on and off for days.

Note to self: Buy something stronger tomorrow.

There was a small, padded bench between the shower and the vanity, and Leslie sat there for what seemed like a long time, her elbows on her knees and both hands pressed to the sides of her head. It *hurt*.

It hurt, and somewhere inside that throbbing pain, inside her aching brain, she could have sworn she heard, very faintly, two words whispered. That was all. Just two words.

But everything in her shied away from listening to those words, even acknowledging what they were, even though the silent battle made her head hurt more. Trying not to moan with the pain, but also trying to hold back those awful words, to pretend she didn't hear them, that everything was normal.

It was just a headache.

She talked to herself aloud, her voice soft.

"I have to sleep. I have to get back into bed with Ed and sleep. Tomorrow, things will be better. Tomorrow, things will be fine. My head won't hurt anymore. The light won't bother me anymore. I won't hear impossible words. And I won't . . . I won't see . . . anything strange. Everything will be back to normal. I'm sure."

She used the vanity to help lever herself upright, and clung to it for long minutes because she felt dizzy and weak. She splashed cold water on her face and dried it with a towel, resisting until that moment any glance into the mirror above the sink.

In the dim light she saw her face, pale but her own. Eyes huge and oddly . . . blurry. Maybe because of the words in her head, the words she refused to hear.

Maybe that.

Or maybe it was something else.

She stared at herself for a long minute, then looked past her left shoulder.

It was her shadow on the light-colored wall. Just that, just her shadow. Except that it had a funny red tint. That was one thing that was wrong.

The other thing that was wrong was that she shouldn't have had a shadow just there, with the dim light in the shower. It was on the wrong side. And, besides, she shouldn't have had a shadow at all. Not like that. Not all . . . distorted.

Not a monster shadow.

Feeling a little sick and a lot shaken, Leslie Gardner slipped back into bed beside her snoring husband, very carefully not looking to see if the shadow had followed her even here into the dark.

WEDNESDAY, OCTOBER 8

In the bedroom of a small but surprisingly cozy cottage on an all-but-deserted island in the Bahamas, Reese DeMarco woke to find himself alone. He woke early out of long habit, but not this early, not without reason.

The reason this time was the empty place beside him.

It was still dark outside, and the muffled sounds of the ocean told him it was approaching high tide only a dozen or so yards from the cottage. There was no light in the bedroom, but when he looked at the nearly closed door, he could see a light coming from the living space beyond.

He got out of bed and found a pair of sweatpants to pull on, then went out to the living room to find what he expected to find. The scent of coffee was sharp in the morning air, a glance toward the compact kitchenette showing him the coffeemaker with a pot already half empty.

Hollis was on the couch, the big coffee table before her covered with papers and her open laptop, which was plugged into a wall outlet. A mostly empty coffee cup sat on the end table beside the couch. She was barefoot and bare-legged, and wearing nothing but a man's white shirt that made her look, even with her recent golden tan and the few pounds he'd managed, with his cooking, to add to her slender frame, deceptively fragile.

"Can't sleep?" he asked, leaning on the back of the couch slightly to one side of her.

"I slept. As long as I could. Sorry if I woke you." She leaned back and looked up at him with a faint smile. And returned his deep and not-at-all-brief kiss with matching fire.

It was one of the things they had discovered for themselves during the weeks away from the job and other people. A passion for each other of rather astonishing ferocity, something that was still a new aspect of their partnership but one very much treasured even more for the long and difficult path that had brought them here, separately and together. And something that had most certainly deepened their already strong connection to each other.

That last fact had also created a few surprises for them as yet untested in the field.

"Don't start something," she murmured when she could.

"Why not? We have a few hours of vacation left."

"Yeah, but right now something about this summoning business is bugging me. And you know how I get when something's bugging me."

He knew.

Looking at the coffee table, he noted a ruler and a red marker as well as a couple of pencils and pens and a legal pad, supplies she generally carried in her laptop case, and realized for the first time what most of the papers spread out on the table were. "We're on an island that's barely inhabited, and you found a map of the southeastern US?"

Turning her attention back to the map, Hollis said absently, "It's amazing what you can find if you need it."

"Are you conjuring things out of thin air now?"

She frowned at him.

"Just asking."

"No, I haven't sprouted a new ability," she said dryly. "At least not one that you don't know about. I just noticed something on the flight over here that my pilot obviously missed."

"I had other things on my mind," he said apologetically. "What did I miss?"

"A whole bunch of rolled-up maps behind our seats in the chopper. So I went and looked. And found these."

He eyed her. "You went out there in the middle of the night wearing nothing but my shirt?" The helicopter sat waiting for them in a clearing some little distance from their cottage.

"Barely inhabited island," she reminded him.

"Uh-huh. But inhabited. You realize that our landlady's teenage son is fascinated by you?" A fact he had noted during the occasions when they'd been out on the beach or zipping around on Jet-Skis or scuba diving in the incredibly clear water. When Hollis's brief swimsuit had shown off much more of her than her normal casual clothing.

Difficult to miss a teenage boy wearing a puppy-dog look of extreme yearning and devotion, even at a distance as he lurked, apparently believing himself hidden. Even more difficult for a powerful telepath to miss the tangled adolescent thoughts practically catapulted their way.

There were only three major structures on their small island: their cottage, a currently empty cottage a couple hundred yards away from theirs, and a much larger building at the other end of the island that served as an inn during the winter months, which were all owned by their widowed landlady, who lived there with her sixteen-year-old son and a small staff of employees who kept the inn and cottages in good order.

Hollis said, "He's fascinated by the chopper. I caught a glimpse of him lurking in the bushes while I was digging around for the maps."

"In the middle of the night?"

"It's nearly dawn. Sun'll be up soon. I guess he gets up early."

DeMarco sighed.

She grinned at him.

"You are a sadistic woman," he told her.

"It'll keep you on your toes," she said, not at all apologetically. Then added, "Come look at this, will you?"

He came around the couch to sit beside her, looking obediently at the big map. The legal pad had been pushed to the side, its top sheet at least covered with Hollis's neat, flowing script in what appeared to be a list, but he leaned forward, elbows on his knees, and focused his attention on the map.

There were numerous small, red circles grouped in a rather small area of the southeast, most in the southern Appalachians. And most of the markings clearly indicated towns.

DeMarco studied them for a moment, then straightened to look at his partner. "The locations of past cases?"

"Yeah. It occurred to me that a disproportionate number of cases these last years have taken place in the southeast. Mostly in little mountain towns, but some as far south as Atlanta and as far east as the coast."

He glanced at her laptop, which was clearly in sleep mode, pushed aside as the legal pad was. Another man might have asked her why she had felt compelled to not only bring along her work laptop on what was supposed to be a completely carefree vacation, but also to actually work.

Reese DeMarco was not another man.

So all he said was, "You keep notes of all the cases the unit works?"

"Nothing classified or even confidential," she assured him. "Just brief notes I make for myself. Started it with the first case I worked, then later on backtracked to study earlier cases and noted those too. And all the ones since, of course. Locations, who was on the team, the bare outlines of crimes, victims, monsters and whether we caught or destroyed them. And how, if I thought it mattered."

He nodded. "Okay. And?"

"Well, I know we seldom do geographic profiles of the cases we work in these areas, mostly because it would be fairly useless in such small towns. And I don't *think* we've ever done a geographic profile of the whole southeast."

"Probably not," he agreed.

"I didn't really know what I was looking for when I got started," she confessed with a slight frown. "Something was bugging me and I couldn't ignore it. So . . . I just kept marking the places where we'd had cases. All those little towns, the few times all the action took place outside little towns, like the church and that really weird case-that-wasn't with Luther and Callie's location up in the mountains and us at Alexander House."

DeMarco nodded.

"I marked everything I could find in my case notes, plus a couple of investigations I knew about but in which the SCU was never officially involved because the unit didn't *officially* exist at the time—yet Bishop was there, and he got involved. Like that town in North Carolina where his cousin Cassie helped catch a nasty killer, and even Atlanta, where Bishop helped his college friend look for his missing fiancée."

"News to me," DeMarco observed. "One of these days you'll have to tell me those stories."

"As much as I know, sure. I only found out because I'm nosy and kept asking questions."

He smiled slightly, his normally rather coldly handsome face both relaxed and softened in a way that would have startled nearly everyone who knew him, but said only, "So you marked all these places in the southeast where . . . paranormal things involving various SCU agents and Haven operatives happened. And?"

She frowned at the map. "There are probably a dozen different ways to do this, but this is the one I picked." She reached for a sheet of clear plastic he hadn't noticed underneath the coffee table, on which were drawn several straight lines in red.

"Where on earth did you find that? Not in the chopper?"

"No." Hollis looked a little guilty. "I took it out of the frame of that print over there." She nodded toward a suitably tropical print hanging on the wall between two narrow bookcases on the other side of the living room. "I wouldn't have if it were glass, but . . . Anyway, we might want to slip Mrs. Clairmont a little bonus so she can replace this sheet of plastic."

"I doubt she'll even notice," DeMarco said.

"Yeah, but we know I took it," Hollis said absently as she slid the plastic over the map and placed it carefully.

He smiled again, but waited until she had the plastic in place and then leaned forward again to study the result for several moments. "Huh."

"Like I said, probably a dozen different ways to draw lines from one place to another and make some sort of pattern. But this is the one that felt right to me."

She had drawn, in essence, an asterisk, or perhaps more accurately a kind of sunburst, with straight lines of differing lengths beginning at a marked location on the outer edge of the large cluster and ending at the opposite outer edge, both the starting point and the end point of each line a location of paranormal events, with several others along the line itself.

Every single case she had noted fell along one of the precisely straight lines she had drawn.

"Look at what's at the center," she said steadily.

DeMarco looked. "Damn. Prosperity."

"Yeah. Prosperity. It looks like it's been at the center of some very bad things for a long time. The very quiet, very peaceful center. Until now."

After a moment, DeMarco said, "By the time we

finish packing and load the chopper, the sun should be up and Mrs. Clairmont as well, so we can turn in the keys. I think we should head for the mountain house ASAP."

"I think you're right," Hollis said.

FIVE

Sheriff Jackson Archer studied what appeared to be the scene of a suicide, holding on to professional detachment as best he could. He was a good cop and a popular sheriff. And though he had spent a few years with the Charlotte police in order to acquire the sort of experience a small, ordinarily peaceful mountain town rarely offered and even more rarely needed, the truth was that Prosperity had been exceptionally peaceful since he'd taken office, and he suspected he'd gotten used to that.

So professional detachment was difficult.

Not that any cop could with complete detachment view a scene in which a man had blown most of his head off.

"Why a shotgun?" his chief deputy Katie Cole asked, her own detachment having long since departed; her voice shook more than a little, and her face was paper-white. That shock looked odd on her, unfamiliar, at least to Archer, because he'd really never seen her anything but calm, professional, and both courteous and pleasant enough to hide the steel inside her from all but those who knew her well.

He had taken some flak for hiring an "outsider" to be his chief deputy rather than promoting from within, but Katie had a background in law enforcement, and both her friendly, easy manner and her solid training—sharpshooter proficiency on the shooting range and skilled physical workouts in the gym that had pushed other, larger deputies to their limits—had mostly quieted the early rumblings in his department. Plus, experience in working with her day to day had convinced even the most jealous of her hiring and rank that she was indeed the best qualified for the job of chief deputy.

Though those same people might have been forgiven for revising their impressions now.

Because right now, her pale face caused her dark blond hair, worn in a casual ponytail that made her look far younger than thirty-two, appear even darker, and her normally sharp hazel eyes were dark and disturbed. She looked a little shocked, a little frightened, and more than a little unsure of what to do next.

He didn't blame her for that. Any of that.

"Why a shotgun?" she repeated when the silence had lengthened.

"Beats the hell out of me," Archer responded grimly.

From her position several feet farther from the body than the sheriff's, Katie said with a stab at professionalism if not detachment, "I can see with those long arms of his he could easily reach the trigger even with the end of the barrel up under his chin like that, and it's obvious he did from his position, but why use a shotgun when he owns several other guns?"

"Guess he wanted to make sure he got the job done."

Katie eyed her superior, in part because it was a far less stomach-churning view than that of the victim. He was thirty-eight, tall, rugged in a way that made him look more like the sheriff of an Old West town than a twenty-first-century small mountain town. (She had caught herself more than once expecting to hear the metallic jingling of spurs.) He had dark brown hair with a bit of silver mixed in, level gray eyes, and an almost-always calm voice that could turn persuasive— or hard as nails—depending on what the situation called for. He had one broken marriage behind him, a not uncommon curse of law enforcement work, but he didn't talk about that and Katie hadn't asked.

He was a good cop, a good boss, and a man the people of Prosperity and the sprinkling of other, smaller towns in Foxx County respected a great deal. The sort of man people would turn to in a crisis.

Katie just hoped that would be the case now. That the citizens of Prosperity would see in him a steadying hand even when things got bad, very bad, as she knew they would during what she could feel was coming. What had already started. And she very much hoped

Jackson Archer could at least accept the existence of something he would quite probably never understand.

Otherwise, what was going to destroy so much would destroy him as well.

Dragging her thoughts back to the here and now, she said, "He chose to blow most of his head off on an otherwise normal Wednesday morning with his wife upstairs fixing breakfast and the kids still getting ready for school?" She shook her head. "I know he keeps all his guns down here in that gun safe, but would a father of three blow his brains out in the basement with his kids in the house?"

Archer drew a breath and let it out in a rough sigh, not impatient with his deputy, but clearly baffled himself. "It seems clear he did; since he kept his other arm across the gun it barely moved when he let go with both barrels. His finger's still stuck in the trigger guard, and it's the right finger on the right hand—that is to say the correct hand, his left. He is—was—a southpaw."

The victim of what appeared to be suicide, Sam Bowers, thirty-three, was seated on an old couch in the basement that was the only real piece of furniture in a space filled with plastic storage bins on homemade wooden shelving and one fairly large obviously home-made table beside the washer and dryer, presumably used for folding clothing when it came out of the dryer. The couch had been pushed up against one of the cinder-block walls, and the area behind what had been Bowers's head was now splashed with blood and bits of skull and brain matter.

A lot of blood and a lot of brain matter.

It was a gruesome sight. It was the sight Stacey Bowers had found when she had come halfway down the basement steps to see what she'd expected to be a repentant husband, one of whose guns had unaccountably gone off at seven in the morning.

One of those people who handled emergencies with calm and then fell apart afterward, she had managed not to scream, hurried back up the stairs and closed and locked the basement door, called a neighbor to take the kids so they'd be out of the house, and then after hustling them on their way, called 911. She had still been calm enough when the sheriff and his deputies arrived to tell them where the body of her husband was and why he'd gone downstairs. Or, at least, why she'd believed he'd gone downstairs. White as a sheet and with a steady voice that had finally begun to break by the time she finished telling them what she had to.

After that she had fallen apart, literally dropping to the floor with an agonized moan, and was now upstairs in the living room still sobbing, her shock and grief deep and genuine, with a sympathetic but otherwise helpless female deputy with her and the family doctor on his way.

Her thoughts clearly running along the same lines, Katie said, "Stacey won't be able to tell us anything, assuming she even can, for a while. I'm betting her family doctor will want to sedate her."

"Yeah, probably. Did you call her sister?"

Katie nodded. "Should be here in about half an

hour. She was already at work, so coming from downtown out here. She said she'd take Stacey and the kids to her house, that they'd stay with her as long as they needed to."

"How did she react to Sam's death?" Archer knew Heather Davidson, who worked at the courthouse, and he knew she was neither easily shaken nor a fool. And the sisters were close.

"Shocked. Genuinely shocked. Said there was no way it was suicide and sounded absolutely positive about it."

Archer's frown deepened. "No note. Not down here, not in their bedroom, not in his briefcase. He's dressed for work at the bank as usual. According to his wife, he just came down here while she was busy with breakfast to get a few things out of that chest freezer over there and carry them upstairs for tonight's supper. Just . . . a routine morning, a common chore."

Until it had turned into something horrible.

JIM LONNAGAN EXAMINED the shotgun carefully, then the revolver, handling both with expert hands. Then the rifle, which looked a lot like the two his father had left him. All his attention was focused on what he was doing, but he became vaguely aware that the gun store's owner, John Robbins, was speaking briskly.

"No problem with the background check, of course. But there wouldn't be, you being a cop and all. But I thought you didn't approve of guns in the house, Jim?

I mean, I know your service weapon has to be there, but in a gun safe when you're off duty, so any kids in the house can't get to it."

Calmly, Lonnagan said, "Don't worry, these'll be under lock and key as well. I've ordered a nice display case for the . . . man cave half of the basement." He laughed a little.

Robbins laughed as well. "She let you have half, then? Well, at least you aren't out in the garage. That's the only man cave my wife lets me have."

Lonnagan smiled at him. "I've fixed it up nice. Big couch, TV, pool table. I'll store my golf clubs down there. And these guns. The cabinet has a good lock, I made sure of that."

"I imagine you did." Robbins finished ringing up the sale, adding in the boxes of ammo Lonnagan had requested—and a thick pack of paper targets that could be pinned up on hay bales or stuffed dummies, or just at the firing range in the basement of the sheriff's department. Robbins assumed one or more of those places would suit Jim Lonnagan.

"There you go." He handed over change and watched Lonnagan stuff it into the front pocket of his jeans carelessly before zipping the shotgun and rifle into a single carrying case and the revolver into its holster. The ammo was bagged up for him, and he picked up everything before reaching over to shake Robbins's hand.

"Thanks, John. See you around."

"You too, Jim." He watched the other man leave,

and it wasn't until then that he realized he was wiping his hand down his jean-clad thigh over and over unconsciously.

He frowned, then shrugged. *Everybody has cold, clammy hands sometimes. Nothing wrong with that. Nothing at all.*

"A CONSIDERATE HUSBAND," Katie said rather mournfully about the late Sam Bowers. "He brought that basket of dirty clothes down for her too." The basket heaped with clothing sat on top of the dryer some feet from the couch and victim.

Archer grunted. "We'll know more when we talk to his coworkers at the bank *and* check into the family's finances, but I never heard they were having any troubles financially."

"No, me either. Never heard there were any marital problems."

"We'll have to talk to friends and family," Archer said. "Outsiders usually don't know what goes on inside a marriage, not all of it at least, but they may have noticed something."

"Something worth Sam killing himself over?" Katie shook her head. "I don't see that."

"Neither do I, but neither one of us was him. Some people handle problems easily, and some don't. It could have gotten to be too much for him. *Something* could have." The sheriff paused, adding, "But I'd expect a note. Most people who commit suicide feel the need to explain why, especially when they have family bound to be shocked and when everything looks good from the outside so there's no obvious reason for suicide."

"Yeah. When I went next door to talk to the neighbor who's keeping the kids, she was completely stunned. Doing her best to keep the kids busy and distracted from what's happened and happening over here, of course. Two of them are too young to understand or have any idea what's happened, and the oldest is only eight, so he's just mostly scared and worried— Where was I going with this?"

"The neighbor was stunned. It's Hannah Seaton, right?"

"Yeah. First time I'd met her. Anyway, she was completely stunned. Said Sam Bowers would never in a million years commit suicide. Said he was devoted to Stacey, adored his kids, and never missed a chance to have family time. Both families often barbecued, she said, their kids playing together, and she's absolutely certain there was nothing wrong with that marriage or their life. Said they were two of the happiest people she'd ever known."

Archer looked at her, baffled. "Well, family and neighbors don't always see, but . . . Unless we find something sticking out in their financial records or phone records, or something bad happening with his job, I'm having a hard time seeing this as a suicide myself, in spite of how it looks. Also having a hard time seeing it as anything else. I'll hand over my pension if his wife had anything to do with it."

Katie wasn't as startled as she wished she could be. "I know if there's any question about a death we have to look at the spouse, always, but . . . this looks like a suicide right enough. And if it wasn't one, all my questions still stand, plus quite a few more. Why here in the basement with the kids upstairs? On an otherwise normal Wednesday morning? Why no note? And if it wasn't suicide, if somebody killed him, who could have managed that here?

"I don't believe Stacey could have done it any more than you do. For one thing, she didn't have a drop of blood on her minutes after this happened, according to Hannah Seaton, and I'm willing to bet the doc will say if anybody but Sam Bowers pulled that trigger, they'd have had plenty of blowback all over them." She tried not to sound as queasy as she was when she added, "You can see some of the spray on his pants and even on the floor close to the couch."

"Yeah, I know. But if it wasn't suicide, if it was somebody else killed him, somebody who didn't belong in the house today, then how'd they get in? This isn't a walkout basement and there's no egress at all, so anybody coming into the house would have had to come from upstairs—actually through the kitchen—to get to the basement door."

Katie nodded. "They have a decent security system, which Stacey said was always on at night, turned off only when she and Sam came downstairs in the morning. No signs any of the doors or windows have been forced. According to Stacey, she was in the kitchen from the time they came downstairs."

It was Archer's turn to nod slowly. "And even supposing a killer managed to get in at some point when the system was off, might have lain in wait down here for God knows how long, with God knows what motive driving him, how was he able to get Sam to just peacefully sit down and let his head get blown off with his own shotgun?"

"No signs of a struggle," Katie offered. "I suppose he could have been hit on the head before he had any sense of a threat; the shotgun blast would have removed all signs of a blitz attack."

Archer nodded again, but said, "Say that's what happened. Say somebody hid down here as long as it took, knew the combination of the gun safe—which also requires the fingerprint of Sam Bowers to gain access, though if he was knocked out that wouldn't have been more than a slightly awkward problem— Where was I going?"

It was a characteristic both the sheriff and the chief deputy shared, though Katie wasn't at all sure whether one of them had caught it from the other.

"Say somebody *did* hide down here," she prompted.

"Yeah. Say somebody did, and then managed to surprise Sam, and knocked him out without making enough noise to alert Stacey. Then he positioned Sam with his own shotgun, stage-managed it to look like suicide, and pulled the trigger himself.

"Setting aside the question of blowback, since for all we know he could have been wearing a fucking hazmat suit, how the hell did he get out? Stacey not only closed the basement door until we got here, she locked it. She was sitting at the kitchen table waiting for us, staring at the locked door. And I've had a deputy stationed at the door upstairs since we got here."

"It doesn't seem possible, much less likely. Even if Sam Bowers had done anything to make an enemy that bad, and from everything we've heard so far everybody liked him."

"I've never heard a bad word spoken of him," Archer agreed, then frowned at her. "Why're you rubbing the back of your neck?"

Katie realized only then what she'd been doing, and forced her hand to drop. The nape of her neck was still tingling, and it felt to her like a warning. A less definite warning than the first one had been, but a warning all the same.

She wanted to reach out with her mind, to probe, but that first warning had been all too definite.

She had to protect her mind with every shield, every barrier she had learned to build around it. She was vulnerable in ways most others weren't. Vulnerable the way those she expected to come help would be vulnerable.

Awful to be so sure this is bad in ways we don't understand yet and worse is coming. And I still don't know how to tell him. Hell, what to tell him. How can I?

All she said in response to the sheriff's question was, "I'm feeling tense, I guess. I've never . . . seen anything like this before, Jack."

He appeared to accept that. "No, me either. Not even in Charlotte." He paused. "Where the hell is Doc Forest?" He was not the Bowers family doctor, but the one Archer had chosen to call out for this because he had worked in an ME's office in another state and knew his way around bodies in ways the average doctor in Prosperity didn't.

Prosperity didn't have an official medical examiner or coroner, because they'd never needed one and because Archer could always draw on the state network of specially trained doctors qualified to serve as medical examiners.

"He's on his way," Katie reported. "Said from the way I'd described it we'd probably have to call in a proper ME, but he couldn't be sure until he sees what's here."

"You told him we're having doubts about it being a suicide," the sheriff said, not accusingly.

"Well, he asked. And I said it looked like it but didn't really make sense to us. But didn't make sense as an accident or a murder, either. He said if it isn't suicide, and he can't find anything to satisfy us that it was, or even that it wasn't, that it could have been an accident or even murder, we'd need to call in an ME because as good as he is, as good as the equipment in the hospital is, we may need somebody more used to looking at crime scenes than he is. Said in his work at that medical examiner's office, he was the one who stayed behind and assisted in autopsies and lab work, not the one who went out in the field."

"He might have told me that sooner," Archer said with a sigh.

"Yeah, that's what I told him. He said there hadn't been any reason to until today."

Archer shifted restlessly, his gaze still fixed on the body. "I don't want to call in an ME from the state network unless I have to. But if I have to, I will. I just sure as hell don't want to declare this a crime scene without anything but my own gut to back me up."

Katie nodded in agreement, but said, "One good thing, if I can call it that, is that *if* this is a crime scene, it's pretty contained. I believe Stacey didn't come more than halfway down the stairs, and since then it's just been you and me here. I mean, we can lock the basement door and seal it, post a deputy, and nobody we don't okay is coming down here."

"Yeah. Look, I don't know if the doc will bring a camera with him, but we need pictures of this whole space, and before anybody disturbs anything. Use your cell phone, and I'll use mine. Just to be on the safe side."

His department didn't have an official photographer either, something Archer made a mental note to change. ASAP.

"Copy." Katie was just glad to have something to do, especially when the sheriff began taking pictures of the body and that area of the basement and she could turn to look elsewhere in the very ordinary basement where something not ordinary had happened.

She did her best to ignore the crawly tingle on the nape of her neck.

The sheriff would have to know, of course. Sooner or later. But right now Katie still wasn't at all willing to try to explain something she couldn't prove—and couldn't even really define. Especially to a man as practical and rational as Jackson Archer. They had never discussed the paranormal, but she was fairly certain his first reaction wouldn't be one of acceptance.

Not, at least, until he was faced with something even his practical and rational mind could accept as much further beyond normal than even an inexplicable suicide.

Katie was just afraid of what that might be.

THE GATHERING

Walking with a friend in the dark is better than
walking alone in the light.   —HELEN KELLER

Life is short and we have never too much time
for gladdening the hearts of those who are
traveling the dark journey with us. Oh be swift
to love, make haste to be kind.

                    —HENRI-FRÉDÉRIC AMIEL

SIX

The "study" of the mountain house was in reality a highly functional command center, its true purpose only betrayed, at first glance, by the massive conference table in the center of the room, which could seat a dozen people in comfortable office chairs without crowding, and more if need be. At second glance, it was clear that various high-tech toys were cunningly integrated among bookshelves and gleaming cabinetry that lined two walls, and at least three workstations were tucked into comfortable niches spaced apart, each with spectacular views of the Blue Ridge Mountains.

Completing the huge room and effectively removing any lingering sense of being in a place designed only for work were several comfortable seating areas scattered about invitingly, including a large grouping of two long couches and a couple of wide, deep chairs in front of a rock fireplace where gas logs burned cheerfully and warded off the deepening chill of an October afternoon.

Olivia Castle was one of half a dozen people sitting there, maybe avoiding the conference table and the tablets and paper files and legal pads already assembled during the day because she wasn't quite ready to truly confront the seriousness—and the scary uncertainty—of what they were going to face but more probably because she still felt chilled and welcomed the warmth of the fire. Rex, curled up in her lap after spending the entire morning exploring and happily meeting new friends as well as greeting old ones, was certainly enjoying it.

Especially since he was out of the hated carrier, and because there was a cook in residence who understood the delicate palate of discerning cats.

Hollis Templeton and her partner, Reese DeMarco, had arrived earlier than expected late in the morning, bearing a map and at least the beginnings of an unsettling theory of why they had all been summoned. Or, at least, why Prosperity. Right now, they were silent, faces thoughtful, possibly considering various introductions made in the last hour or so just as Olivia was; they shared one of the big overstuffed chairs, with Hollis sitting in it and DeMarco sitting on one of its wide arms.

The partners never seemed to get very far away from each other, Olivia noted. Not that they were clingy or anything like that, just . . . connected. Obviously connected.

Hollis was a slender, almost delicate woman of medium height, with short, no-fuss brown hair and eyes of an unusual shade of blue very bright and aware in her lightly tanned face. Her other features were good without being in any way remarkable, but that changed the instant she smiled and animation transformed the ordinary into something more than beautiful could ever be.

DeMarco might have been less well-known among the non-SCU community of psychics than his partner, but that was because his FBI career for some years before he met Hollis had consisted of a number of highly secretive deep-cover assignments. Since leaving that more stealthy life behind, he was definitely becoming better known.

Physically he was rather overpowering on many levels. He was very large and clearly possessed the kind of strength that could never be earned in a gym, but what any woman would notice immediately was his thick blond hair, extremely sharp blue eyes, and perfect classical handsomeness. It was as if his still, watchful face had been carved from stone by a master sculptor.

Olivia had felt just a little frightened of him initially, which tended to be her default response to large, unfamiliar men, but the first time she'd seen him lean down to say something quietly to his partner, his stone face softened and made very human if only for that fleeting moment, her fear had left her.

Galen, another large and powerful man who also made her feel wary, had not made an appearance in the last hour or so; Olivia could remember hearing him say something to Bishop about weapons, and she assumed—without wanting to spend any time at all thinking about it—he was off gathering whatever it had been decided the team would need.

Both Bishop and Miranda were also absent from the room for the moment, called away quietly by a dark man they hadn't introduced for some reason he hadn't explained. Olivia was more than a little worried about that, but she did her best not to think about it until she had to. She considered it a cowardly trait, doing that, but it was the way she'd dealt with scary things her whole life, and she doubted very much that would change anytime soon.

Instead of thinking about scary possibilities, she allowed her gaze to wander from person to person, their scattered positions around the room not, she hoped uneasily, a sign of a team that didn't know how to be one.

Tory—Victoria Stark—stood alone near one of the big windows, not taking advantage of what looked like a long, comfortable window seat as she gazed out at the view without, it was obvious from her preoccupied expression, taking much, if any, notice of it. She was younger than Olivia but seemed older, with all the calm, self-control, and shrewd watchfulness Olivia felt she herself lacked. She was of medium height, on the thin side but much, much stronger than she looked, and possessed silvery-blond hair cut short and expressive green eyes.

Sharing Olivia's couch was Reno, serene as always. She didn't look as if she'd pretty much crossed the country twice in a jet in less than twenty-four hours and with no more than brief stops, neither the least bit rumpled nor seemingly in need of sleep. Nor did she appear at all disturbed that one of the three men who had been aboard that jet when it had landed at the airstrip earlier had been sending her hard glares since they had arrived here—and probably, Olivia thought, all the way from Alaska.

Not quite ready to brave those glares even if they weren't directed specifically at her, Olivia looked across at the other couch, which was occupied by the two other men who had arrived with Reno, the wide space between them more indicative of an automatic reluctance to get too physically close to anyone because of their abilities than of any personal animosity.

Sully Maitland she knew well. Born an empath and a strong one, he was still, at thirty-two, working to strengthen his shields; it was one of the reasons he chose to live on a fairly isolated horse ranch in Montana. He was six-two and powerful, dark hair graying at the temples a sign of struggle more than years, and the most intense golden eyes Olivia had ever seen in a human face.

She had seen something very like them once before, but *those* intense golden eyes had belonged to a tiger. And not one caged in a zoo.

Like Olivia, Sully was cursed with headaches and blackouts, and like her he considered the blackouts something of a blessing as long as they happened in private rather than public and there was something soft to fall on. It was, he'd told her once, the only real peace he had, since otherwise the feelings of every soul within a hundred yards of him battered at his shields like an only slightly muffled, extremely painful tide, whether he was awake or asleep.

Sully didn't have a "frequency" that limited his range; the only thing that limited him was distance. Inside a hundred yards—almost exactly—he felt everything from any person who didn't have a very powerful shield (or rare all-receptive rather than projecting or transmitting abilities, like Reno), and from most animals.

It was one of his unique traits, that he could sense the emotions of animals. Not thoughts, he claimed no ability to communicate with them as such, but he knew what they felt. Not all animals, but most. Including birds, especially, for some reason, crows.

It was why the cattle ranch he had inherited had become instead a horse ranch where not even the chickens were slaughtered and no hunting or trapping was allowed.

Sharing the couch at that careful distance was Logan Alexander, wary and somewhat aloof, as he generally was around other psychics. Olivia knew him, but she wouldn't have claimed to know him well. She knew he didn't want to be what he was—a medium, born with that ability. And since, during the single emotional outburst she could ever remember hearing from him, he had confessed that spirits quite literally haunted him, all the time, everywhere, giving him no peace, she really couldn't blame him.

Logan was a good-looking man and probably, Olivia thought shrewdly, drew women as quickly as his abilities repelled them. He was thirty, six-one, and possessed shaggy black hair and oddly light blue eyes that were almost hypnotic. He was frowning now and had been since he'd arrived, but Olivia had no idea if it was because spirits were bothering him here—or because they weren't.

From the corner of her eye, Olivia saw Reno move restlessly to glance back over her shoulder with a slight frown marring her normally serene expression as she somewhat ruefully eyed the final member of their team.

Or . . . perhaps not.

Dalton Davenport had been born a telepath. And he quite likely would normally have developed at least a shield of sorts by the time he reached his current age of thirty-three. But Dalton was one of those unlucky souls whose psychic abilities had been misunderstood and feared by those around him from very early in his life, before he hit his teens. Abandoned by family when too young to even try to defend himself, he had lived the secretly feared horror of many psychics: Medically diagnosed with supposedly dangerous mental "disorders" that were judged to pose a danger to himself and to others, he had been kept on an ever-changing regimen of strong medications—and institutionalized.

For nearly twenty years, until Bishop had found him.

So nobody could blame Dalton for the fact that he had begun pacing almost from the moment he'd arrived, along with Reno, Logan, and Sully, less than an hour ago. They couldn't even blame him for the fact that he had not stopped pacing for an instant and had remained stubbornly unresponsive while all the necessary introductions had been made, keeping his distance and holding on to the glare that was directed often at Reno, but saying nothing.

The problem was that Dalton not only lacked a shield to protect himself and block the thoughts of those around him: He broadcast his own thoughts and emotions. Strongly. And since anger tended to swallow up most other emotions and thoughts, what was coming off Dalton in almost palpable waves was only that. He was angry. He was so very angry. All the time.

And anger was one emotion most telepaths and empaths could not shut out no matter how strong their shields were.

Looking around at the others in the room, Olivia saw Hollis wince and rub her left temple, her blue eyes following Dalton's pacing with both sympathy and pain.

Then she looked up at her partner, and Olivia barely caught her quiet words as he bent his head attentively.

"Can I just apologize for all the time I spent broadcasting? Honestly, I had no idea it was like this. So painful. Why didn't you tell me?"

DeMarco smiled faintly. "Different situation."

"Yeah?"

"Yeah." Then he straightened and looked across the room, his attention so obviously yanked from his partner that Olivia found herself following his gaze without even thinking about it.

She saw Dalton reaching one end of his pacing path,

turning blindly to start back the other way—and then Victoria moved three quick, soundless steps toward him from behind, reached up both hands to touch his head on either side, and spoke one firm word.

"Sleep."

Dalton dropped like a stone. Victoria sort of danced back a couple steps in a curiously graceful and clearly practiced maneuver, and caught him under his arms before he could hit the floor.

She let out a grunt when she took his weight, then looked at the others. "Little help here?"

DeMarco and Sully were there in seconds, relieving Victoria of her burden and laying Dalton out on the window seat. He looked utterly boneless and totally peaceful, so much so that he was oddly unfamiliar to those who had known him longest.

"Thanks," Victoria said.

"No, thank you," Sully said. "My head was killing me."

Hollis said, "So was mine. How long will he be out, Victoria?"

Since they had been quickly briefed on their journey here as to the abilities of the non-SCU psychics they'd both be meeting for the first time, neither DeMarco nor Hollis was the least bit surprised by Victoria's ability.

She shrugged. "An hour if he's lucky. Ten minutes if we aren't."

"Nifty ability," Hollis noted with a smile as her partner returned to her side. "Is he really out?"

"Sleeping. Deeply. Never tried it on Dalton before, mostly because he wouldn't let me, but it usually muffles whatever the psychic ability is. He's stopped broadcasting, I take it?"

Both Sully and Hollis nodded, the latter adding, "All I was getting was anger. And his aura was going really red. Not good."

Sully, returning to his own place on the couch, said wryly, "It's been a while, but as I remember, Dalton's broadcasting was usually wordless rage. Not that I can really blame him."

"No, not with his history," Hollis said. For a moment, she looked across the room at Dalton's peaceful form, her expression speculative. "I wonder . . ."

Nobody really had the nerve to ask what she wondered.

Olivia spoke up then to say, "Tory put me out once when I thought my head was going to explode. All the pain went away, and it was so peaceful." She sounded a little wistful.

Victoria joined the group around the fireplace, leaning against the back of the couch between Olivia and Reno. With a slight grimace, she said, "It's a temporary relief—and only works really well the first time I use it on somebody."

"What happens when you do it again?" Hollis asked.

"For the same person? The effects taper off more and more with every try. Not such deep sleep, shorter and shorter time periods. Abilities less muffled. By the fourth or fifth time they generally just blink and get mad at me." She glanced over at the sleeping Dalton, adding, "I'd really rather not get that far with him."

Reno looked at the two SCU agents. "Dalton was never willing, but the rest of us . . . experimented a bit over the years. Victoria was able to put all of us out. Like she said, with . . . gradually diminishing returns when it came to the active abilities, and even blocking receptive abilities like mine. It didn't affect any of our individual abilities once we woke up. Even if . . ."

"Even if that's what we hoped would happen," Logan said. He frowned at Victoria. "Did I get mad when it stopped working?"

"Furious," she confirmed immediately.

He looked a bit disconcerted. "Sorry. I didn't remember that."

Victoria smiled faintly. "It was a very tense time. If I remember correctly, you wanted to get away from a stubborn spirit who'd been following you around for days. I think he was standing right behind me when that last attempt failed. So you were probably more mad at him than at me."

"Still," Logan muttered, a tinge of color rising in his cheeks. "Sorry."

She nodded, then looked at the agents. "So the usefulness of my ability is definitely limited. In my real life it's helped with the occasional noisy roommate or bad date, but that's pretty much it. Far as I've been able to tell, it doesn't matter if the person I put out is psychic or not—though psychics remember what happened and nonpsychics wake up confused and wondering why they just suddenly went to sleep. Nonpsychics also tend to be out longer, even up to a couple of hours. Most psychics tend to be grateful for whatever time they're out. They get a restful nap, at least. The first time. After a few times, it just stops working."

"Do you know if the ability can . . . rebuild over time? Like a static charge?"

"So far, no sign of that. I've tried it with a couple of people in this group up to nearly three years after it stopped working. No joy. Whether because I'm limited in that way or they build up immunity or some kind of shield against it, I couldn't say."

Hollis nodded but said, "What about your other ability?"

"I don't have another ability."

Hollis's brows went up briefly, and then she studied the younger woman, her bright eyes narrowed slightly. "Maybe you call it something else," she said finally, "but your aura is shot through with silver on the inside, close to your body, which in my experience means you're holding in power, electrical and magnetic energy. Power that belongs to you. And it's stronger now than it was when you put Dalton out, which I assume would have taken at least some of your energy because any active ability does."

"I have excess energy, that's all," Victoria said. "Not another ability." There was an edge to her voice.

Hollis continued to look at her for a moment, smiling faintly, then shrugged. "Hey, I'm all for holding back a few aces. I hope most of you have more than one ability, because I think we're going to need everything we can get. But I should warn you that intense investigations tend to bring out everything a psychic has, good or bad, and that includes inactive or latent abilities. So it's likely that, assuming we all survive this, your abilities will end up changed in some way. All of them. Maybe even a few you don't . . . know . . . you have."

"That's your deal, your thing," Victoria objected. "Different abilities popping up. It doesn't happen to other psychics I've ever heard of." She was still frowning.

"Well, me aside, if it happens at all, it happens with latent but existing abilities, and during SCU investigations," Hollis said. "Because of the energies of other psychics. Because there's generally a human monster we're hunting, one with all the wrong kind of energy. Because of outside influences producing or using energy, even the weather or other electrical or magnetic fields. And where there's energy involved, especially negative energy, the changes can be . . . rather drastic."

Reno spoke up then to ask, "Do we know if negative energy is involved in Prosperity?"

"It is if something bad is happening there. Or will. We were all summoned, after all," Hollis replied.

Bishop came into the room just then, his wife at his side and Galen just behind them. All three looked grim.

"Something bad just happened," he said. "Something very bad."

WEDNESDAY, OCTOBER 8

"This is not . . . I don't understand this. I don't understand how this happened," Sheriff Jackson Archer said. He rubbed his eyes briefly with both hands, as if he could erase the scene before him. But when his hands dropped, he saw the same impossible things just as he had before. What he had been standing here staring at for more than half an hour. It didn't seem real. Even though he knew it was.

It was a scene of utter carnage.

The normally comfortable and pleasant living room of this nice family home on the outskirts of Prosperity would never be the same again. The Gardner family had consisted of two parents and three children. There were four bodies sprawled around the room, very still, very silent, and very dead.

Blood was everywhere, the acrid, metallic smell of it hanging in the air like smoke.

Ed Gardner, thirty-five, was stretched out on the floor just inside the living room, his head in a large pool of blood, his eyes wide open as if in total shock. His throat had been cut from ear to ear. Three of the fingers on his left hand had been chopped off but left there as if the killer had been interrupted or had just decided it was no fun to chop off body parts if the victim was dead.

Lying closest to her father on one end of a big sectional couch that was unfortunately made of a once light-colored fabric was eleven-year-old Suzy Gardner, the eldest of the three Gardner children. Her eyes were closed, so perhaps she had been rendered unconscious or even dead before the dismembering of her slight body had commenced.

Jesus Christ, I hope she was already dead when that was done. Or out at least. Not aware of what was happening. Drugged, maybe. Or even a blow to the head. Just ... let it be something like that. Let it be that she was dead before she knew what was being done to her. And who was doing it ...

But Archer was afraid she had been alive, even if unconscious, because there was a lot of blood soaked into the couch. Blood soaked around her arms, dismembered at the shoulders. Blood soaked around her legs, dismembered at the hips.

Dismembered ... by a hacksaw. And an axe.

And her limbs lay where they belonged, more or less, as though some demented dollmaker stood ready to sew them back on.

At the other end of the sectional sprawled Bobby Gardner, eight, whose small body had been opened from breastbone to crotch. Blood was everywhere. Too much of what had been inside his body had been pulled out to lie on the couch near him or to ... dangle ... toward the floor. And his eyes were open.

Archer turned his horrified gaze with more reluctance than he could have expressed to the fourth and final victim of this slaughter, on the carpeted floor, nearly hidden between the big coffee table and that section of the couch.

Five-year-old Luke Gardner, not yet in school, had probably been the first victim, he guessed, because the blood on his small body appeared closer to being dried than what was on and around the others, and what lay around him on the pale carpet of the living room had dulled and . . . congealed.

His head was horribly misshapen, some number of blows with a heavy object having caved in his skull in several places. His ears had been sliced off. Each of his fingers had been chopped off with an axe and, even more unnervingly, were nowhere to be seen. His feet had been chopped off at the ankles and stood bizarrely upright in blood-soaked bedroom slippers with the floppy ears of a rabbit.

Most bizarrely of all, on the big coffee table lay a wooden kitchen cutting board, blood-soaked and bearing the deep imprints of an axe. It had clearly been slid under the children so that the axe had been able to chop more effectively.

Archer tore his gaze away and half turned to look at the chair closest to the front door. It were where Leslie Gardner had been found, curled up in apparently peaceful sleep, her hands covered in blood, her face spattered, clots of blood matting her blond hair. Her jeans and blouse had been literally soaked with blood and all the instruments and objects she had used to slaughter her family lay on the carpet near the chair in a neat semicircle. A huge kitchen butcher knife. An axe. A hacksaw. The heavy bronze figurine of a woman holding a child.

They were all covered with blood.

It doesn't make any sense. It just doesn't . . .

"Jack?"

Katie was informal only rarely while they were work-ing, but just as the morning's inexplicable suicide had shaken her, this horrifically inexplicable mass murder had also shaken her. Badly.

Archer turned to face his chief deputy, noting that she had come only far enough to address him, clearly trying not to look down at the body of Ed Gardner, which was closest to her since she stood in the doorway to the entrance hall. And looking Archer square in the eye out of the equally clear determination to not allow her gaze to stray to the other horrors.

Not again, at least.

"Any word from the hospital?" he asked, function-ing on automatic in a situation he had never been trained to handle, his tone queerly detached.

"Yeah, but no real news. Nothing we didn't know, nothing we couldn't see for ourselves. Gabby says Les-lie Gardner is still asleep—and the doctors say she *is* asleep even though they haven't been able to wake her, not faking, not unconscious or in any way injured—and not drugged."

Gabby Morgan was Archer's second most experi-enced deputy, sent to the hospital with EMS and Leslie Gardner, with orders to stick close, follow procedure as far as she was able, and report everything. And not to leave Leslie's side for a moment.

"They're *sure* she wasn't drugged?" It had been a vain hope, he'd known it even as he'd hoped, struggling to find something that might make sense in a situation that was madness.

"The doctors are sure. They're conducting more tests on her blood just in case, tests they don't usually do in . . . normal situations . . . but so far they haven't found a single sign that she was acting under the influence of anything at all. Except maybe a psychotic break, which they can't know until she's awake and shrinks can talk to her. And even if it was something like that, they say there would have been signs people around her would have noticed. Long before it got so bad that something like this could happen."

Katie drew a deep breath. "Everything was photographed at the hospital, her clothing removed and bagged for us. Or for whatever technicians or lab we send it to. Gabby's hanging on to that to preserve the chain of evidence. The doctors and nurses checked Leslie Gardner's body head to toe; there aren't even any bruises, or the . . . normal . . . cuts we'd expect where the knife might have slipped, should have slipped when it got slippery with blood. The blood was all . . . theirs. All belonged to her husband and kids. She didn't have a single wound or cut or even a scratch. I don't have to be a medical examiner or crime scene tech to know that that's weird."

She glanced back over her shoulder, noting that deputies Cody Greene and Matt Spencer, still gray with shock since they had responded to the initial call from a worried neighbor, were standing out on the front porch on the other side of the clear storm door. Neither had ventured any farther into the room than where Katie stood now. They had called the station, horrified and bewildered, and it had been the sheriff and his chief deputy who had discovered Leslie Gardner to be very much alive but weirdly unconscious and summoned paramedics.

Before they'd arrived, Katie had silently taken pictures with her cell phone, focusing on Leslie Gardner and the area around her before she could be moved.

Katie wasn't even sure why she'd done it. And all she knew now was that she couldn't keep silent any longer.

"Jack . . . first that apparent suicide that didn't make sense, that *doesn't* make sense this morning, and now this. The youngest boy was probably killed hours ago, maybe before the other kids were up, maybe even while we were three streets over trying to figure out why Sam Bowers would have killed himself."

"Yeah," Archer responded, his voice sounding hollow.

"There's absolutely no sign anyone else was involved in this. Nobody broke in. None of the doors or windows have been forced or damaged in any way. Nothing appears to be missing. Everything upstairs looks like— like a Wednesday morning with kids in the house. Beds unmade. Used towels on the bathroom floor. It's clear everybody had breakfast, dishes not yet put into the dishwasher. Clear the two older kids had their backpacks ready, their lunches inside.

"The neighbor who called in said Suzy and Bobby Gardner went out to catch the bus just like usual, like her kids did, but then for some reason came back in here before the bus came. She said it looked like someone had called them, or they'd heard something from inside the house. But they didn't come back out, and the bus came and went. Then she noticed that Ed Gardner's car was still here, and she assumed he was going to take the kids to school."

Archer nodded. "Yeah. Yeah, I got that."

Katie kept her voice even. "But when she looked out again, around lunchtime, his car was still parked out in the driveway. That was odd, she thought, because he never came home for lunch. She tried the house phone and got voice mail. Tried Leslie Gardner's cell, and *it* went straight to voice mail. She even called Ed Gardner's work, and they told her he hadn't been in and hadn't called. She knew then something was very wrong over here."

"Wonder why she didn't come over," Archer mused, but absently, as if the question barely touched his mind.

"She was afraid. Word had already gotten out by then about Sam Bowers, and the news was garbled; nobody was sure it was suicide, maybe murder. And she was scared. Too scared to come over here and find . . . horrors. So she called us."

"Yeah."

"Jack . . . this is too much for us. None of us has the training or experience to figure all this out."

"Sam Bowers killed himself," Archer said. "Leslie Gardner killed her husband and kids. That's what happened."

"Maybe. Probably. But Sam Bowers shouldn't have killed himself. And if Leslie Gardner slaughtered her entire family, why did she just curl up bloody on that chair and go to sleep? And why can't the doctors wake her up?"

"What are you saying?" he asked slowly.

"I'm saying we need help. Everything that's happened today was . . . unnatural. Even unreal. Inexplicable. It's not just a suicide and a multiple murder. It's not something ordinary cops can figure out. I feel that, and I know you do too, because we've both been trained to handle crimes and these . . . these are something different. There's something else going on here, Jack. I don't know what it is, but I know the longer it takes us to figure it out, the more people are going to die."

He blinked, stared at her. Finally saw her. "What?"

Softly, she said, "This isn't *natural*. What happened to these people, what happened to Sam Bowers, it's not *natural*. Something . . . outside themselves made these things happen, made them do these things. Something stronger than they were. Something dark. Something we can't see. And it's still here, in Prosperity. It isn't finished yet. I can feel that. You have to feel it. Can't you feel it?"

"All I feel is horror," he said. "And . . . helplessness. I've never felt that before. Not like this."

"Neither have I."

He frowned at her. "I think you know more than I do, Katie. Don't you?"

Katie drew a breath and tried hard to make her voice

steady and matter-of-fact. "What I know is that we're in trouble. What I *know* is that we need help. Not just crime scene technicians and a medical examiner, though we do need those. We need someone able to figure out what's going on here. Someone who knows how to deal with . . . unnatural deaths. Unnatural things. Someone who can see what's happening here."

His short laugh was a rusty, almost broken sound. He cleared his throat before speaking again. "I just . . . I get the feeling you know more than you're saying about this."

Katie shook her head. "What I know is that it's too much for us. And I think I know who to call. But I need to call now. Before things get even worse. And before this scene, before any of . . . this . . . is disturbed."

"Call," Archer said.

THE DARKNESS

It is easy to go down into Hell; night and day, the gates of dark Death stand wide; but to climb back again, to retrace one's steps to the upper air—there's the rub, the task.   —VIRGIL

It is better to conquer yourself than to win a thousand battles. Then the victory is yours. It cannot be taken from you, not by angels or by demons, heaven or hell.   —BUDDHA

"'Come,' he said, 'come, we must see and act. Devils or no devils, or all the devils at once, it matters not; we fight him all the same.'"

—BRAM STOKER, *DRACULA*

SEVEN

It was a winding road, a two-lane blacktop like so many in the scenic mountains, with very little shoulder but the occasional overlook where tourists could pull safely off the road and look at the view.

Their black SUV was just approaching one such overlook when Hollis said suddenly, "Hey, Reese, pull over up ahead."

The valley below them was already partially shadowed, the late-afternoon sun beginning to sink behind the western mountains, but DeMarco didn't hesitate to pull the SUV off the road and onto the wide overlook. No other vehicles were there.

He parked and shut off the engine, looking at his partner. "I can feel it too," he said.

She looked at him, nodded, then opened her door. "I want to see if it's visible."

DeMarco got out as well, following her to the waist-high rock wall that looked natural but had clearly been built to prevent a careless tourist from taking a deadly fall down the mountain while admiring a truly stunning view of a lovely valley far below.

The mountain slopes below the overlook were unusually sheer here for the Appalachians; the very old mountains shouldering up against one another tended to be given more to gentle, rolling hills and rounded peaks blunted by time. For the most part, the only raw, jagged features were due to the activities of man, the blasting of slopes and tunnels to provide for roads.

But what DeMarco saw appeared natural rather than carved by man. And the first thing he noticed when he joined Hollis at the wall and really looked around was that the same thing appeared to be true all around the big valley sprawling below them. None of the mountains he could see almost completely enclosing the valley ended near the valley floor in gentle undulations, tumbles of grass, or tree-covered hills, as was usual.

As much as he could see of the valley, wherever the mountains met the flatland, there were what looked like granite cliffs, sheer and towering.

DeMarco was about to comment on the weirdness of that when his easy connection with Hollis told him she was seeing or sensing something even weirder. He looked at her, recognizing the narrow-eyed, intense gaze of utter concentration as her striking blue eyes roamed slowly over the valley.

Even so, almost absently, she said, "I wonder if one

day we'll go into a case and *not* find yet another very strange and new thing almost right off the bat."

"From the sound of what Bishop got from the sheriff and his deputy down there, we'll be seeing plenty of strange. Plenty of crazy."

"Uh-huh." She turned her head and frowned at him. "You see anything strange?"

"Other than sheer cliffs rising above as much of the valley floor as I can see from here, no. What do you see?"

Her brows lifted slightly in question. "There weren't any bad things on the island for us to use in practicing, so no way to know if it'll still work with something I think is *very* bad. You game?"

"Of course," he replied without hesitating.

Hollis smiled, then reached for his hand, their fingers twining instantly, and returned her gaze to the valley below. "Look again. You see what I see now?"

It took a moment during which his vision seemed to waver just a bit, but only that long before DeMarco did see what she saw.

"Jesus."

"Yeah. I'm thinking that's in no way natural."

The entire valley appeared to be almost encased in a kind of . . . dome. Even though it was not close and they were still well above it, he could see it was high and curved, and that it . . . flashed here and there faintly, close on the underside of the dome-like shape, tiny sparks from this distance but what could easily have been like shimmering patterns of lightning lacing across the sky and hissing high above the town. High above the whole valley.

"Like an aura," he said slowly, frowning. "Is it?"

"Damned if I know. Never seen one cover an entire town, much less an entire valley. The only thing I'm sure of is that it's energy. A hell of a lot of energy."

"Positive or negative?"

"If I had to guess," she replied slowly, frowning, "and I do, I'd say it's both."

"Why does that sound bad?" DeMarco wondered, just as slowly.

"I dunno, but it does, doesn't it? At least more . . . worrying, somehow. Maybe because dark energy is easier to sense, and almost always drives or enhances negative acts. An absolute. Something we've faced and fought before."

"What about the positive energy?"

"If it's had any reaction at all it's helped most of us, usually. But . . . if positive *and* negative energy is caught down there, trapped together, I have no idea what effect it's having on the people in the town, in the valley. Or what effect it'll have on us. If what's happened down there today is because of the energy, then it really is unlike anything we've ever faced before."

"Hence the summons?"

"I'd guess yes. Though not knowing what actually did the summoning is still bothering me."

"And me." DeMarco stared at what Hollis's abilities were showing him a bit longer, his gaze roving, then said, "Am I wrong, or is the outer edge of it more sharp and delineated than a normal aura? Almost like an actual dome made of glass or something."

"You're not wrong. It really does look like a glass dome. Like it's holding the energy in, trapping it. Maybe just that, to keep it here. To keep it more contained. To keep it more powerful, more focused." She shook her head. "I've only seen something similar with the auras of psychics who were fighting off attacking energy. And in those cases, I could see the energy battering at their shields. I don't see anything outside this . . . dome. Just the energy inside it."

"Is it increasing? Building up?"

"I think so."

"Can you see a source?" he asked, still frowning slightly at the unique capture of sheer energy.

"Not from here." She looked at her partner. "The thing is, whatever's holding in the energy does seem to have made a dandy shield for it, not as tangible as actual glass but every bit as . . . enclosing. No telling how strong it is, how impenetrable, until we're down there. I'm assuming we can get through unless and until we find out differently. But once we're down there, once we're inside, all that energy is bound to affect us even through our shields. I just don't know how."

He looked at her and smiled. "Once more into the breach."

"You never used to say things like that," she observed with her own faint smile. "At least, not that way."

"Complaining?"

"No. Oh, no. It's been interesting to hear more just-outside-New-Orleans in your voice these days." Then, more soberly, she said, "I think we'd better use the phone in the SUV and call Bishop before we get any closer to that thing. I've got a hunch that communicating with Base may prove to be even more of a problem than usual."

"The chief deputy and sheriff got through," he noted.

"Yeah. From a landline in the sheriff's office. I could be wrong, but I'm betting electronics are already being affected, especially communication. Which means it's a good bet cell phones, if they work at all, won't reach outside the valley even in the short amount of time we generally have to use them. I'm not even sure the sat phones will work. We may be restricted to using landlines ourselves."

"And landlines are becoming more scarce in these days of cell communication. Could be a problem," De-Marco noted thoughtfully.

"Yeah. And we're likely to have problems using our tablets, laptops, and other equipment as well, especially if we need to use Wi-Fi or otherwise connect to the Internet or FBI databases. It's something Bishop needs to know before he sends the others in. Something they all need to know. Be as prepared as they possibly can be. Protect themselves as far as they possibly can. What I said to Victoria is . . . probably going to be an understatement, at least for some of them. That energy, positive or negative, is awfully strong. And except for Victoria, none of them has a really strong shield to protect them from it."

"Think Bishop may think twice about sending them in?"

Hollis shook her head immediately. "He wasn't all that forthcoming—as per usual—about whatever he and Miranda saw when the rest of us got blasted, but I'm willing to bet he's certain we all have to go down there, no matter what the risks are, to any of us. As certain as we are. We all have to be in Prosperity."

DeMarco looked at her a moment, then glanced back out over the very peculiar valley and the dome of energy they both could already feel. "I guess we'll find out if there's anything . . . sentient . . . about all that energy," he said. Then he returned his gaze to his partner, brows rising slightly. "Or do you already know that? I'm not picking up anything, but I've never been able to read anything other than human minds."

"From here, it's almost impossible to say much of anything definite about it, not the source or sources, not whether there's any kind of mind behind it, or why it's only now causing trouble." Hollis paused. "Except that it's energy, strong energy. And growing stronger. And that it's going to cause more very bad things to happen."

"You're sure of that?"

"Positive."

"Clairvoyance?" His tone was matter-of-fact.

"Not sure. Which is a little unsettling, but not all that surprising. I haven't really learned to differentiate between the newer abilities. So maybe it's something I'm feeling. Or maybe it's something another sense is trying to tell me." She sighed. "Dammit, I hope I get the hang of this soon."

"You will."

Darkly, she said, "It's more likely something else will pop up to confuse me even more and you know it. I just don't want precognition. Seriously. I think I can handle just about anything but that."

"I," he said, "think you can handle anything you have to."

"Yeah?"

"Yeah."

Still in a dark tone, but with bright eyes, she said, "In the future, when we speak of this, and we will, just remember that I've given you many chances to escape."

"I appreciate that. But I'm not going anywhere except with you." He smiled, thoughts and awareness flowing easily between them below the level of words.

Hollis drew a breath, muttered something under her breath about rotten timing, then said briskly, "Okay, then let's call Bishop. And tell him stuff he probably already knows *anyway*."

YOU KNOW YOU *want to, Elliot.*

Elliot Weston blinked, frowned, and shook his head a little, trying to ignore the voice in his head that had been a whisper at first, a nagging little thing like a tune stuck in his head.

It was louder now. More distinct.

More . . . tempting.

He tried to concentrate on his job, on the virtually automatic spiel as he led the young couple through the carefully staged, nice little suburban home he was trying to sell them.

"As you can see, the three bedrooms are a nice size, and there's a full basement that could easily be converted into whatever extra space your family might need—"

You always want to. Such silly questions they ask. Wasting your time . . .

"How is the school district?" Lorna Simmons asked somewhat anxiously.

Elliot looked at her. She had a clipboard and had been making notes, clutching pens of four different colors in one hand. He smiled. "It's excellent. Prosperity may be a small town, but the name is accurate, and the town council feels strongly about education. So the schools get the best of everything, from the best teachers to the latest equipment."

Stupid cow.

Charles Simmons, walking into the master bedroom to explore, asked, "Is there enough hot water in the showers? I really hate running out of hot water."

"No problems there," Elliot replied, still smiling. "The house has one of those newer systems that heats water instantly as it's needed. Even if clothes are being washed and more than one person is taking a shower, there's plenty of hot water."

Stupid bastard.

"Electric or gas?" Simmons asked.

"You have an efficient combination in this home. The cooktop and water heater are gas, while the HVAC system is electric."

"Is there an HOA?" his wife asked, still anxious, as she made a note in blue on her clipboard. "I mean, are there rules about what colors we can paint the outside, and what flowers we plant, like that?"

"There's no official homeowners' association in this neighborhood," Elliot assured her. "Just the usual ordinances and zoning common in any residential neighborhood. I can assure you the people who live here are very laid-back, very easygoing. I live a few streets over myself. Terrific neighbors."

Come on, Elliot. You know you want to do it.

Trying to ignore that increasingly insistent, even seductive voice in his head, Elliot said quickly, "Beautiful tile work in the master bath, as you can see. And plenty of closet space. And the master's here at the back of the house, of course, so it's very private, and you can hardly hear anything from outside, not traffic or the neighbor's dog, or anything troublesome."

"There's a leash law, right?" Simmons demanded.

"Certainly. No roaming dogs; we have a strictly enforced leash law. This development was carefully planned so that all the backyards are fenced, with plenty of room for the kids and for the family dog. And there's a nice dog park just outside the development where neighborhood dogs can play and get to know each other. We also have several good vets in town who can take excellent care of family pets."

"I hope the people on either side here don't have dogs that bark all night."

He's one of those. Those assholes who believe whatever they want should be law.

"No, I can assure you it's a very peaceful neighborhood." He wondered why the other man looked more and more ugly, with eyes a weird color and too many teeth in his mouth.

He's an animal, Elliot. You can see that.

Lorna Simmons, her voice increasingly strident to Elliot's sensitive ears and her face beginning to remind him strongly of an aunt he'd disliked his entire life, said, "I couldn't bear living in a cookie-cutter neighborhood, I just *couldn't*. I have an artistic flair, Charles always said so, and I'm very *particular* about my surroundings. They have to work for me. Colors we choose, and I have to have my garden gnomes in the flower beds!"

Elliot, listen to her. That voice could cut glass. You know you don't want them anywhere near your family. You don't want them anywhere. You know that.

Charles Simmons rolled his eyes slightly at the mention of gnomes but said, "Long as nobody tells me I can't wash my car in my own damned driveway and play music while I do it, I'm fine with neighbors. There are services available to cut the grass? I'm a busy man."

"Several lawn services work in this area of town, very good ones," Elliot promised, his smile beginning to feel horribly unnatural and an odd, red mist sort of drifting between himself and the very demanding couple.

"The kitchen really is lovely," Lorna Simmons said, a pleading note adding to the stridency as she looked anxiously at her husband. "Just what we've been looking for, darling."

"I'm not sure about that carpet in the living room," he countered.

"Carpet is easily removed," Elliot murmured, wondering if his teeth were gritted the way they felt. Why did everything seem to be turning red? Why could he feel his own heart beating, harder and harder?

"Hardwood floors underneath?"

"In this particular home, no, but—"

"So there's another added expense," Charles Simmons said bitterly, his very ugly face even more ugly wearing a grimace.

Go on, Elliot. Do it. You know you want to.

"The price will have to come down quite a bit to cover the cost of laying hardwood—"

You know you do. That's why you brought your gun.

HAVING BEEN TOLD by the FBI unit chief he'd spoken to that a team was very nearby, Archer had asked that the feds come directly to the Gardner home, the same request he'd made when he spoke to one of the state medical examiners who worked, she told him, out of Asheville and could get a lift at least partway to Prosperity in one of the MAMA—Mountain Area

Medical Airlift—choppers. So the help he had called in was near.

Near enough that there was still some sunlight when a big, black SUV pulled to the curb in front of the house not more than a couple minutes after a discreet white van parked in the driveway behind Ed Gardner's car. A man and woman got out of each vehicle, all casually dressed without a suit or tie in sight, and only Archer's experienced gaze could detect that both feds wore guns under light jackets.

The guy fed wore a big, silver cannon in a shoulder harness.

The four newcomers met in the center of the yard, obviously acquainted.

"Hey, Jill," the slender brunette said as she and her tall, blond partner reached the other pair. "Didn't expect to see you again so soon."

"Hollis. Reese. My assistant, Austin Messina."

As Archer approached them, he saw the feds nod to the ME's partner, who was fiddling with some piece of equipment and who nodded with an absent smile in return, and then the brunette asked, "What happened to Sam? That last case make him rethink his career options?"

"Sort of. He's with your bunch at Quantico for a few months. Special training. After the last time, we figured it wouldn't hurt." She wasn't very big, was very pretty, and didn't look like messing about with dead bodies would be her specialty, but it was clear the two feds obviously respected her and felt comfortable with her.

Archer wished he felt comfortable. About anything. He wished he felt something other than the queasiness that lay in the pit of his stomach and an overwhelming sense of dread.

"Sheriff Archer," the brunette fed said when he reached them, rather discreetly flashing her credentials in perfect sync with her partner, then reaching to shake his hand with a good grip. "I'm Hollis Templeton. My partner is Reese DeMarco. Sorry for the obvious Fed-mobile sticking out in this nice neighborhood, but we tend to carry quite a few supplies and such, so it couldn't be helped."

Archer, feeling a bit swept along in her briskness, merely nodded as he shook hands with her partner, then nodded again and shook more hands when Dr. Jill Easton introduced herself and her assistant to him.

"Do you want to get started first, Doctor?" he asked her.

"I imagine Hollis and Reese will want to study the scene for a bit first, Sheriff. We'll be getting our equipment out and getting suited up in the meantime." Her partner was already sliding open the side of the van, which was clearly crammed—neatly—with more rather enigmatic equipment and supplies.

As she stepped away to join him, Archer looked at the two feds. He had never shared the hostility toward federal cops that some of his peers so often felt and too openly displayed, but he had also never worked with feds on a case, so he looked at them a bit uncertainly. "I'm not sure what the procedure is from this point,

Agents," he told them. "Then again, I'm not sure of anything today."

Hollis Templeton nodded, her expressive face showing rueful sympathy. "More often than not, we tend to play it by ear. The sort of cases we get invited to assist in tend to be of the very weird variety, Sheriff. Beyond horrible. Not something local or even state cops have much experience with. Sometimes the usual law enforcement training just doesn't cover it."

"My chief deputy said you belonged to some kind of special FBI unit, and I talked to your unit chief, but . . . I guess I never figured there were enough . . . weird crimes to call for that."

"You'd be surprised," she told him earnestly. "There's a lot of strange and crazy in the world. The Special Crimes Unit teams tend to be pretty busy." Her very bright eyes, their blue color definitely unusual, studied him for an instant as though looking for something.

Archer had no idea whether she found it.

"You've kept the scene intact?" Her voice was brisk again.

It wasn't really a question, but Archer nodded. "Except for the removal of Leslie Gardner to the hospital, everything inside is . . . just as we found it."

"She's still out?"

He nodded. "I have a deputy staying with her, and so far the report is she's sleeping. Just sleeping. Except that the doctors can't wake her up."

Reese DeMarco said thoughtfully, "It might be a good idea to ask the doctors that they not try any . . .

extraordinary means to wake her up. Let it happen naturally if at all possible."

"Why?" Archer asked blankly.

"Because we don't yet know what we have here," the big blond man—former military, Archer was willing to bet, just from the way he stood and the knife-sharpness of his blue eyes—said in the same quiet, pleasant voice.

His partner added, "Memory's a tricky thing. If she's forced awake before she's ready to be, we may lose information we badly need to understand all this."

"I hope somebody can understand it," he muttered, then gestured slightly and led the way to the front porch of the home. "I have two deputies sitting in their cruiser across the street, but so far none of the neighbors have tried to get closer. Just standing out in their yards, most of 'em, staring."

"Yeah, we noticed," Templeton murmured.

"Should have put crime scene tape up, I know," Archer said, trying not to sound defensive.

"Why didn't you?" she asked, her tone interested rather than in any way critical.

"Honestly? Didn't think of it right away. None of us did. Shock, I guess, as unprofessional as that is. Too many years living in a town where crimes that require tape just don't happen. And when I did think of the tape, it seemed . . . to add more obscenity to this. This was a very quiet, very peaceful neighborhood. I just . . ." He shook his head, adding in a more certain voice, "I hope you both have strong stomachs."

Matter-of-fact, DeMarco said, "We've seen the initial

photos your chief deputy took, Sheriff. We know what to expect in there."

Archer wondered if they did, photos or not, but simply nodded and led the way into the Gardner house. He stopped a foot or so outside the doorway to the living room. "I'll stay in here, if you don't mind," he said. "They have a landline phone here in the front hall; I'll use that to relay your request to the hospital about Leslie Gardner."

Hollis Templeton gave him another very direct look, then said, "Radios and cell phones aren't working?"

He grimaced slightly. "Not reliably. Been having trouble with both off and on for the last few days, maybe a week, and it's been getting worse. Cell company says there's some interference, and they're working on the problem. My technical people are flat-out baffled about the radios. But they're trying to figure out the problem with those, and we're in contact with specialists—who seem just as confused as we are. In the meantime, only landline phones are dependable, and we're lucky to have one here. Lots of people just rely on the cells nowadays."

Having not looked into the living room once, he moved away from the feds toward the phone.

Hollis braced herself, something no one but her partner would have known since there was no betraying outward sign, and then the two of them moved just inside the living room.

There was, really, no way to brace the mind and senses against anything in that room, and it was emotionally devastating as well. Even for strangers who hadn't known the family.

The photos, horrific though they were, had not really shown the truly shocking amount of blood and the utterly senseless, brutally twisted slaughter. The scene was literally an assault on more than the senses.

They both stood just inside the room, near the door but to one side, moving no closer to the bodies than necessary to see what they needed to see. Because they didn't want to disturb the scene Jill and her assistant would minutely examine and photograph. And because neither of them needed to get any closer.

After a moment, quiet, Hollis said, "First time I've had to study the scene of a multiple homicide. Just realized that. Or kids."

"Makes it worse that it's a family with kids," De-Marco said. "Not something you'll ever get used to." His voice was steady with the kind of control Hollis understood and shared.

"Not something I'd ever want to get used to." She glanced back over her shoulder to make sure Archer was still using the phone, then lowered her voice. "Are you sensing anything?"

They were both shielding, but DeMarco was using only half his double shield, and Hollis's shield was still a bit undependable.

"Just what we both felt from the time we reached the valley," he replied just as quietly. "My skin's crawling faintly and there's a sense of pressure. It's bearable right now, not really a distraction, but if the effect gets stronger or is cumulative . . ."

"You should probably use both shields," she told him.

"I'd rather not just yet."

She looked at him and managed a faint smile. "I'm fine. If it comes to that, you can extend your shield to cover me too. But in the meantime, one of us needs to use all the protection possible. This . . . isn't sane. Whatever's behind it. We need to make sure we have at least one sane and protected mind on our side. Just in case."

"It's the *just in case* that bothers me," he told her. "If we're right about at least part of what happened here, what's continuing to happen, it's also possible, maybe even probable, that neither one of us is immune, shields or not."

"Reese, we need to know if the connection is still there even through both your shields. Just because it worked on the island doesn't mean it'll work here. Especially with all this damned energy, never mind the horror of all this." She resisted an impulse to rub her arms. She wasn't cold, but her skin was faintly tingling, crawling, just as DeMarco had described. It was a distinctly unpleasant sensation.

He nodded reluctantly, and a moment later she was more relieved than she wanted to admit to hear a familiar mind-voice.

Okay. Both shields. My skin isn't crawling anymore. I'm aware of that faint pressure, but just barely. Normal

senses seem to be working. And I can still feel our connec-
tion. It feels strong to me. How about you?

Yes. Thank God. Your other senses really are okay?

Seem to be.

Telepathy? I mean outside our connection?

Some static, but I can read Archer clearly enough.

Panic underneath the horror?

You're getting that through me?

Yeah.

Better than I expected, then.

Same here.

Archer stepped back to the doorway, keeping his gaze on them rather than looking into the room. "The doctors have stopped trying to wake Leslie Gardner. They said it was probably best to wait and see anyway. They're baffled as hell, that's clear."

Without looking at him, Hollis said more than asked, "All her vitals are normal, I take it."

"Yeah. By every measurement they know, she's asleep." He waited, watching the two feds as they stood only a few feet away and studied the room. As far as he could tell, neither one of *them* had a queasy lump of horrified sick fear in the pits of their stomachs.

It might have been easy to resent their control, their seeming indifference to this scene of slaughter, except that they exchanged glances just then—and he could, for a brief moment, see the sick emotions that training and experience hid beneath control.

They felt it too.

Agent Templeton looked at Archer steadily. "Normally—if I can use that word—we'd want to check out the entire house. Look for signs of behavior to explain this. Profile the scene."

"But not this time?"

"No. We don't believe doing that would help us to understand what happened here. Why it happened."

"Why not?" he asked, mostly because he couldn't think of another question.

"You had another violent death today, a suicide," she said, maybe answering his question. "Sam Bowers?"

"Yeah. Nice, ordinary family man blew his brains out with a shotgun this morning. Just sat down on a couch in the basement, dressed for work, put both barrels of his shotgun under his chin, and . . . In the basement, with his wife and kids upstairs." Archer drew a breath and let it out slowly. "What's left of him is at the hospital morgue, waiting for Dr. Easton. The local doc I called to the scene said he wasn't up to the job. I didn't blame him. He'll assist her if needed, but the last time I saw him, he was throwing up everything he'd ever eaten in his life."

"I can relate." She nodded, then immediately added, "Bowers didn't leave a note?"

"We thought he didn't. Looked for one in the basement, the rest of the house. None of us were too eager to touch the body, and there didn't seem to be any question as to who he was, so his body wasn't searched at the scene. But then when he was lifted to go into the body bag, the doc heard something. Paper. It was in the inside pocket of his suit jacket. It's at the station now. Bagged."

She nodded again. "What did it say?"

"It didn't make sense," Archer told the two feds. "It was . . . crazy. The same sentence repeated over and over, all down the page, with the handwriting getting worse and worse. All it said was . . . *Just me, not them.* Over and over again. *Just me, not them.*"

EIGHT

Galen had come into Prosperity separately from Hollis and DeMarco and a bit earlier, in an ordinary light-colored sedan that didn't scream *fed* or anything else to attract attention. As per orders, he drove around the town of Prosperity and surrounding neighborhoods, seeing what he could see in the daylight that was rapidly becoming twilight.

His psychic ability—if it could be called that, and he had often doubted so aloud—was not one that required any sort of mental shield. But in his work for the SCU, he was most often cast in the role of watcher or guardian, and both suited his innately guarded, watchful nature, all of which had built or intensified a pretty impressive shield.

He was, other psychics had told him, buttoned up tight.

But that natural shielding had failed him during the SCU's extended investigation of a deadly, charismatic cult leader more than a year before, and though not another soul blamed him for what went down, he still blamed himself for the terrible toll taken when everything hit the fan, the loss of innocents, and the blows dealt to the SCU.

No matter what Bishop said to the contrary.

Galen had taken time away from the SCU after that, time he'd badly needed to come to terms with what had happened because the blows to him had been both unexpected and deeply personal. And time he'd needed to also come to terms with his own once-latent and now-awakened abilities.

Bishop hadn't said anything about that, about new abilities, and neither had Galen. All Bishop had said, mildly, was that Galen's natural shield had developed into one that was "nearly seamless."

Seamless or not, Galen's shield had not stopped the blast of sensations that had summoned other psychics to Prosperity. Even though he had not been summoned himself. And yet he had been. Galen hadn't explained it to anyone, least of all himself; all he knew was that he needed to be here. That he had a part to play as well in whatever would happen here.

And once in the valley, he had felt the energy. His skin wasn't crawling, but he was nevertheless aware of it. The longer he drove around, minding the speed limit and not otherwise calling attention to himself, the more aware of it he became. It was . . . pressure. Something bearing down on him.

And on Prosperity.

It was not pleasant.

At first glance, both citizens of Prosperity and obvious tourists looked and seemed perfectly normal. But Galen looked closer, and he observed signs that virtually everyone he saw was both a little tense and almost imperceptibly distracted. He noted a few arguments breaking out here and there, nothing violent but . . . tense. Unusual sort of thing to see out in public in a small town like this one.

Then again, he was also aware by the time he had completed a very thorough exploration inside the town limits of Prosperity and around the periphery that details of the morning's inexplicable suicide had gotten out, that details of this same day's multiple homicide were also spreading rapidly, so it was no wonder people appeared tense.

They were quite likely scared shitless.

Galen had not contacted Base or the team of Hollis and DeMarco in order to learn about the multiple homicide; there was a single radio station in town, and even though the local news report had been interrupted frequently by bursts of static, Galen had heard what he needed to over his car's radio. He'd already tried his cell, but, as Hollis and DeMarco had suspected and warned Base before coming into town, it proved to be useless. There should have been a strong signal given the four very tall cell towers he'd seen well placed in the valley, but on his cell the bars indicating signal strength were literally dancing up and down, from absolutely no signal to a full-strength signal—the entire end-to-end dance lasting for about three seconds. Not nearly long enough to even attempt a call or text.

He turned it off and tossed it over his shoulder to land on his go bag in the backseat.

Then, having explored as much as he could before darkness made that a fairly useless proposition, he turned his car toward the sheriff's department to meet up with Hollis and DeMarco, as previously agreed.

His timing was perfect. He pulled into a parking slot beside the newly arrived hulking black SUV before its brake lights could go off.

Getting out of his car, he spared a long moment to study the Foxx County Sheriff's Department. He found it to be a newish, fair-sized two-story building two streets back from Main and occupying most of a block if you included the sizable parking lot beside and behind the building.

It looked more than adequate, especially since Prosperity was the only town of any size in the county.

He joined Hollis and DeMarco on the sidewalk in front of their vehicles. "Local radio reported the multiple homicide," he said.

Neither of them appeared surprised that he hadn't bothered with a hello.

Hollis said, "Yeah, we heard the report on the way over here, even if the SUV's radio *was* crackling with static. How's your shield?" she added, not bothering to lower her voice because there was no one within earshot.

"Pressure," he replied.

"Nothing else?"

Galen shook his head in a slight movement.

Hollis eyed him for a moment, then looked at her partner and said dryly, "It's a good thing you've started to be more talkative. Otherwise I'd mostly be talking to myself."

"I thought you did that anyway," Galen said.

Refusing to take the bait except with a brief narrowing of her eyes, Hollis merely said, "The medical examiner is someone we've worked with before, Jill Easton. She's clairvoyant, one of those Bishop wanted but didn't get—except occasionally as part of the state networks of docs trained to serve as MEs. She's still at the scene of the multiple. We only had a minute to warn her to shore up her shields, but she seemed calm enough before the warning, so maybe she won't be adversely affected. Hopefully, anyway."

Galen nodded.

"We're supposed to meet with Sheriff Archer and his chief deputy inside. Unless the plan's changed or something happens along the way to change it, Bishop's sending Victoria and Logan in tonight, and the rest tomorrow."

"I know Victoria's supposed to have a strong shield," Galen said. "But Logan?"

"We think it's a good idea to find out how a medium reacts to the energy in this valley."

It was Galen's turn to eye Hollis. He had a couple of questions but asked only one. "You don't already know?"

"Afraid not. My primary ability, but not my only one, so I can't really be sure. I'm trying to keep my shield up, but my skin's crawling a bit. My guess is that what I'm feeling isn't spiritual energy, but Logan's the only one who may be able to tell us that for certain, because that's definitely his whole focus. And it's something we need to rule out—or rule in. To help define this energy."

"Have you seen any spirits?"

"No." She frowned suddenly. "Though, to be honest, I haven't been looking for them. Maybe my shield is stronger than we thought. Or maybe this energy is interfering."

DeMarco said, "Probably both. You said the spirit who told you we had to come here was . . . different somehow."

"Yeah. Sort of . . . wavery. Sort of like heat off pavement. But since she was crying I was too busy trying not to cry to figure out what else might be going on."

Galen said, "The downside of multiple abilities."

"One of them," she agreed ruefully. "And the empath thing is newest and was triggered in a different way, so it's giving me more trouble. This whole valley is filled with freaked-out people. And not just spooked, but scared and tense and irritable as hell. A state of affairs I expect to get worse before it gets better." She drew a breath and added calmly, "So if I start snapping at you guys, don't take it personally."

Galen glanced at DeMarco and noted that Hollis's

partner was a bit tense himself, something he rarely showed. "Both shields?" he asked.

"Yeah. And holding. A sense of pressure, apparently what you're sensing, but it's not bad."

"Then she's the one you're tense about?"

"*She* is standing right here," Hollis snapped. Then she closed her eyes briefly, lifting both hands unconsciously palm-out in a "hold it" gesture. Then she shoved her hands into the pockets of her jacket, settled her shoulders, and stared at Galen. "Sorry. Since we don't know just how this energy is going to affect us, especially over time, we thought at least one of us should be as protected as possible. That means Reese keeps both shields up. But he's still aware of how I'm feeling. Which, yes, is very tense."

"Got it," Galen murmured.

"So, right now, you and Reese are as protected as any of us are likely to be from this energy. And from whatever it's doing to people. We hope. We also hope Victoria's shield will be solid here, and will protect her."

"And Logan?"

It was DeMarco who said, "Risky as hell, but we need to know if this is spiritual energy. If it is, he should know quickly enough. And even though he hasn't been able to shut out spiritual energy, Bishop believes he does have a kind of shield."

"A *kind* of shield?"

"His words, not mine."

"And," Hollis said, "Logan *was* summoned. They all were."

"By some . . . force . . . we know nothing about," Galen reminded them. "I don't like it when I get invited to a party by somebody I don't know. It stinks. I still say it could be a trap."

"Of course it could," Hollis said. "But considering that only eight psychics were summoned, it seems like an odd way to go about setting a trap for only a handful of us. There are a hell of a lot more than eight just here in our country, quite a few arguably quite powerful. And why invite us here at all?"

"That's true of this whole damned thing. Why are we here?"

"That's what we're here to try and find out," she reminded him. She began to turn toward the walkway to the front doors of the sheriff's department and stopped as though she'd run into a wall, her slender body racked with a sudden, visible shudder. Even in the deepening twilight, it was obvious she went pale.

"Hollis?"

She looked at her partner, for a moment almost blindly, then said in a very steady voice, "We need to hurry."

Neither of the two men asked questions.

ARCHER MET THEM just inside the sheriff's department, in the lobby, which was fairly spacious and contained a couple of benches for anybody who needed to wait and a high desk, behind which sat a very alert deputy. Glass doors opened on either side of the lobby, both, as typical of most law enforcement buildings given the current troubled times, guarded by coded locks, the number pad beside each mute evidence of security measures.

Hollis introduced Galen, aware by the fact that the sheriff looked no worse than he had at the Gardner home that news of another event had not yet reached the station. But she knew it was coming, and soon.

She had felt it, two sharp bursts of pain tangled with shock and confusion. And then nothing. Whatever she'd felt wasn't close, she thought. At a guess, whatever had happened had been on the outskirts of Prosperity. At another guess, they were beyond help.

She knew Reese was aware of what she had felt, but they had decided on the way from the multiple homicide scene that the mind talk that was so much a part of their connection now should be used only when they were alone or needed to communicate something privately. Otherwise, things were apt to get confusing.

It was confusing enough for the two of them; though thoughts were clear and easy, Hollis's uncertain control over her newest ability meant that DeMarco was sometimes slammed by an emotion that wasn't his or hers.

Which tended to disconcert even DeMarco.

Archer indicated the door on their right, saying briefly, "That leads to stairs and the second floor. Administrative, the main communications center, and other technical areas my deputies don't need to access regularly are all up there. This other door is the one we'll use most often. Bullpen, offices, conference room, break room, locker rooms, restrooms. Plus interview rooms and a dozen cells in the back."

"We don't have to swipe a card, do we?" Hollis asked a bit distractedly as she looked at the number pad.

"No, and it's a simple code. Nine-one-one-oh-one. Easy to remember. To be honest, I've always thought the security for this building was tighter than necessary, at least here in Prosperity, but we followed the recommended security setup for law enforcement buildings in this state." Then he frowned. "A card would have been a problem?"

She smiled quickly. "I'm one of those people who affects things like magnetic cards, especially those for hotels and other door locks. I've been known to screw up ATMs too."

"Katie's the same," he said, nodding, then added, "Chief Deputy Katie Cole. She's getting things set up in the conference room. If you'll all come this way?"

They followed him, through the bullpen that was mostly deserted except for three deputies, two of them talking on landline phones while taking notes and the third frowning in obvious frustration at his computer console. It was a sizable bullpen holding more than a dozen desks, and they could see the adjoining conference room, since the wall between the two spaces was glass from about halfway from the floor to nearly the ceiling.

When they went into the conference room, they found a scene that was familiar to Hollis and DeMarco and less so to Galen since he tended to spend more time out in the field, often literally outside, during a case. There was an oval conference table that could seat about a dozen people in relative comfort, with a power strip down the middle and a conference phone sitting in the center. Whiteboards had been set up along the wall opposite the glass partition to the bullpen, blank but with markers and erasers ready.

Archer introduced his chief deputy, Katie Cole, and if her smile was welcoming and easygoing when she greeted the feds, there was definite strain in her hazel eyes.

Hollis knew immediately that she was psychic but wasn't sure of the specific ability.

"We don't have much in the way of a start in here," she said to the feds a bit wryly. "The photos we took this morning at the Bowers' house and the ones from the Gardners' are being printed out now—if one of our techs can fix the printer. We have deputies out talking to people related to or friends with both families, and with neighbors. We haven't called in anyone to give a statement yet. The notes taken by deputies are being printed out—or just copied with a bit more neatness and detail *from* their notes." She grimaced slightly. "Our printers and computers are being as temperamental as the cells and radios."

"Getting worse?" Hollis asked.

"Yeah, seems to be. It was just the cells and radios at first. Now it's electronics in general." Katie started to reach for the nape of her neck but quickly stopped herself.

Hollis knew the feeling. She wanted to rub the nape of her own neck, which was not only tense but a bit crawly, worse than it had been earlier.

"I don't get that," Archer said, frowning. "We've never had any trouble before, and it's not like the equipment we're using is either too old and breaking down, or too new and still full of bugs."

Hollis hesitated, still unsure of how the sheriff would react to what he needed to know, but there was a clock ticking in her head and it was getting louder. Any minute now, they were going to be called to the scene of yet another baffling, violent event he would most certainly find inexplicable, and she just didn't know . . .

Making up her mind for better or worse, Hollis half sat on the conference table and looked squarely at Archer. "Sheriff, how much do you know about energy? Electrical, magnetic?"

His frown deepened as he returned her gaze. "About as much as any layman, I guess. We use a hell of a lot of electrical energy every day to run our homes and offices, all our gadgets. Magnetic energy . . . Hell, I don't know. Are we talking about the cells and radios not working right? Equipment not working right?"

"Yes. And why it's getting worse. And why people are dying in your town." Her voice was calm and matter-of-fact.

"It's connected?" He didn't look or sound disbelieving, just startled and baffled.

"We believe it is. For some reason we don't—yet—

understand, there's an abnormal amount of electrical and magnetic energy in this valley. Highly abnormal. We don't know the source, don't know if it's more than one source. We don't know if it's permanent or temporary. We don't know if it's a naturally occurring phenomenon or something being . . . manufactured."

"Deliberately? By a person?"

"It's been done before. You know about EMPs—electromagnetic pulses?"

"Yeah, they're supposed to knock out electronics."

"Right, they do. Electrical energy can be overloaded. Shorted out. The current can also be unstable; it can surge, become much, much stronger as well as much weaker, suddenly."

"Okay, I get all that. I even get—sort of—that something like that could be interfering with cell service and our radios, the computers. Hell, sunspots do that. But the murders today—"

Hollis kept her voice calm and matter-of-fact. "The human brain is basically an organic, electromagnetic computer. Our thoughts, our actions, our emotions, all are created, triggered, controlled, by electrical impulses in our brains. Synapses firing off all the time, faster than thought. Different areas of the brain responsible for different things, lighting up when active and going dark when not. If a specific area of the brain is stimulated by an electrical current, or influenced by a strong enough magnetic field, then the brain . . . responds."

"With suicide and murder?" There was, now, disbelief.

"Remember when I told you there was a lot of strange and crazy in the world? We've seen a fair amount of that. Enough to not discount something that's scientifically possible—even if wildly unlikely."

"Like energy that—drives somebody to kill?"

"Yeah, like that."

ELLIOT WESTON SET his gun down on the kitchen counter and looked at his two clients in a sort of vague curiosity. Former clients. Charles Simmons had a neat, round hole in his casual shirt just above his heart and a very surprised look on his ugly face.

One or more of the bones in his burly chest must have stopped the bullet, Elliot realized, because there was no sign of blood from an exit wound underneath his sprawled body.

Lorna Simmons lay beside him, her mouth open, wide eyes blank, her clipboard flung aside. There was a neat, round hole in the center of her blouse, and beneath her body a pool of scarlet blood was spreading slowly.

Smaller bones, Elliot supposed. Or just a smaller body.

Elliot knew, on some deep, quiet level of himself, that he had done something horrible. Something beyond horrible. But wherever that level was, it was unreachable right now. All he knew was that he was finished here, and he needed to make a few notes in his cell phone.

He turned and went outside, sitting down on one of the white wicker chairs of the nicely staged front porch, and pulled his phone from his pocket.

No bars at all, he noted, but he didn't need to make a call. He just needed to make a few notes on his schedule, that was all. Notes that this house was still available, that maybe they should look for less demanding clients next time.

He made his notes and put his phone away, then just sat there staring peacefully into space. He felt very calm.

ARCHER MOVED A little way around the conference table, pulled out a chair, and sat down. He could see all of them from his position, his gaze roving from one calm face to another. Even Katie's face, he noted, was calm. Until a fleeting wince tightened her features, and she reached up absently to rub the nape of her neck.

She'd been doing that a lot lately, he realized.

"So . . . electricity made Sam Bowers kill himself. Electricity made Leslie Gardner slaughter her entire family. Her *kids*. That's what you're telling me." Archer knew he sounded incredulous. He felt incredulous. And it was sort of good to feel something other than sick horror.

Hollis moved to take a seat directly facing the sheriff, and the others pulled out chairs as well. She said, "No, that isn't what I'm telling you. It isn't that simple. Not exactly electricity. Energy."

"There's a difference?"

"Electricity is only one form of energy. There's nuclear energy, for instance. Atomic. Solar. Wind. It can all be converted to what we call electrical energy, and used by us that way. But there's also energy we don't . . . actively use. There's an electromagnetic field around most living things. Around this planet. The sun. Around the electrical devices we use every day."

Seemingly without being aware of it, she reached up a hand to rub the nape of her neck, her unusual blue eyes remaining fixed on his face. "There are even some people who claim that if we can ever learn how to . . . understand, really understand energy, we'll find that it really does make up most of our universe. Even, perhaps, that part of us we choose to call our souls."

For just an instant, Archer was tempted to follow that interesting tangent—at least, he hoped it was a tangent—but then he shook off the temptation. Carefully, he said, "I've never heard of energy influencing people to kill."

"We have," Hollis said simply. She appeared to realize she was rubbing her neck, and stopped, clasping her hands together on the table before her with a fleeting frown.

"Some of that weird and crazy you mentioned?"

She nodded. "Up until now, what we've seen has been . . . relatively minor. People manipulating energy to affect other people. Generally one-on-one."

Archer blinked. "That's possible?"

"Very possible. There are scientists studying it all over the world, with various . . . implications in mind. But actual cases we've had to deal with have been, as I said, relatively minor."

"And what's here isn't minor."

"Definitely not. We're talking about energy capable of affecting the thoughts and actions of human beings. People's minds are not that easily influenced, at least not directly, not like this. Not to do something so drastic and horrific as kill, especially kill family. But the energy that appears to be trapped in this valley is very unusual, as I said. And becoming stronger, more intense. It's likely to affect a great many people as it does that. With luck, most of the effects will be minor: temper tantrums, fist fights, arguments. If we're not so lucky, more people are going to die."

Since Archer appeared stunned, DeMarco spoke up then to say, "We believe it's what's also disrupting radios and cell service; that's a common enough occurrence with any spike in electricity, any energy surge. As you said, even sunspots can affect communications. Affecting electrical equipment takes a stronger surge, a more intense energy field. The most sensitive and sophisticated would be affected first. Like computer equipment."

"First?" Archer said uneasily.

"We're afraid the intensifying energy could have an

increasing and even cumulative effect on equipment. And on people, as Hollis said."

"This is nuts." He shook his head. "Not weird or crazy, just *nuts*. Insane."

Quietly, Hollis said, "More insane than Sam Bowers blowing his brains out this morning for no apparent reason? More insane than Leslie Gardner slaughtering her family—and then just going to sleep?"

Archer stared at her.

"There are more things in heaven and earth," she murmured. Then she added in a stronger voice, "The Special Crimes Unit has encountered a lot of weird and crazy, as we've told you. That's one of the reasons the unit was formed, one of the reasons the FBI, not known for fanciful beliefs, far less insane ones, was convinced the unit was necessary."

That reminder of something official and solid he could understand and hold on to seemed to steady Archer.

"The FBI. Right. So . . . how does law enforcement fight something like . . . energy?"

"It depends on the source, but generally energy is fought with a different kind of energy, stronger or more focused, maybe more under control. In our case, it's fought by law enforcement officers and others who understand energy and who have been trained to use their abilities to deal with it."

"Their abilities?" He felt himself going adrift again.

Hollis glanced around the table, at her partner, at

Galen, and lastly at Chief Deputy Katie Cole, who was studying her thumbnail very intently. Hollis smiled faintly, ruefully, then met Archer's suspicious gaze directly.

"We in the SCU have a lot of tools in our investigative toolbox," she told him calmly. "We've all been well trained. So we have the usual law enforcement skill with weapons and observation and interrogation techniques. Defensive driving. Knowledge of law. Some of us are profilers. Most of us, really. We have some . . . fairly esoteric skills for cops. Reese is a pilot. I'm an artist. We can both pick a lock with a certain amount of skill, and Galen can disarm most security systems—in the dark."

Archer looked at the other two very calm men, frowning, then back at Hollis. "Okay," he said slowly.

Her smile widened just a bit at his wariness. "We're cops, bottom line, just like you. We were all trained by the FBI, standard Bureau training as a solid base, and if we have more unusual tools for the toolbox than most agents, it's because our unit chief saw the potential years ago, and decided there was talent being wasted. So he went out and found us. People with abilities that could help investigate crimes and catch criminals, of course, as well as abilities to deal with things most cops or federal agents were never trained to deal with."

Archer zeroed in. "*Unusual tools.* Exactly what sort of unusual tools are you talking about? Specifically?"

Hollis sent a pained glance toward her partner. "I don't dance around a subject well, do I?"

"Not your strong suit," he agreed with a faint smile.

"Agent—" Archer began.

"Hollis. We're very informal. Though if you forget names, *Agent* is fine too." Her glance sort of lifted away from him suddenly and seemed to be fixed on something in the distance, the very blue eyes going even brighter, almost luminous, narrowing. "We don't mind," she added absently.

"Okay, then. *Hollis*, what the hell are you talking about?" His voice might have been a bit sharper than he'd intended.

She blinked, looked at him, then smiled. "Sorry. Things are about to get even crazier, so I couldn't really dance around it even if it *were* my strong suit. Sheriff, the Special Crimes Unit is made up, mostly, of psychics. We're all cops, we're all trained, we're all experienced, and we've been working with law enforcement agencies all over the country, particularly here in the southeast, for quite a few years now."

Archer opened his mouth, but Hollis went on before he could say a word.

"You talked to our unit chief, Special Agent Bishop; if you want to call him back he can furnish you with a list of references as long as your arm, other sheriffs and chiefs of police and detectives, city cops and county cops and state cops, quite a number of them within a few hundred or so miles of Prosperity, all of whom will be happy to furnish testimonials or just talk to you awhile about their own experiences with . . . strange and crazy."

After a long moment, Archer said slowly, "I always heard my grandmother had the Sight. Never knew her, though."

"We've found that sort of knowledge or awareness common, in these mountains especially," Hollis said. "They're old mountains, and people have been here a long time. Long enough to accept that . . . there are more things in heaven and earth than they teach us about in school."

After another long moment, Archer said with commendable calm, "You didn't really change the subject with all this, did you? It's still about—energy."

"It's still about energy." She frowned briefly, then said, "I hate parlor tricks, but . . . Any minute now one of your deputies is going to come rushing in here to tell you that two more people have been killed. Inexplicably. Horribly. Strangely."

"How do you know that?"

"I felt it. Just a few minutes ago. Two people dead. And . . . a killer you'll find inexplicable."

Archer opened his mouth, beginning to look angry, but was prevented from saying what he obviously wanted to when a deputy rushed in, face white, and burst out with words that tumbled over themselves in a hurry to get out.

"Sheriff—we've got another one. At least it has to be— In that new development on the outskirts of town. A real estate agent shot and killed the couple he was showing a house to. A neighbor heard the shots and went to see and—and the guy's just sitting on the front porch, smiling. Like nothing happened. The couple is dead in the kitchen. The real estate guy's gun is on the kitchen counter. And—and he's just sitting on the front porch. Smiling."

NINE

The neat little house in its neat little planned development was lighted from top to bottom, and this time Archer had ordered crime scene tape surrounding the whole house and yard.

Neighbors in the mostly full development remained in their own yards, but some had migrated toward fences with other neighbors, to talk, to exclaim, to wonder. And to stare toward the inexplicable.

Inside the perimeter that only law enforcement and their acting medical examiner and her assistant had entered, a few uneasy deputies hovered here and there, staring at the lighted front porch where a murder suspect sat in a white wicker chair, hands cuffed but still smiling, a faintly inquiring expression on his pleasant face as he looked at the sheriff and two of the feds.

Chief Deputy Katie Cole was inside the house with their acting medical examiner and her assistant.

Archer had sat down in the neat wicker chair that was separated from the other one by a small table and which made up the attractively staged front porch.

It seemed surreal to Archer. It *was* surreal.

He looked at Hollis and DeMarco, both leaning back against the white-painted railing side by side, only a couple of feet from the chairs, studying the murder suspect with calm, thoughtful eyes.

"He sold me my house," Archer said to them, wondering vaguely if surreal was going to be his new normal.

"And I know you're happy with it," real estate agent Elliot Weston said with his pleasant smile. "I'm very good at my job."

Archer drew a breath and tried again, as he'd already tried several times, to get the answers he needed and quite desperately wanted. "Elliot, why did you kill them?"

"Kill who, Jack?" He looked puzzled.

"The couple you were showing this house to. The couple lying dead on the kitchen floor, shot with what appears to be your own gun. Why did you kill them, Elliot?"

Weston shook his head, clearly puzzled. "I don't know why you'd say something like that, Jack. I'd never kill anybody. You know I'd never kill anybody." His voice was mild, his eyes guileless.

Trying a different tack, Archer asked, "Then what are you doing here, Elliot?"

"Well, this house is one of my accounts. And I stopped by here on my way home just to make a few notes on my phone," Weston explained, pausing a moment because he lifted a hand to gesture, perhaps even to produce the cell that Archer had earlier removed—along with everything else in his pockets—from his person. It was only then that he seemed aware of the handcuffs. "Why am I wearing handcuffs, Jack? Is this some kind of silly joke?"

"Christ, I wish it were." Archer looked at the agents. "You two haven't said much."

Hollis frowned slightly as she looked at Weston. She kept her voice quiet as she said, "Well, he's feeling pretty much the way he looks and acts. Calm and a little puzzled. But his aura . . ."

Archer blinked. "His aura?"

"Mmm. One of the tools in my toolbox. Everyone gives off an electromagnetic aura; some of us can see that. Tends to show me someone's mood even if I can't read them any other way. And whether they're holding in too much emotion, too much energy. Or fighting off some kind of attack."

"Attack?" Archer really wanted this day to be over.

"Energy, usually. The really odd thing is . . . he doesn't have an aura."

"Sure?" her partner asked her, his voice quiet as well.

"Yeah. The energy doesn't seem to be interfering with that. I mean, I can see everybody else's, so if he had one I should be able to see it. I don't. And I haven't a clue what that means." She looked at DeMarco. "Are you getting anything?"

"Same as you. He's calm, he's puzzled. Not really thinking about anything. In fact, his mind is almost completely blank, at least as far as surface thoughts go. He forgets about the cuffs until something draws his attention to them. And he has no idea what the sheriff is talking about. Even more, he doesn't really care."

Archer looked at them a moment, then rose and gestured toward the nearest deputy. "Matt, you and Kayla take Mr. Weston back to the station. Don't talk to him. Don't ask him any questions. Just put him in a cell and keep an eye on him."

"A close eye," DeMarco murmured. "I wouldn't leave him alone, Sheriff. Not until we figure out what's going on here."

Archer nodded to his deputies. "Somebody keep watch. Don't leave him alone at all."

"Copy that, Sheriff."

Somewhat gingerly, Deputies Matt Spencer and Kayla Nelson each took an arm, helped Weston to his feet, and led him off toward their cruiser. He could be heard asking them if they could stop for coffee.

Weston was smiling as if he didn't have a care in the world.

When they were out of earshot, Archer stared at the feds, his gaze roaming from one to the other, finally settling on Hollis. "Auras? I know people give off energy, plants, all living things, but—you can see that? Colors around people's bodies? And you're seeing that around everybody else but not around Weston?"

She nodded, utterly matter-of-fact. "And about what

I'd expect. The colors all mean different things, different emotions. There are a lot of colors around everyone else I've seen today, and more now because everybody is tense, edgy, and feeling a lot." She frowned again and rubbed the back of her neck suddenly. "I'm sensing those too. Neighbors are scared, your deputies are horrified, and—you don't know quite what you're feeling."

"Good guess."

Hollis offered him a faint, rueful smile. "Not a guess. We all have a primary ability; most of us have at least one more, and some of us more than one more. My primary ability is as a medium. And I can see auras. But I'm also an empath."

"You see dead people." His voice was stony.

"And talk to them."

"Empath. Empathy. You feel what other people feel?"

"Yeah. New ability for me, so not really under control. Sometimes it takes us a while to adjust." She rubbed the nape of her neck harder.

Archer stared at her a moment, then looked at DeMarco. "And you?"

"Telepath."

"So you read minds."

"Not all minds. None of us can control our abilities a hundred percent, and none of us can read every single individual we encounter. We've theorized, and science has pretty much backed us up on it, that each individual human mind has its own frequency, as unique as a fingerprint. Virtually all telepaths have a limited range. Think of it like a radio. I can pick up . . . stations . . .

within a certain range of frequencies, but there are frequencies beyond my abilities to tune in."

"Can you—"

"Yes, I can read you." DeMarco didn't offer more, just looked at his partner, a slight frown drawing his brows together. "If the effects of the energy don't lessen at all even after dark, then more than one of us is likely to be affected with or without shields."

She stopped rubbing her neck and straightened, frowning up at him. "Well, I don't feel the energy lessening, but not intensifying either, not the way it was before dark. Thing is, I'm not sure I could tell at this point, at least not unless the difference was really strong."

"Emotions getting in the way?"

"Oh, yeah. And that crawly feeling all over, especially on the back of my neck, is worse. Distracting." She drew a quick breath. "On top of everything else, I don't think we're done, even for the day. Something else is going to happen."

Archer, pushing aside the intense discomfort of even the *possibility* that his thoughts might well be an open book to one or both of the feds, spoke up then to say, "You can predict the future too?" He was a little surprised at the mildness of his voice, since he wanted to yell and break things.

"No, thank God," she said with definite feeling. "It's . . . I think it's still the empathy. There are so many emotions it's hard to sort through them, but . . . I can . . . feel somebody out there struggling. Fighting against whatever he's being urged to do."

"Urged?" Archer managed.

She stared at him. "Sam Bowers blew his brains out, leaving a note that said, 'Just me, not them,' as if arguing with someone who wanted him to kill the rest of his family too. Leslie Gardner slaughtered her entire family and then went to sleep and remains asleep; I'd say she lost the argument, and it might just have broken her mind. For good. Elliot Weston shot and killed two clients—and can't seem to remember a thing about it. Or care at all. Please tell me you don't believe things like that are just happening, randomly in a single day in your nice little town, without being driven by something external."

KIM LONNAGAN STUDIED her husband rather anxiously across the supper table. She hadn't been a cop's wife all that long, and in a normally peaceful little town like Prosperity the job wasn't nearly as dangerous as it would have been somewhere else, so anything other than brief worry was somewhat alien to her. But this day had been unsettling and more than a little frightening.

Talk had been flying 'round all day, carried by mail carriers and the checkout people at the grocery store and neighbors, and even if nobody was clear on details, it was definite that people had died today, died horribly.

So Kim was worried and anxious, and not a little bit scared.

Her husband's preoccupied air and expression weren't helping things.

"Jim?"

He looked at her, his normally clear gray eyes sort of . . . odd. Holding a kind of flat shine. For no reason she could have explained, a cold shiver rippled up Kim's spine.

"What is it?" he asked politely.

"You've hardly touched your supper." It was the only thing she could think to say, the only thing that seemed normal.

He looked down at the plate of spaghetti, the crisp garlic bread, the nice salad on the side. Then looked back at his wife. "I'm sorry. You went to all this trouble. And it looks great. I'm just not that hungry right now. I'm sorry."

Kim had the scary feeling that he wasn't really apologizing for not tasting his supper, or for the "trouble" she'd gone to fixing it for him. As she did every single night.

"Jim, you don't sound like yourself," she said a bit unsteadily.

He blinked, then smiled. "Do I sound like somebody else?" he asked in that odd, polite tone.

"What?"

"Do I sound like somebody else?" The flat shine that seemed a veil over his gray eyes increased. "Do I sound like your lover?"

Kim literally felt the color drain from her face. Not from guilt, because she'd done nothing to feel guilty about. But because infidelity was something she was abnormally sensitive to; she'd watched her parents' marriage break up because of her father's chronic cheating. But not before they'd torn each other to emotional shreds and hurt their children dreadfully in all the turmoil.

And Jim knew that.

Finally, she managed to force words out, hearing them shaking. "Jim, I don't have a lover except for you. I love you. I would never betray you like that. I *couldn't.* You know I couldn't."

His head tilted slightly, and though his strangely veiled gaze was fixed on her, he seemed to be listening to something else. "How could I know that?" he asked almost absently. "I'm at work all day. Sometimes all night. And you're here alone."

"Jim—"

"Alone. And so tempting. Tight jeans and a blouse I can almost see right through."

"Jim, sweetheart, listen to me." She held her voice as steady as she possibly could. "I love you. I don't want anybody else. I swear to you, I don't want anybody else."

He didn't seem to hear her. "I have to work tonight. I have to leave you alone. For hours and hours. But you won't be alone, will you? Because I've seen them watching you. The men in the neighborhood. I've seen them. They want you."

"Jim, I would never cheat on you. You have to believe that." It was just a whisper, all she could force through a throat clogged with fear and misery.

He rose slowly from the table, almost as if every

muscle hurt, and his distant gaze saw right through her. "I have to go to work," he said. "But . . . I can't leave you here alone, can I, Kim? I can't trust you here alone."

She was on her feet as well, moving instinctively to put herself between the kitchen and his work gun belt and service weapon, lying on the living room coffee table. Even though there was a small gun safe on his nightstand for his service revolver, something required by his job, they didn't have to be so careful with his other guns when it was just the two of them in the house, he had explained to her. Not yet. Not until they had kids.

"Jim, you trust me. Just like I trust you. It's so important to both of us, that trust. You know it is."

He moved around from his side of the small table, stopping less than an arm's length away from her. "I don't think I want to leave you here alone," he said. "I don't think I can trust you. Or them. The men all around, watching you with their lustful eyes."

It took all the courage Kim had not to back away from him, and her own fear of him hurt her. "No, Jim. None of them watch me. And I don't care about them. I love you. I love you so much."

She had come home from afternoon errands full of horrified gossip and speculation.

He had come home from his own afternoon errands with something unusual, with more guns, saying only that they couldn't be too careful with all the craziness going on in Prosperity, that he planned to buy a big gun cabinet and keep it in the basement, safely locked. While she had gotten supper ready, he had spent nearly an hour in his den with the guns, saying he had to clean them.

Kim had been only vaguely surprised then.

Now she was terrified.

"Jim—"

He stared at her, his hands coming to rest lightly on her shoulders. "You love me?"

"You know I do. More than anything."

His hands slid upward until they closed gently around her throat, and he smiled almost sadly. "I wish I believed that, Kim. I really wish I did."

ARCHER DREW A breath, trying to fight against the insanity of this. "External. Okay, I'll buy that. Maybe it's . . . some new kind of disease, making people crazy. Something that's contaminated the water or the food supply. Something only some people are affected by. I could call the CDC, and—"

Hollis cut him off. "And before they did anything else, they'd ask Jill and your local doctors about symptoms, and they'd be told that Leslie Gardner appears to be fine, normal bloodwork, just sleeping. That bloodwork on Sam Bowers came back normal. That Elliot Weston, when his bloodwork is done, will also appear perfectly normal. No drugs. No pathogens. No signs of any organic disease or infection."

She held her voice level. "It isn't a disease, Sheriff. It

isn't something in the water or the food supply. The CDC is no more equipped to handle what's happening here than you or your excellent deputies are. Because what's happening here is nothing natural. Not even some new disease. What's happening here is weird and crazy. And that's our specialty. It would help a lot if you could believe that."

"I don't know what I believe," he said, holding his voice quiet with an effort that showed. "Just . . . tell me you and your team can do something *about* this."

"We're going to do our best," DeMarco said. Then he surprised Archer somewhat when he reached out and took his partner's hand, holding it firmly.

Hollis immediately looked less tense but frowned up at her partner. "You shouldn't—"

"I know it'll interfere with what you can pick up, but you need a break," he said. "And if whoever you've sensed is still struggling, maybe we have a little time."

"I'd hate to bet his life on that," she said. "And the lives of whoever else he might be struggling not to kill."

"You still need the break," DeMarco insisted. "This thing's just getting started, and it'll be a lot worse before it's better. I'm betting you're the one who's going to hold the team together for the duration."

"Oh, shit, don't say that."

"You know it's true. You're team leader."

"They don't even know how to *be* a team."

"Which is why they need you. You can—forgive the term—empathize with most if not all of them because of your own abilities and experiences. I can't even

empathize with Dalton, even though he's another telepath."

"I still think he may have the best defense of us all,"
she said, then frowned and said, "or the most vulnerability. Just depends on how his rage is affected by all this
damned energy. Bishop didn't give him a gun, did he?"

"Of course not. None of them will be armed until
we have some idea of who might be affected and how.
And possibly not even then."

"I'm worried about Reno. Her ability is wholly receptive, and unlike Sully she's never needed a shield.
She's wide open. If all this energy is looking for vulnerable minds, it won't find one in hers, I know that, but
it's bound to have some kind of effect on her. And it's
likely to be a negative effect."

Archer drew their attention, silently making a "time-
out" gesture with both hands. His face was very calm.

Hollis wasn't tempted to laugh. "Sorry. I know it's
confusing," she told the sheriff. "Baffling, crazy,
unbelievable—whatever you want to call it. But it's *real*.
What's happening here is real. You get that, right?"

"I've got seven people dead since daybreak," he said
in a very, very steady voice. "One killer sleeping and
another one who is clearly unaware he's done anything
wrong, much less shot two people to death in cold
blood. Believe me, I know this is real."

"Okay." Her voice remained calm as well. "We're
real too. Nothing we do is magic. Nothing is beyond
the realm of science or the limits of the human mind.
We've just learned to use energy because we have the

natural abilities to do that, and because we've spent years working to understand and use those abilities. To . . . home in on frequencies beyond the range of our normal hearing. To see further than most people, and see more sharply, even around the next corner sometimes. To focus our own energy and use it in very specific ways. Because these abilities are *natural* to us."

Archer made a slight, helpless gesture. "Okay. Fine. I don't have to understand. If you can stop these killings, stop whoever or whatever is causing them, and get Prosperity back to normal, I don't give a shit if you *do* use magic."

Chief Deputy Katie Cole came out onto the porch in time to hear that, holding a bagged pistol and looking a bit queasy. But all she said was, "Oh, good, you told him the rest."

"You should have," Hollis said somewhat severely.

"Didn't know how."

Archer was staring at her, and Katie managed a rather weak smile. "Sorry, Jack."

"You too?"

"Yeah, since I was a kid. That's how I knew which unit in the FBI to call. I'd met Bishop a couple years ago, even considered joining his unit." Her voice was casual, though the hazel eyes were watchful on her boss's face. "I'm clairvoyant."

"Which means?"

Hollis answered. "It means she knows things, picks up bits and pieces of information without really being able to explain how."

He frowned at his chief deputy. "Anonymous tips," he said somewhat bitterly. "You always said they were anonymous tips."

"Sorry, Jack," Katie repeated, then went on quickly. "The doc's assistant had a print kit, so this has been printed; I think we'll find only Weston's prints on it, and that we'll be able to match the registration number of the gun to Weston. So far, nobody's tried to hide anything, so I don't know why he would have used somebody else's gun."

"Probably wouldn't have," Hollis agreed. "And that means, if it's his gun, he brought it along today. I don't think real estate agents normally show homes while armed."

"No," Archer said almost absently.

Hollis, aware that the sheriff's entire world was in the process of being adjusted rather drastically, looked at him with sympathy as she said, "Which means someone or something told him to bring his gun. And I'm betting that someone or something was . . . whispering in his mind while he was showing the house. Telling him whatever it took to cause him to kill them. And then to forget he'd done it, or care about that or anything at all."

"Why?" Archer demanded. "I don't have to understand how, maybe, but *why*?"

"That's one of the questions we have to answer," Hollis told him. "And we've assembled a . . . unique team for this investigation. Galen stayed behind at the station to wait for the first two, arriving tonight. The rest will be coming in tomorrow. Four more."

Archer blinked. "Agent Bishop said there'd be more following you three, but didn't say how many. Um . . . all psychics?"

Hollis nodded. "With differing abilities and differing strengths and weaknesses. The idea is to complement each other, each supplying another tool or two for the toolbox. So we can cover all possible bases in terms of abilities."

She studied the sheriff and decided to keep things brisk and businesslike. No need to mention the energy . . . dome . . . which she had discovered was eerily visible to her even after dark: a faint reddish glow to the night sky, and softly hissing strands of energy moving high above them like lacy patterns of sheer electricity.

More weird and crazy.

No need to mention that. And no need, she hoped, to go into anything but the briefest details about the rest of her team.

"The other members of the team," she told him, explaining what they had decided would be cover for the non-SCU members, "have been attached to this investigation because their tools are needed. They're members of our civilian sister organization, Haven."

"The FBI has one of those?"

"The SCU has one of those."

He stared at her. "I've never heard of that."

"Most law enforcement officials haven't until they have need of Haven's investigators and operatives—or until we do. Haven operatives and SCU agents have worked together a lot. They're all licensed investigators.

And part of this team. They wouldn't be if our unit chief wasn't convinced they need to be here."

Archer might have said something else, but Jill came out of the house just then and joined them on the porch.

"Preliminary report?" she said to the sheriff.

"Yeah. Yeah, maybe it'll help us."

"Help you to convict Weston, sure, assuming he's fit to stand trial if any of this gets that far. Otherwise, not so much."

She had examined Elliot Weston briefly when she'd arrived, finding normal vitals and nothing else that had appeared out of the ordinary. Except, of course, for his smiling unconcern.

Archer nodded. "Okay, got it. Your report?"

"What you saw in there is what I expect to find in the posts. Two victims, each killed by a single gunshot from the weapon found on scene. No defensive wounds at all. No sign that they were anything but completely surprised and didn't have time to run or even try to defend themselves."

Archer drew a deep breath and let it out slowly. "You think you'll find the same with the other victims killed today, don't you, Doc? That they were killed just as it looked like they were."

She nodded. "I'd rather not speculate too much until I get them all on the table, especially the apparent suicide victim I haven't seen yet, but it all looked pretty clear to me at the Gardner house that the victims either were subdued by fairly lethal blows before they were mutilated and killed, or else—as seems the case with Mr. Gardner—were taken by surprise. No sign of defensive wounds."

Archer looked toward the end of the driveway behind the ME's white van at the dark hearse parked there. They had never needed a coroner's wagon in Prosperity, so one or the other of the local funeral homes generally transported bodies to the hospital morgue—or directly to their own, if victims had died naturally and there was no suspicion attached to their deaths.

Which had virtually always been the case. Until today.

The sheriff sighed. "A couple of my deputies will help load the bodies as soon as they're in body bags. They'll be taken to the hospital morgue, like the others."

Jill Easton nodded. "Good. Sheriff, the chances are I'll only be able to get one of the posts done tonight. I'd like to start with the apparent suicide, since that was the first scene you were called to. I'll get you that report ASAP, then start on the other posts first thing in the morning."

"Long day for you," he murmured. "Today and tomorrow."

"I'm used to it."

Katie Cole spoke up then to say, "We've reserved rooms for you and your assistant at the largest hotel in town, the Jameson. It's about halfway between the sheriff's department and the hospital, just off Main Street. Very comfortable, good service and food."

"Thanks," Jill said. "It'll probably be midnight before we can get checked in, but I definitely want a good night's sleep before tomorrow."

Katie nodded. "They have room service until midnight; if you think you'll be later, call the front desk and they'll be happy to leave meals in your rooms. Sandwiches, salads, soup—whatever will keep best if you're delayed longer."

"Appreciate that." Jill looked at the two feds. "Are you guys staying there?"

Hollis nodded. "Bishop called ahead and arranged for us to have the entire top floor. Since the team is larger than normal, we'll need the space. Apparently, most of the rooms on that floor have connecting doors, plus there's a comfortable lounge common space we can use if we need to."

"Thinks of everything, our Bishop, doesn't he." It wasn't a question. Jill smiled faintly, then said to the sheriff, "You can send your deputies inside for the body bags in about five minutes, Sheriff." She went back inside the house.

"She knows Agent Bishop too?"

Casual, Hollis said, "Bishop knows a lot of people, especially in and associated with law enforcement and support services. Jill was part of the last case Reese and I worked on, and Bishop joined us at one point."

"Does he often show up himself?"

"No, not very. He's a field unit chief, so he tends to be out working cases just like his teams are."

Nodding an acceptance of that without much interest, Archer looked at his watch and grimaced slightly. "Hardly later than suppertime. Christ, this has been the longest day of my life." He rubbed his face with both hands wearily, then looked at Hollis and De-Marco. "We still don't have much in the way of reports or evidence for your team to get started on tonight. I say we go back to the station long enough for me to meet the two team members arriving tonight, toss around a few ideas if anybody has 'em, and then we all should try to get some rest. I don't know about you, but I'm not looking forward to tomorrow. Just going over autopsy reports takes a lot out of me."

"Same here," Hollis murmured.

He's forgotten about the other potential killer you felt struggling.

Yeah. But no need to remind him right now—he's got enough on his mind. Especially since I can't even point him in a specific direction toward that person, far less give him a name. Let's find out what Victoria and Logan have sensed. If anything.

Probably best.

Oblivious of the mind talk, Archer said to the agents, "I'm assuming we keep Weston in a cell tonight. Should I call a doc to take a closer look at him?"

"I sort of doubt any of your doctors would find much," Hollis said. "But he needs to be kept under someone's eye all the time; we should try talking to him again tomorrow. And, if you don't mind, Sheriff, could you have the deputy with Leslie Gardner notify either you or one of us when she wakes up? Even if it's the middle of the night? We'll definitely need to talk to her."

He looked at her with mild curiosity. "What do you expect her to tell us, assuming she says anything at all?"

Prompt, Hollis replied, "If anything at all, I expect some version of what we got from Elliot Weston. No memory of what happened to her family and no awareness that she did anything at all. I don't see how she could have just gone to sleep otherwise. I think her own mind put her to sleep to protect her from the horror of what she'd done."

The sheriff winced. "I was afraid you were going to say that. Dammit. Okay. Gabby was due to rotate off shift hours ago; I'll send somebody to relieve her."

"Sounds good. Meet you at the station," Hollis said.

Archer nodded again, following them far enough off the porch to beckon to two more of his deputies to come to the house.

Hollis caught a slightly wary, slightly surprised glimpse from one of them as she and DeMarco walked past headed for their SUV, and murmured, "Feds holding hands. That's what they're thinking, right?"

Calmly, her partner said, "One of them is thinking it must be nice to not have to pretend there's no personal involvement between partners."

"I thought I was picking up a little envy from someone close."

"So you can sense emotions even through my shield?"

"Just the people really nearby, I think. And probably not many of them. You know, we've never discussed whether our personal relationship will affect how we're viewed and treated by any of the law enforcement people we'll have to work with."

DeMarco opened the passenger door of the SUV and helped her in without releasing her hand. "Do you care?" he asked politely.

Hollis grinned faintly. "Nope. The married couples in the SCU don't seem to have any problem, so I don't see why we would. Will. You're planning on keeping me inside your shield all night, aren't you?"

"I am. You need whatever break I can give you from all this energy trapped with us, and you need to sleep tonight. You'll have more than enough to deal with tomorrow." He released her hand finally and went around to the driver's-side door.

The loss of physical contact, however brief, brought Hollis's abilities back into sharp focus, and as DeMarco got behind the wheel, he both saw and felt that she was picking up something she did *not* like.

"What?" He frowned slightly as he looked at her.

"Don't shield me for a minute," she murmured, staring straight ahead. "I think . . . whoever was struggling is . . . terrified almost out of his mind. Maybe out of his mind. All I'm getting is a sort of desperate terror."

"Then maybe he can resist."

"I dunno, maybe." She turned her head and looked at her partner. "I can tell you he's not where he was before. Feels like he's closer. And still moving. Let's get back to the sheriff's department. If something happens or has already happened, that's probably where we should be."

"Agreed." DeMarco started the SUV and put it in gear, only then reaching for his partner's hand. "Between here and there, take a break."

"Do I have a choice?" she asked dryly.

"No," DeMarco said, and headed for the sheriff's station.

TEN

They found Galen, as expected, in the conference room at the sheriff's department, seated at the far end of the big table, slumped and apparently sleepy as he watched the two other people sitting along one side of the table, Victoria Stark and Logan Alexander.

As Hollis and DeMarco walked into the room—not holding hands any longer—they came in on what had apparently been a rather tense discussion.

"All I'm saying," Victoria told Logan, "is that maybe you need to *try* to see them."

"I don't want to try," Logan responded sharply. "All this energy in the air is bad enough without adding in spirits."

"Hey, guys," Hollis said, rather glad that no deputies were near enough to overhear. Although she wasn't at all sure the psychic abilities of her team wouldn't be an open secret, among the deputies at least, very soon. They'd all learned in their everyday lives to hide or at least keep quiet about their abilities, her non-SCU team members, but they had never been called upon to work as a team, or work with law enforcement without giving away the details of how they acquired the information they did, and they didn't have the experience the SCU agents had with a whole lot of strange and crazy.

She and DeMarco sat down across from them, and Hollis smiled faintly at Logan's stubborn expression. Her gaze turned to Victoria, who was looking a bit impatient but otherwise not giving away much.

Without wasting time, Hollis asked both of them, "What are your impressions of the energy?"

"I can barely feel it," Victoria replied. "Sort of a tingle on the back of my neck, and I'm more tense than usual for me, but that's pretty much it."

Hollis nodded. "About what I expected. Logan?"

"What?"

She laughed under her breath, undisturbed by his snapped response. "I gather you haven't seen any spirits since getting here?"

"No." He eyed her, then added, "It's been a nice break."

"I hear that. You can obviously feel the energy in this valley; could either of you see it on the drive here?"

Victoria said, "Bishop asked us to stop at one of the overlooks when we could see the valley and find out if we could see what you did, but it looked normal to me."

"Logan?"

"Normal."

"Okay. What about now? What, exactly, are you feeling?"

"Not much," he answered. "Skin's tingling a bit. And there's pressure, I think. Faint."

"But no spirits."

"No spirits."

"Correct me if I'm wrong," Hollis said, "but you always see spirits. Right?"

"Yeah, since I was a kid." He could remember the very first instance. He'd been three, and his grandmother had been smiling at him. Standing beside her open casket.

"Everywhere you go? In a broad range of places and circumstances?"

"Yeah." He hesitated, then said, "Didn't see any on the jet, which is usual, but there were some around the airport in San Francisco, also usual. And—that's the last time I saw any. None at the airstrip near Bishop's base, and none at the house. None along the drive here. None here."

"Have you gotten any sense at all of spiritual energy?"

Logan frowned. "I generally don't. I mean—I don't really differentiate when it comes to energy."

"How do you know you're looking at a spirit and not a living person?"

"I just know. Look, Bishop wanted me to learn about some of this shit, but I wasn't all that interested because I didn't believe it would make a difference for me. I see dead people. They talk to me. They follow me around. Usually they want me to do something for them."

"And do you?" Hollis asked.

"Sometimes. If I can, which is pretty much limited to anonymously alerting officials of something or other." He grimaced. "I've spent a hell of a lot of time over the years calling police departments all over the country to tell them where to find bodies. First using pay phones and nowadays using burners. Probably spent a fortune on the damned things. But the last thing I wanted was to get involved in some murder or missing-persons investigation just because a spirit told me where to find their bodies."

Hollis was frowning slightly. "You've moved around a lot, according to Bishop. When you saw spirits in whatever town or city you were in, were they local?"

It was his turn to frown. "Now that you mention it, yeah, they were. Or, at least, what they asked me to do was local. I hadn't thought about that before. Why? Is that important?"

"I don't know what's important yet," she told him frankly. "But this is a big valley holding several thousand people. And the town was founded over two hundred years ago. That's a lot of people living and dying here over time."

Galen spoke up then to say mildly, "Graveyards at every church I saw while I was driving around. Half a dozen or more. And two big cemeteries outside the city limits, one north and one east of the town. Everything very well tended, both the church grounds and the cemeteries. Nothing neglected. Even the oldest graves look to have been taken care of."

"So, respect for the dead." Hollis was frowning. "I don't know if that matters either. I've only ever seen one spirit in a cemetery, and she wasn't buried there. Logan?"

"I stay away from cemeteries and graveyards," he said flatly.

Her frown faded, and she smiled at him. "Unless you're different from every other medium I know, you don't have to avoid graveyards or cemeteries; the dead don't seem to want to hang around those places. Although you generally see a few in churches, and definitely hospitals."

He blinked, and asked almost unwillingly, "Do spirits always ask you for help?"

"A few have. A very few have helped in investigations. But mostly I just see or sense them around. Off in the corners, the shadows of some house or building usually. Not really coming forward. I think most of them aren't interested in interacting with the living. Unless, as you've discovered, they need the help of the living."

"At any hour of the day or night," he said somewhat bitterly. Then he eyed her. "Maybe it's different for— You aren't a born medium, are you?"

"No, I was triggered a few years ago." She could say it easily now, without horrific memories clawing through her mind. And other than a couple of nightmares when she and Reese had first arrived at their island, those had stopped as well.

Hopefully for good.

Thoughtfully, Hollis added, "It probably is different for born mediums, though every one I know is unique in some way. I didn't have any kind of a shield at first, and I broadcast, which was . . . disconcerting. But other members of the SCU helped me. And it got better."

He lifted an eyebrow at her. "Recruitment speech?"

"Of course not, Logan. Would I do that?" Her tone was mild.

"I have no idea what you'd do," he told her. "But if Bishop couldn't persuade me, I doubt you could."

DeMarco murmured, "Don't be so sure."

Logan looked at him, but before he could say or ask anything, Hollis was speaking again, briskly.

"Okay, look, guys. We were all summoned here, and there is definitely something weird and crazy going on. Something very deadly weird and crazy. Since nothing else has stuck out so far, we can be fairly certain at least for now that the energy in this valley has to be the cause. And since neither Logan nor I have seen any spirits, we probably aren't dealing with spiritual energy."

"Have you before?" Victoria asked.

"Dealt with spiritual energy? Oh, yeah. But if the spirits want to get involved in this, they aren't saying."

Politely, Logan asked, "Then why are we here? Why am *I* here? I don't have a secondary ability. I see spirits. If there are no spirits here, if none are involved in— whatever the hell this is, then why am I here?"

"It's a good question," DeMarco said.

Hollis looked at her partner. "Yeah. But I still don't know what it means. A very upset spirit told me I had to come to Prosperity. I'm guessing Logan was told the same way."

He nodded. "Yeah. Although he wasn't initially upset. I mean, not about that. He was upset because his girlfriend had been wrongly accused, he said, of poisoning him."

It was Hollis's turn to blink as she looked at him. Then she turned her gaze to her partner again. "How come I don't ever get stuff like that?"

"Give it time," DeMarco said.

"Something to look forward to," she murmured.

Logan, frowning, brought them ruthlessly back to his original question. "Okay, so the two mediums involved were told to come here by spirits. I don't know about yours, but mine pretty much stopped talking in midsentence and then looked anxious and afraid. In less than a minute, he looked terrified. Said something about both the living and the dead being in trouble or being hurt by this—by whatever *this* is. That I had to come to Prosperity, that I had to help *them* stop *it*. All of you, I assume. Then he disappeared. Then there were a whole bunch of dead people all around me in the park, just standing and staring at me, which has never happened to me before and which was creepy as hell. Felt like the fucking zombie apocalypse, except they all looked normal—for spirits. Just staring at me. And then there was a girl spirit, a young woman, who also begged me to come to Prosperity. Said I was needed here. So. If this energy has nothing to do with spirits, if the threat here has nothing to do with spirits, then how am I needed here?"

"I hate to have to repeat myself," Hollis said, "but I have no idea. Yet. We're very much at the speculation and information-gathering stage of the investigation. But it definitely bothers me that neither of us has seen a spirit in or around Prosperity."

"Due to the energy here, maybe," DeMarco said. "Or the pressure. Maybe whatever's holding energy in this valley is also holding spiritual energy *out*."

Hollis nodded slowly. "Could be. And, if so, it might explain why two mediums were summoned. It may well take both of us, if that's what we have to do."

"I'm not following," Logan said.

"We open doors," she said. "It's what mediums do. We open doors between the world of the living and the spirit realm; that's what allows the communication. *If* all this energy in the valley is somehow blocking or otherwise holding out spiritual energy, maybe we're the only ones who can let it back in."

Politely, Logan said, "And why in hell would we want to do that? If the spirits stay away, I'm seriously considering moving here to live. A nice, peaceful place where no dead people talk to me."

DeMarco said, "Where seven people have died today under very mysterious circumstances."

Still truculent, Logan said, "Well, none of them has shown up asking for my help, so why should I care?"

Hollis said, "It's all about balance, Logan. The dead have their parts to play just like we do." She looked at her partner suddenly. "Maybe that's the common denominator we've all missed."

"What do you mean?"

"What summoned us. And the way we were all summoned. No matter what our abilities are, we all heard, in some form, voices telling us to come here. Logan and I saw spirits who were very upset, distraught, who clearly felt threatened. You heard a voice telling you to come here. Olivia said she heard whispers, then voices telling her to come to Prosperity. Reno had a vision of a hellish place filled with hideously deformed creatures that might once have been human—and Shadow People, one of which offered her a pretty chilling warning of what could happen if we can't stop whatever's going on here."

"I've heard of them," Victoria said suddenly. "Shadow People. They seem to keep turning up in— popular lore. Supposedly where people are experiencing the ugly side of the paranormal. I've seen self-proclaimed mediums on TV saying the Shadow People are demonic."

Almost absently, Hollis said, "More of those TV mediums than you might think are genuine."

"Talking about demons?"

Hollis looked at her, saw her. "Dark energy. Negative energy shaped into a . . . recognizable form. Maybe even negative spiritual energy, originating from very evil dead people. Calling them *demons* is probably as accurate a term as any."

"You mean they don't go straight to hell?" Galen sounded disgusted.

Still in that preoccupied tone, Hollis replied, "Sure, some of them do. Maybe most of them."

DeMarco glanced at the end of the table, a little amused to note that the answer had visibly disconcerted Galen. It wasn't often that his hard face showed any emotion. It was even rarer for him to be disconcerted. By anything.

Victoria looked disconcerted as well. "There's a hell? An actual fiery pit?"

"Something like that," Hollis replied. "A place of judgment, punishment. Not necessarily a fiery pit, though probably for some. For others . . . punishment fitting the crime, would be my guess. I think most of us, as long as we try to make it through life in a positive way, have another chance, maybe a lot of chances, to get it right, but the truly evil find something very different waiting for them after death."

Victoria gazed at their team leader in unconscious fascination. "Wow. I . . . did not know that. Never been very religious."

"Me either. Religions mostly just try to explain things," Hollis said. "In terms people can understand. Most every religion has some form of hell, limbo, purgatory. So people are warned that there are always consequences. In this life. In an afterlife. And in whatever comes after that."

———

ARCHER RETURNED TO the station less than five minutes later, and was introduced to Victoria and Logan. He felt more weary than he could ever remember feeling, far too tired to want to get into another baffling discussion about psychic abilities, so he wasn't about to bring up the question of what psychic "tools" had been added to the team of pretty ordinary-looking people.

He tended to weigh people quickly when first introduced, but he didn't even try with these two. Something else claimed his attention almost immediately.

Hollis had introduced the two newest team members, her voice just a bit distant, and after making professionally polite noises at the newcomers, Archer realized that everyone in the room was watching Hollis with varying degrees of tension or concern. She wasn't looking at any of them, just sort of staring into space as he'd seen her do earlier.

And her unusual eyes were . . . luminous.

Afraid to ask, more afraid not to, the sheriff finally said, "Somebody want to tell me what's going on? Hollis?" He was hardly aware that it was the first time he'd used her given name unprompted.

After a moment, she blinked, then looked at him. "Hmm?"

"What is it?"

Hollis abruptly rose to her feet, startling him, and

turned her gaze, frowning now, through the glass partition dividing the room from the bullpen, and past that to the lobby and the front desk.

Before Archer could ask again, there was a commotion in the lobby, a confusion of thuds and bangs combined with an unnaturally loud voice he didn't immediately recognize. Cody Greene, the deputy manning the reception desk, was sort of scrambling to turn around, his hand on his gun in a movement that looked more instinctive than deliberate.

Matt Spencer and Kayla Nelson were the only two deputies in the bullpen, having delivered Elliot Weston to a cell in back and made sure he was being watched at all times. Both had been relaxed but rose quickly to their feet the instant the commotion began, hands also coming to rest on the grips of their service weapons.

Before anyone could react in any other way, a uniformed deputy with an armful of guns pushed open the glass door of the lobby and rushed into the bullpen—and straight back to the conference room, his wide-eyed gaze fixed on the face of the sheriff.

"Here!" He thrust the guns, several rifles and what looked like a shotgun, into the sheriff's surprised arms, then immediately unloaded two pistols from his pants pockets onto the conference table with a clatter, and began unbuckling his belt, his service weapon still securely fastened in its holster.

"Jim, what the hell?" Archer half turned toward Hollis, the closest to him, long enough for her to reach out silently to take the rifles and shotgun from him and place them on the table.

"You have to take them. You have to keep them." Jim Lonnagan's voice was low, hurried. "Keep them away from me. *Away.* I nearly killed her, Jack. I nearly killed Kim. I had my hands around her throat, and—and the voice said to kill her, said I had to, and I was *listening*, Jack, I wanted to *do* it! Just like I wanted to buy these damned— Take the guns, please, lock me in a cell before I hurt her, before I hurt anybody—"

His face was ghostly pale and beaded with sweat, fear and desperation coming off him in waves.

DeMarco, who had risen as the others had when his partner did, saw Hollis lift one hand and rub her left temple hard, her gaze fixed on the deputy and her expression holding both pain and anxiety. He could feel it through her, the emotions so powerful they were like a punch in the gut. And even so, she was trying to probe, to understand what was fighting so hard to influence this deputy.

Archer accepted Lonnagan's gun belt, almost tossing it onto the table, then snapped out to the deputies standing stock-still a few feet away in the bullpen, "Go check on Kim, *now*."

Both started, jolted out of their frozen bewilderment, and hurried toward the front door.

Lonnagan was still babbling, virtually unintelligible now, his voice a desperate tumble of words chased by terror. He grasped fistfuls of Archer's slightly open jacket, the plea for help obvious even if coherency was beyond him.

"Jim—Jim, calm down. It's all right. Jim—"

Both Victoria and Logan had jumped up when Hollis rose, and both had instinctively given way to the distraught deputy, backing away from him and the table. Almost directly behind him, Victoria stared at the deputy for just a moment, then met Hollis's gaze.

Hollis nodded once.

Immediately, Victoria stepped close enough to Lonnagan so she could reach up and touch either side of his head with both hands.

"Sleep," she said quietly.

The babble was cut off as though a switch had been thrown, and Lonnagan dropped, caught expertly by Victoria. Logan stepped forward to help automatically, and Galen moved around the table toward them.

It all happened within the space of a few seconds.

"There's a couch in the sheriff's office across the hall," Hollis told them, the pain and anxiety no longer gripping her features. "Take him in there for now."

Archer stared down at his deputy, his face still holding shock, and watched as Galen and Logan carried the unconscious man out of the conference room. He looked blankly at Victoria. "What did you do?" he asked.

"It's all right, Sheriff, he's just sleeping," Victoria replied, calm. "I think he needed to, don't you?"

Archer stared at her a moment longer, then looked at Hollis. He obviously wanted to ask a dozen questions, but only one emerged. "What the hell?"

"Sit down, Jack," she said.

The sheriff found himself sitting down at the table just where his deputy had stood, hardly noticing that Victoria silently pulled out the chair for him. He looked at the pile of guns before him and repeated, "What the hell?" rather helplessly.

The others were reclaiming their seats, joined in less than a minute by Galen and Logan. Hollis waited until everybody was there again before she spoke to the sheriff, and even though the words were somewhat flip, her tone was anything but.

"Good news, bad news," she said to Archer. "The good news is, your deputy didn't murder his wife or anyone else."

"And the bad news?"

"He almost did."

Archer was staring at her. "Jim Lonnagan is a good man."

"I don't doubt it. Did you listen to what he was saying, Jack? A voice told him to buy the guns. A voice told him to kill his wife. A voice he very badly wanted to obey. I seriously doubt he's in the middle of a psychotic break none of you saw coming. Any mental illness would have presented with symptoms long before now. So this is new. This was sudden. This was something no one, not you and not Deputy Lonnagan, could have seen coming. What I know, what I feel, is that he's the one I've felt struggling so desperately not to give in. If he'd lost that struggle, he would have killed his wife. And maybe himself. Maybe others."

Archer wearily rubbed his face with both hands in what was becoming a familiar gesture. "And if he'd killed Kim, but not himself? Would we have found him on his front porch smiling and blank like Elliot Weston? Or asleep like Leslie Gardner?"

"Probably one of those," Hollis said in that steady voice. "Though more likely another successful suicide. He fought so hard, I doubt he could have lived with it if he'd been forced to kill his wife. But he fought it, Jack. And he won. That's important. It's the first real evidence we've had that whatever's doing this *can* be fought, and not by resorting to suicide the way Sam Bowers did. It can be fought. And it can be defeated."

"Energy?" There was no longer even disbelief in his voice.

"Some kind of energy. But energy alone can't speak, not words. It can't urge, command. Not without a guiding mind behind it, focusing and controlling it."

"What does that mean? Somebody's doing this? Somebody's driving people to murder others?"

Hollis barely hesitated, knowing that the sheriff would be able to accept a some*body* as an enemy far more easily than he would a some*thing*. Especially when the some*thing* pretty much defied description, far less definition.

Besides, she wasn't absolutely positive a person or people weren't behind it all. Somehow.

"That's what it means. We'll find out who's behind it, Jack, I promise you. It's what we do."

He stared at her for a moment, then half nodded,

something in his expression telling everyone in the room that he had reached his limit, at least for the day, that he literally couldn't absorb any more of the weird and crazy.

"What about Jim? Will he wake up?"

Victoria replied, "In a couple of hours, probably. Unless—" She looked at Hollis, abruptly worried.

But Hollis was shaking her head. "I don't think he'll stay asleep longer than the nap you gave him. He resisted. He didn't kill his wife or anyone else." She looked at Archer. "It might be a good idea to have a doctor standing by for when he wakes. If he's in the same state he was, sedation or an antianxiety med might be the best thing for him."

"You don't want to talk to him?"

"Definitely, assuming he's up to it. Not tonight, though. He needs to be a lot calmer when we talk to him, and I don't think that's going to happen in the next few hours. Hell, it may not happen at all. But I'd put him in a cell, Jack. If possible, not close to Elliot Weston. Both need to be watched."

"Yeah, okay." He glanced toward the empty bullpen.

Galen got to his feet. "Logan and I will carry him back to the cells, Sheriff. If you'll lead the way."

In the same numb voice, Archer repeated, "Yeah, okay." Then he got up and led the other two men out.

Hollis noted that Logan had looked a bit pale, and she said to her partner, "I think he's just realized."

"Yeah, he has," DeMarco responded quietly.

Victoria frowned at them. "What?"

"Logan never really had much luck building a shield," Hollis said.

"Yeah, I know that. He's never been able to keep out spirits. So?"

"The energy in this valley is affecting nonpsychics, obviously, if all our theories are right. It's driven people to suicide or murder even if we don't exactly understand how. Lonnagan fought it and didn't kill, but we don't know what damage may have been done to his mind during that struggle. The energy is also affecting us. Reese has a double shield, and he can still feel it. I can feel it. You and Logan have been aware of it."

Victoria frowned a moment longer, then went a bit pale herself. "You think— You're saying that the same thing that happened to that deputy could happen to us? That we could be . . . urged . . . to kill someone against our will?"

"I'm saying it's probably more likely than not that we'll be targets. That one or more of us will be somehow negatively affected. Anybody with a weak or nonexistent shield is more likely to feel it first. We don't really know what symptoms to look for; there must be a period before these people heard that voice, when the energy was first taking hold, but so far none of them has been able to tell us much about that."

"Then—"

"Keep your shield up, Victoria. And if you start experiencing any unusual symptoms, tell us immediately."

ELEVEN

Hollis attempted to use the phone they carried, but since it only crackled loudly she had to use the hotel landline in their room to report in to base nearly two hours later.

"Communications are really screwed up," she told Bishop. "My tablet's already dead, and I had to plug my laptop in for more than ten minutes before it would even boot up." She was on the bed, leaning back against pillows banked behind her. "Wi-Fi's useless, but this hotel kept their earlier data ports feeding into a ground line, so it looks like we'll be able to send and receive information that way. Not sure about the Internet yet."

"Log on as soon as you can and go through the handshake process with the databases we use. Remember that?"

"Yeah, pretty sure, even if it's been a while. If not, Logan's an IT guy, right?"

"How he makes his living." Bishop paused, then said, "The real estate agent who killed his clients. He was completely blank?"

"Pretty much. I mean, he could talk, he could respond to questions, more or less, but he was clearly out of it, didn't have a clue what was going on. Even forgot he was wearing handcuffs unless he moved his hands. And even though Archer didn't seem to notice, Reese and I both believe Weston got . . . worse . . . just in the time we were there. Tomorrow morning, we may find him asleep, catatonic, or, if we're lucky, no worse than he was. Which would be smiling, pleasant, and with absolutely no memory of what he did."

"So no help in understanding what's happening."

"No, I think we've gotten all we're going to from Elliot Weston, and Reese agrees. We checked the hospital just before calling you, and Leslie Gardner is still asleep. I'm not at all sure she's ever going to wake up, but we'll go to the hospital tomorrow anyway and see if Reese can read her. Not sure what we're going to have when Deputy Lonnagan wakes up, and I don't know what I fear more—that he'll still be wild with terror, or that he'll be mindless."

"Which do you really expect?"

Hollis paused for a moment to consider, gazing at her partner, who was leaning back on the bed near her feet. "Well, that depends on whatever's behind the energy. We can't know yet whether the aim is to destroy the mind—or take control of it just because tools are needed to kill and cause chaos, and leaving a wrecked mind behind is just a side effect of the process."

"But there's a definite goal or goals."

"Oh, yeah. Lonnagan was raving about the voices in his mind telling him to kill his wife. He fought, he resisted, and she's still alive. Not sure how long ago it started for him. For any of them. I mean, how long do you have to work at a woman's mind before she'll butcher her own kids?"

"That probably depends on whether the energy found a weakness in her somehow. A vulnerable place."

Hollis frowned. "We were thinking that. The deputies who went to check on Lonnagan's wife came back just before we left the station. Said they found her hysterical, terrified, and that she didn't say much they could even understand. They called her sister to come stay with her, waited for her to get to the house, then left. The thing is, Reese was able to read one of the deputies, someone who's been fairly close to the couple, and one thing *she* got from Kim Lonnagan, hysterical or not, was that her husband had accused her of infidelity, which is apparently a very sensitive thing between them. Both saw their parents' marriages torn apart by infidelity, and both had always sworn it wouldn't happen to them."

"A vulnerability."

"Yeah. Which, if you ask me, makes this energy thing a lot more dangerous and scary. It not only got into Lonnagan's head, it apparently knew exactly which button to push—or found it once it was in his mind. That's not just energy, that's energy being directed, by a very clever, very devious and ruthless mind."

"But is it a human mind?"

"I have no idea, and neither does Reese. So far we haven't sensed anything to tell us if it is. Or if it isn't. Look, we all know it's more than possible for a single evil mind to do a hell of a lot, but . . . Assuming this destructive energy is supposed to balance the scale with the positive energy that summoned us, which I really hope is the case, I'm wondering if the positive energy I can sense here is what summoned us, or was left over when we were summoned. And, if so, will it come into play at the right time to help us."

After a thoughtful moment, Bishop said, "That may depend on how much of the energy was required for the summoning."

"True. But the negative energy is being used or expended at a very high level. I mean, at the very least this thing has been affecting and controlling people during overlapping time periods. I'm really hoping it's limited in that way and can't go after all the people in this valley at once, but we're all feeling the energy, so who knows? Maybe that's what it's building up to."

"That's probably more likely than not."

Hollis had been wondering if he knew more than he'd told them about this. She thought she had her answer. But all she said was, "Then finding the source or sources and sealing whatever doorways or portals are there is the only way to stop the energy buildup."

"I would expect that to be a first step. Later, we can send people to make those seals as strong as possible, but the most important thing is to close them as best we can as soon as we can."

"Yeah. Well, Reese and I need to get out and explore the valley tomorrow; the energy is still visible to me even tonight, but it's a lot clearer in the daytime and a lot more likely to help show us whatever it is we need to know. Hopefully we'll find those doorways or portals before more people are killed and/or driven mad."

Bishop was silent for a moment, then said, "You said Logan and Victoria were shaken by the deputy."

"Not when he first rushed in, I think. They took that pretty calmly, on the whole, and Victoria was quick to act. Looked to me first, which was a bit reassuring; I still don't know how many of them are going to accept a team leader. Or even being part of a team. Anyway, when Victoria and Logan realized after they saw Lonnagan that it was at least possible the same thing could happen to one or even all of us, that we could be forced to fight just to keep control of our own minds . . . Yeah, that shook them. Shakes me too."

"You handle energy better than any psychic I've ever known," Bishop said.

"Be that as it may, until we find the source or sources of the energy I don't think there's a lot for me *to* handle. Or, at least, not a lot I *can* handle. So Reese and I both feel that's the priority. Unless one of us in some way senses someone in trouble, someone we might be able to help, finding the energy source has to be our priority. Otherwise, we're just sitting around uselessly speculating or else racing to reach a murder scene too late to do anything about it. Profiling a killer isn't what this is about, so what we normally do isn't going to help."

"I'd agree."

"I hope Archer does. He called for help and what he got was a group of psychics who are turning his belief system completely upside down. Pretty sure he's not going to be happy when most of us are *just* out roaming around this valley looking for the energy source."

"Do you want me to call him?"

"No, not yet. But he may call you. Depends on whether he gets any sleep tonight and how clear his head is tomorrow."

"I'll be here if and when he calls."

"Good. Now, what about the others? I don't know about Sully's shield, how strong it really is, and I know he's limited by distance, but there are a hell of a lot of very freaked-out people around here, and I'm fairly sure that's going to be difficult for him, never mind the energy. I'm worried about Olivia because she's so fragile; I'm worried about Reno because she's so open; and I'm worried about Dalton because—well, I'm just worried about him."

"So am I," Bishop said wryly. "Miranda and I have done what we could in the little time available, but each of these people is pretty much coming to Prosperity with the abilities they had when they were summoned. They may well be affected by the energy, and their abilities could evolve to help them fight. Which I hope was the intent of whatever or whoever summoned all of you."

"Bishop, be straight with me. What did you and Miranda see?"

He was silent for so long Hollis wasn't at all sure he'd answer, which would be fairly typical of him, but when he finally did offer an answer, she almost wished she hadn't asked.

"We saw . . . something of what could happen if the team isn't successful at stopping this. It was a lot like Reno's vision, except we saw the beginning. Saw the darkness spreading outward from Prosperity, destroying everything in its path. That's the line your team has to hold, Hollis. If whatever it is escapes that valley, stopping it becomes pretty damned close to impossible."

Hollis drew a breath and let it out slowly. "Next time, just tell me I really don't need to know," she said.

"This time you did. You can handle this, Hollis."

"Yeah. Right. When are you going to send the others?"

"It'll be late morning when they arrive. Since it sounds like Sheriff Archer has all he can deal with for the moment, I'll have them meet up at your hotel. They can get checked in and then wait there for you and Reese. Plan to be there around noon."

"Okay. What about Galen?"

"What about him?"

"You told me he wasn't summoned, but he felt he had to be here. Fine. But what's his part in all this? I'm not complaining, mind you, because I'm sure he'll be an asset in any kind of fight—any kind of normal fight, at least. And he and Reese have the strongest shields against this energy, so another plus. Still, if he wasn't summoned, *does* he have a part to play?"

"I expect you'll all find why you're meant to be there, including Galen. He may want to spend more time prowling alone, or he may be . . . drawn . . . to a member of your team."

Hollis held the receiver away from her ear for a moment, staring at it, then put it back to her ear and said, "I knew Yoda had to come back sooner or later. Listen, do you think maybe this isn't the time to be all cryptic and mysterious?"

"It's just a hunch," Bishop said calmly.

"One you're not going to explain."

"Best not. I could be wrong."

Hollis absorbed that for a moment. "Um. Okay. Well, Reese and I have agreed it probably isn't wise for any of us to be roaming around Prosperity at night, at least not until we get a better handle on what's happening here. Which we need to do as quickly as we possibly can. We don't know how many other people have already been affected, or are being affected now, and for all we know the voice could be telling half the town to shoot cops and feds. And it's a well-armed town."

"You expect to be targets? Specific targets?"

"I think we wouldn't be smart if we assume otherwise. The whole town is so freaked out I haven't been able to sort through all the emotions to sense whether anybody is struggling now the way Lonnagan did a few hours ago. Right now it's just waves of emotion from just about everybody. Not fun. Reese wants to keep me inside his shields all night, especially since my iffy shield is even less dependable when I sleep."

"A smart precaution, I'd say. Take breaks from the energy whenever you can, Hollis. I don't believe *your* mind could be affected by it, not controlled by it; you've faced evil and negative energy too many times. But until you know what the source is, you won't know what it's going to take to transform or disperse that energy."

"Transform or disperse. Step one is to find the energy source or sources. Step two is to seal those portals. And step three is dealing with the energy here in the valley, transforming or dispersing it. Because energy can't be destroyed."

"We know this. You know it better than anyone. And you can handle it, whatever it is. If the barrier over the valley is indeed holding the energy inside, then discovering the source, fighting it, defeating it, may not destroy that barrier. You may have to punch a few openings in it. But take care, Hollis. That energy *must* be rendered harmless before it's allowed to escape the valley. Even without a guiding consciousness it could do an incredible amount of damage."

"Right. Right."

"Hollis, don't think you have to handle it alone. You have Reese and you have the rest of the team. I have to believe you were all summoned because everyone *does* have a part to play. Don't focus on protecting them."

After a moment, she said, "It's hard not to do that.

This sort of thing is new to them. Using their abilities in a situation like this with so much at stake. Being a team. How can I not worry?"

"You're bound to worry, just as any team leader would. But you can't let worry pull your focus away from the source of the energy. And you have to remember they need to be there just as you do."

She sighed. "Yeah, copy that. I take it you expect my instincts to kick in at the proper moment and tell me just *how* we can transform or disperse the energy."

"They always have," Bishop pointed out.

"But no pressure."

"You can handle it," he repeated.

"Right. Right." Hollis paused, then added, "I had a moment to speak to Katie Cole, and she told me the slam of information *she* got included a warning for her to shore up her shield, to protect herself as much as possible. So she's doing that, and she seems to have a fair shield. She agreed with me that the best place for her to be in all this is with the sheriff.

"He's a good cop and doesn't need his hand held, but Katie's known him long enough and well enough that I believe she can help him accept all this. She thinks so too."

"So do I," Bishop said.

"Seven murders today. I'm counting Bowers, since he was forced to do what he did."

"Yes."

"I doubt all the killing just stops, Bishop. For all we know, tomorrow could be a bloodbath."

"Yes, it could be. But you're there, first, to find and deal with the energy source and the energy itself. Nothing stops until that's stopped."

Hollis wished that reassured her. She wished it very much. "Okay. I'll report in tomorrow night. Sooner if anything breaks, or the situation changes."

"Copy. Get some rest," Bishop replied.

Hollis hung up the phone and looked at her partner. "You got all that, right?"

"Yeah. Handy thing, our connection."

"Seems to be."

"Bishop's right. We need to rest while we can. *You* need to rest while you can, and take a long break from the energy. It could make all the difference when we find this thing."

"And you have no doubt that we *will* find this thing."

"Absolutely none." He smiled faintly. "But it's been a very long day, and ours started before dawn with packing and flying nearly a thousand miles. So, for tonight, I say we order room service, have a shower, and then go to bed."

Hollis eyed him. "You're planning on finishing what you started *very* early this morning, aren't you?"

"I thought we could."

"You're trying to distract me."

"Well, that too."

"Not exactly restful," she pointed out thoughtfully.

"I certainly hope not. But I've noticed you do sleep better afterward."

She couldn't really argue with that. Not only did she sleep better, it was a very deep and restful sleep. And no nightmares, not when she slept in his arms.

"Sounds great to me," she told her partner, adding briskly, "Where's the room service menu?"

THURSDAY, OCTOBER 9

Whitney Neele slapped at her alarm early Thursday morning to stop the maddening buzz, trying to pry her eyes open. She had not slept well. In fact, she had not slept well for at least the past week.

Nightmares. Extremely vivid, almost visceral nightmares in which she was always trying to get away from something terrible. To run, to hide. Terror clawing at her mind, at some primitive sense deeper than thought that understood real terror.

And knowing, always knowing, that whatever horrible thing was after her was right behind her, getting closer. Always knowing she couldn't escape.

Always knowing she was doomed.

Waking exhausted every single morning.

She forced herself to sit up in bed and swing her legs over the side, wincing as the dull throb in her head seemed to swell and pulse with a life all its own.

Goddamn headache.

At first it hadn't been bad. Just a faint throb, a vague sense of pressure that made her want to yawn the way you do on airplanes. Whitney had figured she was coming down with something, maybe some bug, or just a cold. But the headache was getting worse, and it really didn't feel like some bug or a cold.

It felt . . . oddly alien.

Something outside herself.

And yet . . . something inside herself as well.

She tried to shake away that feeling, telling herself it was nonsense, that a normal, irritating headache only felt weird now because of everything that had happened yesterday.

The suicide, the murders. The sort of stuff that never happened in peaceful Prosperity. Never. So everyone was naturally on edge, anxious. Afraid. And the talk was already wild. She'd heard at least two people discussing the possibility of *magic*, for crying out loud.

Whitney sat on the side of the bed for a couple of minutes, elbows on her knees and her hands on either side of her head. It hurt. It hurt and throbbed, and felt like it weighed a ton.

She tried yawning a couple of times, but it didn't help the sense of pressure. Sure as hell didn't help the throbbing pain.

Eventually, she got herself out of bed and into the shower, thinking she'd feel better afterward, like she always did. She even washed her hair, less worried about being late than about massaging her head and hoping that would help.

It didn't.

Worse, the sound of her hair dryer was an oddly muffled roar, and made the throbbing become a pounding.

By the time she finished in the bathroom and returned to her bedroom to dress, she felt like banging her head against a wall until the pain stopped.

But she didn't, of course, and the throbbing continued.

She put on underwear, a pair of nice slacks, and a pretty blouse that didn't leave too much flesh showing. Couldn't look too sexy in her job. Nope. Just wasn't the thing.

Not appropriate.

Which was why she pulled back her hair in a neat, simple style, and used only moisturizer on her face. She'd use the lipstick in her purse later. Lipstick was okay.

She loved her job.

Well, just lately it had been a little annoying, but . . .

She loved her job.

She wondered vaguely why her face looked so flushed in the mirror. So pinkish. Decided it was the fault of the shower's hot water. She really needed to be more careful about that. Or speak to the super, who also owned the building and didn't stint on things like hot water.

Maybe too hot.

There was a fine line between water hot enough to wake you up and water hot enough to burn you.

She went into the kitchen and considered options for breakfast. She loved breakfast. Best meal of the day.

Though, lately, her coffeemaker seemed to take forever.

Lately, she didn't much like even the idea of eggs and turkey bacon, her favorites.

Lately, breakfast was more of a chore.

Her queasy stomach couldn't face much on this bright—really too bright—coolish October morning.

Probably that bug she was coming down with.

Damned headache.

Goddamned headache.

So she toasted a couple slices of bread while the coffeemaker took forever to do its job. By the time coffee was ready, she'd nibbled about half of one slice of plain toast.

The coffee tasted bitter.

Dammit.

She remembered to turn off the coffeemaker and left the unfinished toast on a bread plate on the kitchen counter.

She had to look for both her work bag—which her father insisted on calling a briefcase—and her keys. The keys she got, everybody mislaid their keys now and then, but she couldn't figure out how her rather large work bag could go missing so often.

Just lately, it seemed to happen every morning.

Lately, it had gotten really annoying.

She found what she needed, finally. Put on the lightweight, tan trench coat that was her only nice coat because it was just about cool enough for a light coat. Left her apartment, being sure to lock the door behind her. Went down the two flights of stairs to the lobby, wishing there were an elevator. Not that she minded stairs, and of course it was healthier.

But just lately, she would have preferred an elevator.

There was no one in the lobby when she reached it, and she didn't see any of her neighbors as she went out to the parking lot along one side of the building.

Her head was really hurting.

And why did too many things outside look red?

A tree whose leaves, she was almost certain, had not been red the day before. A red tricycle and red wagon somebody's kids had left nearly blocking the sidewalk. And when had so many of her neighbors' cars been red? She hadn't noticed that before.

It made her head hurt even more.

Whitney found her car, vaguely surprised it wasn't red. Unlocked it, got in. Started the engine. Obeyed the annoying beep telling her to fasten her seat belt. Then headed out for work.

There wasn't much traffic, and since this was her second year in her job, the way was so familiar she almost didn't have to pay attention to the drive. So she let her mind wander, absently reminding herself to not forget the daily chore of going by her father's house after work to feed his cat since he was down in Florida visiting family.

She thought she wanted to take a look at her father's gun collection. It hadn't interested her before, but just lately, she had noticed the gun cabinet. And she had thought about maybe borrowing a gun or two from the case.

She knew how to use them.

And with strange things happening, scary things, maybe having a gun or two would make her feel better. Safer. More able to . . . take care of things on her own.

Absently, she realized she was at work, the Prosperity Elementary School looming up before her. Odd. She hadn't thought the bricks were so red. Really red. That was odd. She was almost sure it was odd.

Whitney Neele pulled her car into the teachers' parking lot, and looked for a place, irritated when she couldn't park close to the building. It was a long walk. Funny, but there seemed to be an awful lot of red cars. She hadn't remembered that so many of her fellow teachers drove red cars. Not that it mattered. Not that it was *important*.

She loved her job. Loved the kids.

Though, just lately, the kids had been a handful.

Lately, they were misbehaving a lot.

She needed to do something about that.

THURSDAY, OCTOBER 9

Hollis had suggested that her team members eat breakfast at the hotel, just as she'd suggested they eat supper there the night before. She knew only too well that gossip had certainly already started about them, at least about her and Reese since they'd arrived in the unmistakable Fedmobile, but she'd told the others that keeping a low profile would be best. For as long as they could.

Staying out of restaurants and attempting to be unobtrusive was at least something, she had told Reese privately. If this energy *was* being directed toward specific targets, not calling undue attention to themselves might prevent them from becoming victims. Or at least delay that threat.

So they all met up at the sheriff's department a bit after eight thirty on Thursday morning. There were more deputies in the bullpen than there had been the evening before, and they all looked very tense, though Hollis didn't sense any hostility aimed at them as she and Reese walked back to the conference room.

All the murders made them tense and anxious, no question about that. Some were still shocked and horrified, others just baffled. But their strongest emotions, Hollis knew, were focused on Deputy Lonnagan.

One of their own had nearly killed his wife the night before, and was even now in a cell in the back, sedated.

Hollis had called in first thing to check, unsurprised but concerned when Katie had told her that Weston was even more of a smiling blank this morning, and that Lonnagan's terror and anxiety had returned as soon as he'd awakened from his Victoria-induced nap. So the doctor Hollis had suggested had put him back out, chemically this time.

It was a short-term solution.

And she wasn't at all sure that even finding and fighting the energy would repair the damage already done to those living victims. They might well remain on the *destroyed* side of the ledger.

The cost of this battle could be very, very high.

They found the others already seated in the conference room, which was different today only in that a large map of the valley had been tacked up onto one of the boards. Her team had obviously been talking to Katie, and the chief deputy immediately pushed a closed folder toward Hollis and DeMarco as they sat down.

"You might want to take a look. Jill's report on the first death yesterday morning. Or at least the first one we were called to. Sam Bowers."

"Let me guess," Hollis said without opening the folder. "Probable suicide, with nothing to indicate the involvement of anyone else."

"Yep. No forensic evidence anyone else was involved. Only his prints on the gun and on the gun cabinet. She said there was no sign of drugs or alcohol, though she sent blood and tissue samples to the state medical examiner's office in Chapel Hill to have that verified. Protocol." She paused, then added, "Jack and I are going to talk to Stacey this morning. She should be calmer now; she's the sort who will always try to be strong for her kids. Maybe she can tell us something useful."

Hollis glanced out the open door of the conference room to see the closed door of the sheriff's office but didn't ask if he was in yet. Instead, she said, "I know you know this, but try to find out if Mrs. Bowers noticed anything unusual in her husband's behavior in the week or so before. If he seemed unusually tense or preoccupied. If he said anything that seemed weird to her, out of character. If he complained of headaches or pressure in his head. We need to know if there were any warning signs. I doubt if he was convinced to kill himself over a single night, especially since he clearly struggled against the urges to do more."

"Just me, not them," Katie murmured.

Hollis nodded, then looked at them one by one, noting that none of them looked more tense than they had the previous day. But not exactly more relaxed either. "How are you guys holding up?" she asked generally.

"I didn't sleep much," Katie confessed. "Probably more because of Jim than anything else. He came out of his nap while I was still here last night, so . . . that's the memory I went home with. It was not a pleasant memory."

"I slept okay," Victoria said. "Never cared much for hotels, but my room was comfortable. Room service was good too."

"Same here," Logan said, though a slight frown lingered.

Hollis studied him a moment, then turned her gaze to Galen, who merely said, "I'm fine."

She was pretty sure Galen would say he was fine no matter how he actually was, but since he was still buttoned up very tightly, she got no sense of his emotions. And since he was in that relatively small percentage of people Reese couldn't read, she had no idea what he was thinking. He was an experienced agent, and she had to respect his judgment of his own condition. At least unless she saw anything to worry her.

And she really hoped she wouldn't do that.

Hollis returned her attention to Logan. "Still no spirits?"

"No spirits." He hesitated, then added, "I can't believe I'm saying this, but it's beginning to bug me." He actually looked a bit embarrassed, which, given his protestations in the past, made perfect sense.

She totally understood. There had been a few times in her SCU career when spirits had, for one reason or another, stopped popping in for a while, and it had bugged her.

"It does feel weird," she agreed with him calmly. "Once you get used to having spirits around, no matter how much they affect your life, the absence of them just doesn't feel . . . natural. Like a kind of warning flag from the universe that everything's out of balance. Probably stronger with you, since you're a born medium."

"But I wanted them gone."

"Yeah," Hollis said, "but them being gone right now has nothing to do with you getting rid of them."

His frown deepened as he considered that, and then he sighed. "I guess. A lesson from the universe? Be careful what you ask for, because you might get it?"

"Probably," Hollis agreed. Then she said briskly, "The others will be arriving later this morning, and the plan is to meet up with them at the hotel around noon. Until then, I think we should be out searching this valley."

"For what?" Logan asked. "I mean—specifically. Victoria and I can't see the energy the way you can."

It was Hollis's turn to frown. "When Reno told us about her vision, didn't she say she was warned that the very earth here in Prosperity was about to . . . heave itself open and spill out evil?"

"Yeah. That wasn't symbolic?"

Victoria spoke up to answer that. "Reno doesn't have symbolic visions."

"She doesn't?"

"No. Always literal. Often . . . exaggerated, she says, but always literal."

"I hope that one was exaggerated," Logan muttered. "A lot."

Hollis nodded a wry agreement, saying, "But we take it literally. Which means we need to be looking for . . . disturbed ground. And that could be anything from a plowed field to an old well, a cave, or any other type of opening in the earth. Especially if it seems recent or just doesn't look right. Listen to your instincts."

She turned her chair to face the board and the map hanging there. "I asked Katie to mark the locations of the multiple homicide, the suicide, the Lonnagan house, and the house Weston was showing prospective buyers. Notice anything?"

It was Galen, who had driven all over Prosperity the day before, who answered. "Every location is on the outskirts of town. All outlying neighborhoods."

"Yeah. And if you draw a line from where the killings began, starting with the Gardner house—since both the sheriff and Katie believe Leslie Gardner killed at least one of her children before Sam Bowers killed himself—you can see that each location is a little closer to town."

"Oh, man," Victoria said. "I hope that isn't as bad as I think it is."

"This whole damned thing is bad," Logan reminded her.

"Yeah, but that . . . makes me feel hunted."

"You should feel that way. Just in case we're being hunted. Fear sharpens the instincts." Hollis turned back to face them. "The point is, it doesn't look as random as we all thought it might be. In spite of how large the total energy field is, whatever is picking targets in Prosperity could have its source outside the town, at the other end of the valley."

Katie said slowly, "There are a lot of farms and ranches on that end of the valley."

DeMarco said, "It would probably be a good idea to contact those people. Call if they have a landline. Visit if they don't. But don't send a single deputy. Always at least two."

"To keep an eye on each other," Katie said.

"It would probably be best. None of us should really be alone out there." He didn't look at Galen, even though he and Hollis both knew Galen had never worked with a partner in any true sense and was unlikely to want company while he prowled around.

"Okay. A lot of our people have asked to put in overtime. After Jim . . . Well, they don't understand what's happening, but they want to help."

Hollis said, "Understandable. Problem is, they want

to find a bad guy they can put in cuffs and then in a cage. And we just don't know if that's what's behind all this."

"We've got plenty of the *normal* casework," Katie said. "Still friends and family of the victims to interview. Neighbors. And now checking on all the places out in the valley. But if we don't end up with that bad guy, if our people are left with nothing except a lot of unanswered questions, I don't know how it'll affect them going forward."

"Let's jump off that bridge when we come to it," Hollis suggested. "Keep your deputies busy doing the work that needs to be done. My team will start searching the valley looking for . . . anomalies. Anything that might point us to the source of the energy. Even places where the very earth might be showing signs of trying to heave itself open. With a little luck, we won't have to knock on any doors out there, but you might want to alert whoever needs to know that there'll be strangers out in the valley."

"I'll make sure whoever's on the desk knows, so they can handle any call-ins."

"Thanks. If my sense of direction is right, the hospital is on the way out of town toward that end of the valley. Reese and I want to stop and see Leslie Gardner. Even if she's still sleeping—"

"I don't think that'll do you much good." Archer had emerged from his office and stepped into the doorway of the conference room, catching them all by surprise. Which actually bothered Hollis a lot.

She looked at his very calm face—and more closely at the sickened expression in his eyes. She rose without thinking about it. "What is it, Jack?"

"I just talked to the hospital," he said in a level, controlled voice. "In the last hour, Leslie Gardner's vitals have begun to show signs that she's slipping into a coma. But that's not why they called me. Apparently, some of their test results showed something . . . odd . . . in her digestive system. So they did X-rays. It took three different techs and two doctors to figure it out, but they finally realized what they were looking at."

Katie said in a voice that almost wasn't there, "I'm afraid to ask."

Archer looked at her. "The youngest Gardner child, Luke. His fingers were missing."

"Jesus," Victoria murmured.

"They aren't missing anymore," Archer said.

TWELVE

THURSDAY, OCTOBER 9

"I wonder if Archer is ever going to be the same after this," DeMarco said as he drove their SUV through the downtown area of Prosperity.

"You know he won't be." Hollis was looking down at their copy of the map with rough "search" grids marked on it. "He grew up in this nice little town. Never expected to have to deal with suicide, murder, filicide, and cannibalism. It's not exactly all in a day's work for us either. And that's saying something."

"Filicide?"

"I had to look it up."

"Uh-huh. Your headache's back."

She stopped absently rubbing the ache between her eyebrows. "Yes, it is. But starting small today. Maybe it'll take a while to really begin pounding."

He sent her a quick, searching glance, then returned

his gaze to the road in front of them. "You're still sure we're not stopping by the hospital?"

"I don't even want to get close to the hospital. If you do, let me off somewhere first."

"She's pretty much in a coma," DeMarco reminded his partner.

"Yeah. But I don't think there's much research into what coma patients do or don't think, and do or don't feel. And I'd rather not start it off with what has to be in *her* mind."

"We've never had to deal with cannibalism before."

"No. A psychic able to feed off the energy of another person, which is horrific enough. But a person consuming the flesh of another person, the flesh of her *child*, is beyond evil."

"It wasn't a decision she made. Or a sick need driving her. She wasn't in control."

"No. Which is why she went to sleep, and why she's in a coma, and why she'll probably die. I don't want to get close enough to her to have it confirmed, but I think she was aware, Reese. I think whatever this thing is that took over her mind and her actions made her watch what she was doing. Made her know. Made her understand. And when it was over and it let her go, she curled up in a chair and went to sleep."

"We'll stop it, Hollis."

"God, I hope so. And, you know, as horrible as it would be to find some*one* behind it, I'd rather we found just that. Because transforming or dispersing energy won't send it to hell."

"It will if there's a consciousness guiding it, which seems to be the case. Whether it's holding the energy or the energy is holding it, removing the energy releases it. One thing you've taught me is that there *is* a hell waiting for evil. This thing is evil. One way or another, it's going to hell."

She looked up from the map finally, frowning as she gazed ahead. Then she turned her head and looked at her partner. "That's true."

"Yeah. Do me a favor?"

"Sure, what?"

"Stop closing the door on your side." He glanced at her in time to see her blink.

"Um . . . sorry. It's just that when I knew what Archer was going to say, the feelings, mine and his . . . I didn't want you slammed by them too."

"We're connected for a reason, Hollis. We share. The bad as well as the good. Remember?"

"Yeah. You're right. Sorry."

Thank you.

You're welcome. Seriously.

DeMarco smiled faintly, then said, "How did Victoria and Logan handle it?"

"You can read Logan. Can't you?"

"Yeah, but not once Archer began speaking."

"Horror throws up its own barriers?"

"That's what he was feeling?"

"Oh, yeah. Both of them. Horrified and sickened beyond belief. I picked up Victoria's emotions even through her shield."

"Then I guess horror throws up its own barriers. At least this time."

"They were both shaken last night after Deputy Lonnagan ran in. They're even more shaken today. And they didn't look at bodies yesterday."

"Probably best," DeMarco said.

"For all of them, yeah. They might have been able to handle a more . . . conventional . . . investigation their first time out of the gate. And they'll find a way to handle this one. But not both, I think. Not yet."

"So we keep them away from bodies and postmortems."

"If we can. Neither one of them looked at Jill's report on the Sam Bowers suicide, you know."

"I thought they probably didn't. They didn't want to be cops. The fact that they answered the summons says a lot about their characters."

"Well, they both seem driven. Maybe just by the need to get this done and over with. Not that I really care, as long as they can focus on the job."

"They should have time to check out the first grid on their search list before we all meet up back at the hotel. So should we."

"Yeah. But before we head there, I'd like to get up as high as we can out in the valley. And you should get a really good look at the layout now that we're inside all the energy. I don't know if either of us will see anything, but if we do your sense of direction is better than mine."

LOGAN RATHER GINGERLY replaced the large piece of plywood and bundle of barbed wire over the ground-level opening of the old well. "This is not a very safe barrier," he noted.

"No," Victoria agreed, using a handy tree stump as a desk while she marked the position of the well on their search map. "It's not in a pasture or near a trail, though, so I suppose the landowner thought it was good enough."

"The sheriff might feel differently."

"Yeah. May be one of the reasons why Hollis asked us to mark anything like this on the map. Plus, she might just be worried that if we *do* find the energy source underground, something like an old well could provide a ready-made escape hatch."

"You both talk like the energy is alive. I mean, that it can think, make reasoned decisions."

"Because it is. And you know it. Energy can't be a voice in someone's head, not without an intelligence of some kind guiding it. Energy can't force people to kill. There's an agenda behind all this, and that means a mind, a consciousness, behind it."

He eyed her. "Haven't evolved into a telepath, have you?"

"No. Still the same, just the naps. But a while back, I asked Bishop if I could have access to SCU case files—important names and sensitive information redacted, of course."

"And?"

"And . . . the SCU has had some very serious, very deadly battles with energy over the years. Especially negative energy. And if there wasn't a consciousness behind it, there was one using it."

Logan frowned as they began to make their way back to the Bronco they were driving. "Didn't Hollis say this energy is both negative and positive?"

"Yeah. Which is more than a little weird given what's been happening here. Negative energy must be what's being used to control people, to make them kill. So what's the positive energy?" She absently rubbed the back of her neck.

"Maybe it really is what summoned us? Or what's left of what summoned us?"

"Maybe. Still weird, though. If that's what summoned us, it also must have a consciousness behind it. The good side of good versus evil, I guess."

"You're not saying God summoned us." It was almost a question.

"No. I don't think any version of God would have needed our help. But positive has to balance negative, good has to balance evil. And people, at least here on our little orb, tend to be behind both. We cause balance; we cause inbalance. The balance can be upset, the way it is here, now, but not for long because the Universe wants balance. So maybe we were summoned by a . . . universal consciousness."

"A benevolent universal consciousness?"

"Maybe."

"Hollis doesn't seem all that interested in finding out what summoned us."

"No. I think she's always going to be more focused on taking care of the threat. I also think she's had a *lot* of experience with energy *and* a lot of experience in facing evil. My guess is, she's just glad we were all summoned here before things really got out of control."

"Seven bodies, one killer-victim in a coma, one a smiling blank, and one in a continual state of terror sounds pretty out of control, Victoria."

"Yeah. But I think all that's just the beginning, or at least the beginning of the . . . plan. Otherwise, why summon us here when we couldn't get here in time to stop any of that?"

Logan was silent until they were in the Bronco. He started the engine, then looked at her. "You sound almost . . . comfortable with all this."

"I wouldn't say that."

"I would."

"The next area we're supposed to take a look at is a bit north of here. The service road we've been using should take us there."

"Victoria."

"What?"

"Are you thinking of joining the SCU?"

For a moment he didn't think she was going to answer him. But then she looked up finally from the map and shrugged. "I dunno. Maybe. I never thought I could handle any law enforcement work, but Bishop was right in telling us years ago that the SCU isn't your conventional law enforcement agency."

"No, but that doesn't mean it isn't a very dangerous life."

Victoria frowned, green eyes thoughtful. "The dangerous part never bothered me. I mean, just living is dangerous and, besides, having something worthwhile to do with your life—and our freakish psychic abilities— puts a lot of points in the plus column."

Logan put the Bronco in gear and began driving slowly along the barely there service road. They were in an area immediately north of the town, an area with a forest and the sheer cliff walls of the mountains surrounding the valley to their left and farm and pasture land stretching off toward the center of the valley to their right.

"Haven't you been tempted?" she asked suddenly.

"I never wanted to be any kind of psychic."

"Yeah, but you are one. You've been dealing with your abilities for most of your life, and you've been helping spirits. Telling law enforcement agencies where to find murder victims and missing persons. Hell, you're already doing some of the work. Why not get paid to do it?"

"I haven't thought much about it."

"Of course you have. You wouldn't be human if you hadn't. Why not do useful work *and* use your abilities with a group of people who understand, who don't look at you like you're a freak, and who can help you learn to control those abilities?"

"It isn't that simple."

"Maybe it ought to be."

Logan continued to drive the Bronco slowly, his eyes scanning their surroundings rather than looking at her. "Maybe it should. But it isn't."

"We're getting a taste of the work. Both of us might feel differently about it when this case is over."

"A taste? Victoria, that's like knowing you should start out wading in ankle-deep water and somebody throws you into the deep end of the pool. This is the deep end of the pool we're in. Along with sharks we can't see."

"I gather that's fairly typical of SCU cases. I mean, encountering the unexpected. Not really a guidebook or a rulebook. Call me crazy, but that sounds sort of appealing."

"You're crazy."

She smiled faintly, studying him. "Well, we'll see. In the meantime, how are you handling all this energy, really? Because it's bugging me even through my shield."

"My skin's sort of crawling," he admitted. "But I'm not hearing a voice in my head telling me to buy a bunch of guns or to kill somebody, so I'm grateful for that."

"So am I."

It was his turn to smile faintly. "Honestly, I expected to feel a lot more. With no shield, it just seemed reasonable I would. Maybe whatever's blocking spirit energy is helping protect me from all this negative stuff."

"Maybe. Or maybe you have a natural shield you've just never used before. One that only protects you against energy."

"Unexplored territory for me," he admitted.

"The sort of challenge that helps abilities evolve, maybe. That seems to be the rule rather than the exception."

"We'll probably know more about that once the others get here and get involved. Considering the range of abilities, I mean."

"Yeah, probably. Hey—up there to the left. Does that look like a big tree down, the roots showing?"

"Yeah. The 'very earth heaving'?"

"Disturbed ground, at the very least."

"So let's take a look."

"WHAT DO YOU think?" Hollis asked.

DeMarco studied the very odd sky above them, the energy visible to him because Hollis was showing him what she saw. It was an odd color for an otherwise clear October sky, shading toward a grayish navy, brightened weirdly as threads of white energy hissed almost inaudibly across it in a lacy pattern.

"I think it's a good thing most if not all the people in this valley can't see what you see. Is this how it looked yesterday before it got dark?"

"Pretty much. Except there are more threads of energy visible. I think. The field feels stronger, and whatever is holding it in feels more solid. I know that."

"Which would explain why the local radio station is nothing but static; yesterday we could at least hear some of the broadcast."

"Yeah. And the pressure is a bit more intense."

"Hence your headache."

"Not sure." Hollis shrugged as he looked at her. "It could be that, of course. Probably is. But it's almost like I'm catching a glimpse of something out of the corner of my eye. Do you get any sense that we're being watched?"

"I don't get any sense of a threat."

"I'm not sure I do. I mean, I'm so conscious of the energy and so aware of all the horrible things that happened yesterday, I may be half blocking myself."

"Wouldn't be the first time," DeMarco noted.

"No, it wouldn't. But I really need to be able to count on all my senses here. And I'm not at all sure I can." She turned her gaze to their view of the valley; it was a good one, since they had found a bit of higher ground about half a mile into the sprawling, faintly bowl-like shape of the valley floor—a shape that was far more evident once one was actually down in the valley.

There were farms, several of which showed fields with the remains of harvested crops plowed under, and the entire valley was dotted by pastureland. It was clear that the human population was very scattered here, most certainly outnumbered by the cattle and horses grazing peacefully.

Peacefully. That bothered her.

"No sign any of the animals have been affected," she said slowly. "Why does that strike me as strange?"

"Maybe because animals are generally affected by energy fields before people are," DeMarco offered.

"Mmm. Sully feels what animals feel, right?"

"Yeah."

"Then maybe he can answer that question. Or maybe it doesn't matter, and I'm reaching."

"So soon? We've barely settled in."

Hollis narrowed her eyes at him, but all she said in response was, "We usually have some idea of an enemy's agenda by now, even if the agenda is a sick and twisted one. Maybe especially then."

"We know this enemy's agenda. Death and destruction."

She smiled wryly. "True. Now tell me evil is easier to fight when it's not poured into a recognizable human shape."

"Well, we've only dealt with the human-shaped variety of evil," he noted thoughtfully. "But I will point out that this evil is at least contained here in the valley. And given its all-too-destructive potential to reach outside the valley, I'd say that puts us one up on it."

"For now."

"We're always working against the clock."

"Stop backing me into logical corners," she said with sudden irritation.

"I usually don't have to," he responded mildly. "You're the most ruthlessly logical woman I know."

"I'm not sure that's a compliment."

"Fishing?"

"Well, of course I'm fishing."

He smiled slightly, but his gaze was a bit more watchful than usual. For Hollis to become irritated, at least momentarily, wasn't at all unusual, but he was all too aware that this particular evil seemed bent on invading human minds and influencing both thought and behavior. Like Bishop, DeMarco did not believe his partner could be deceived by evil, far less taken over by it, but that wasn't to say it might not have a destructive effect on her.

Especially when she was standing in the middle of it, and was distracted by unspoken worries about what horrible thing might be happening in town. Or out here, behind closed doors.

Worried that there could be a bloodbath today. Or tomorrow.

Worried about her newly fledged team.

"It's a compliment," he assured her. "One of your strengths. You always find the logic in madness. Which is what we're dealing with here."

"Madness. That's true enough."

He turned more to face her without releasing her hand, studying her slightly abstracted expression, the way her gaze roved restlessly around the valley. "So, find the logic."

"Maybe I can't this time."

"You already have. You were very clear with Bishop, the others. We have to find the source of this energy. Before we can do anything to stop it, we have to cut it off from its source. Preventing it from intensifying, building. That's logical, isn't it? When you don't know the reach of your enemy but do have some warning of increasing power, you have to define that reach yourself. Impose limits, and as quickly as possible."

"That sounds military."

"I'm not surprised." He was former military. "Hollis?"

"Yeah?"

"Look at me."

She did, her abstracted expression slowly fading, her normal sharp awareness returning. She blinked. "What just happened?"

"You tell me."

After a moment, she said slowly, "Damn. That was . . . stealthy."

"The energy?"

"Yeah. I didn't even realize it had got in. Why didn't I know it had got in?"

"Had it? Or was it just . . . trying to get in?"

Hollis nodded, realizing. "Yeah, that's what it was doing. If you hadn't made me focus—"

"You would have done it yourself. You were just distracted for a moment."

"And a moment is all it took. Jesus. I know I don't have much of a shield yet, consistently anyway, but I'm supposed to be sensitive to energy. Especially negative energy. I really should have felt what was happening."

"You will next time," he said.

Rather grimly, she said, "Thanks to you, I had a warning. This time. I have a feeling not many people here will get that. We have to warn the others, Reese. And we *have* to find the source."

"We will," DeMarco said.

"I DON'T KNOW what the fuck I'm doing here," Dalton said.

"Yes, you do." Reno kept her attention focused on the road that wound down from the mountains to Prosperity. She was driving their Jeep, in part because Dalton did not have a license.

One of his small rebellions. Or just another attempt to impose control on his surroundings. Probably both.

"I don't—"

"Can you feel the energy?"

He was silent for a moment, then said reluctantly, "My skin's crawling, and there's pressure. You?"

"The same. I sort of wish I could see it the way Hollis does. On the other hand, seeing it might freak me out even more."

"You *should* be freaked out. We both should be. This is not our job, Reno."

"Maybe it should be."

He frowned at her. "What's that supposed to mean?"

She was silent for a moment, then said, "We're here because we were summoned, like the others. Because some . . . universal consciousness, or God, or the devil decided we had the right tools to fight this—this evil."

"Reno—"

"Do you ever think in absolutes, Dalton? I don't

believe I ever did. Right or wrong, black or white, good or evil."

"I don't believe there *are* absolutes," he said finally. "There isn't a clear, dividing line between good and evil, Reno. There are endless shades of gray. Just like there are between other extremes."

She frowned. "I suppose that makes sense. But something else I'm feeling now that we're here, now that we're actually going to Prosperity, is darkness. Evil. I can *feel* that."

"After that goddamned vision of yours I'm not surprised."

"Maybe, but my point is that we were given these tools, tools most other people don't have. Doesn't that also give us the responsibility to use them? To fight the darkness?"

Suddenly dry, he said, "It's a little late in the day to be questioning that, don't you think?"

"I don't just mean this time. I mean all the time. I sell real estate, Dalton. You and Logan do IT work from home. Sully's a rancher. Olivia works at a bank. I'm not sure what Victoria is doing right now, but it's a good guess it's something . . . ordinary, like all her other temp jobs have been."

"Most people do ordinary," he said.

"We aren't most people. That's the point. Look, if my vision was right—and they always are—and if Hollis and Reese are right, which I hear they mostly are, then this thing we're going to fight has been building up a long time."

"So?"

"So Hollis and Reese have been fighting it, or pieces of it, for years. Bishop, Miranda, the SCU. They go into really dark places, and they fight monsters. Monsters most of the rest of the world doesn't even know about."

He waited with uncharacteristic patience.

"So maybe we could have made a difference before. If we'd been in the game, I mean. Maybe this darkness would never have been able to build up. Maybe those people yesterday wouldn't have died."

"Regrets are useless," he reminded her. "We can't fix what's behind us, only what's ahead of us."

Reno sent him a faintly surprised glance. "I didn't think you had any regrets."

"They're useless. You heard me say. Look, I'm not a cop. You're not a cop. Neither one of us has any experience with law enforcement. We've been living our lives—"

"—hiding from the world—"

"—day to day, just like most everyone else. Nobody asked us to suit up and get into the game, and if we're honest we'll admit that neither of us was even paying attention. Like most people."

"Bishop asked us."

"Actually, he didn't. Or, at least, I never heard him ask any of us. He found us, and he wanted to know if we were up to joining the SCU or that civilian outfit of his, Haven. Clearly, none of our little group was. But he still kept tabs, didn't he? He put us up in that so-called group home. Where we didn't feel quite so much like freaks. He visited when he could. Couple other SCU and Haven people visited. They offered advice, talked about their experiences. We did a few experiments of our own. But in the end we all went in different directions, and for most of us it took less than a year. Does that sound like a team to you?"

"It sounds to me like we were mostly scared," she replied.

"I wouldn't argue with that. Scared, anxious, wondering how on earth we could possibly fit into the world."

Reno decided to leave personal matters out of it for the moment. "And now?"

"Now something other than Bishop forced the issue. Maybe it took a cosmic kick in the ass to get us here, but we're here. Maybe we're even a team."

Surprised, she said, "If you knew that and were willing, why the hell have you been a pain in the ass about it?"

"I didn't say I was willing. I said I was kicked in the ass and now I'm here. In the game. I don't know any more than you do about what happens next. Or how I'll feel about *being* in the game when this is over with, assuming we survive. And neither do you."

"Huh," Reno said slowly.

"Turn left ahead," Dalton told her.

THIRTEEN

Archer didn't immediately realize that the SCU team he'd called in to help had more or less vanished. He didn't realize for several hours, in part because he and Katie went to talk to Stacey Bowers and that took time because neither of them wanted to make the awful situation even worse for her.

Not that she was able to help them. She had not noticed any sign from her husband that suicide was in any way on his mind, or even that anything was bothering him, and she maintained with absolute assurance that Sam would never kill himself. Never.

When they returned to the station, both discouraged and both tensely anticipating bad news of some kind since the overwhelming events of the day before could *not* be the end of it all, Archer met briefly with the doctor and okayed moving Jim Lonnagan to the hospital, where he'd be kept sedated and under restraints, at least for the present.

A temporary measure, the doctor had noted.

Archer didn't know what the hell a permanent measure would be, and hoped to God he wouldn't have to make that call.

After supervising the transfer, via ambulance, of Lonnagan to the hospital, Archer went into the conference room, where Katie was sitting with postmortem reports spread out around her and her gaze fixed on the big map of the valley pinned to one of the boards.

As Archer came into the room, she said, "Jill's working fast. She's done the postmortems on the three Gardner kids."

"Anything we didn't already know?"

"Not really. Though she does agree that Luke Gardner was probably killed at least a couple hours before the other kids were killed. Says Ed Gardner was killed last; she's working on his post now."

"And when was the other stuff done?"

Steadily, Katie said, "All the postmortem injuries happened within a couple of hours of death."

Archer tried not to imagine how horrifying that scene must have been. And had to imagine, of course.

"Leslie Gardner is now officially in a coma," Katie continued. "And the docs say it's a deep one. Beyond that, they aren't offering anything we didn't know before. They don't know if or when she'll come out of it, or what shape she'll be in if or when she does. Though

I guess we can make some educated guesses based on Elliot Weston and on Jim."

"Yeah. I guess." He looked around. "Where are our federal friends?"

"Looking for the bad guy," Katie replied.

Archer lifted a brow at her. "The bad guy? You mean the bad guy who apparently used some kind of crazy energy to *persuade* a woman to murder and dismember her husband and kids, a real estate agent to murder two strangers, Sam Bowers to kill himself, and Jim Lonnagan to nearly kill his wife? That bad guy?"

Katie nodded, and said immediately, "I had to put two deputies and the front desk on incoming calls. A *lot* of calls, Jack. People are scared. They have a lot of questions and no answers. Except word seems to have gotten around that as horrible as the deaths have been, the killers weren't in their right minds when they committed the crimes. People are asking if it's something in the water or the food supply; I guess that's a lot more likely than . . . energy."

"You think?"

She cleared her throat. "We have reports of the same sort of things we already know about: tension, headaches, the feeling that their heads are stuffed full of cotton. A few have mentioned their skin crawling. Tempers seem to be unusually short, and we've had some calls about loud disagreements and fistfights. Other than recommending that everyone be . . . cautious and vigilant, skip the caffeine, and see a doctor if they're worried, there isn't a whole hell of a lot we can tell them to help them protect themselves. Even assuming the threat's still high, so far we have no idea if there are any visible symptoms to watch out for."

"I hate assuming," Archer muttered.

"Yeah, me too."

"Hollis and Reese didn't have anything to say?"

"I told you, Jack, they're out looking for . . . the cause. The rest of their team should be getting settled in the hotel, and then they'll be out searching as well."

"For this energy monster." It was clear that, today at least, Archer had had second thoughts about what he'd been told the night before. With rest and time to think, he was far less likely today to just accept whatever he was told.

Katie sighed. "Jack, I know how hard it is to believe something like that. But we both know what happened yesterday was not in any way normal. And absent some other explanation, doesn't it make sense to listen to people with a lot more experience than we have with— weird and crazy?"

"Nothing in this entire situation makes sense." He sighed. "But you're probably right. Now tell me how we're supposed to write this up in our reports."

That actually hadn't occurred to Katie, but she was nothing if not quick on her feet. Even when she was sitting down.

"Let's . . . not put speculation in our reports. Just the facts. I mean, unless and until we have more than speculation."

"Uh-huh." He sighed. "Every car we have out patrolling?"

"Like we decided last night, yes. Everybody is under orders to look for anything that sticks out to them as different or unusual. And the guys on the call-in lines know to take any complaint as serious. The last half-dozen deputies are still out talking to friends and family of the victims. The dead victims and the ones still alive."

"I know Jim's still out, and the doctor apparently means him to stay out for the time being. Weston?"

"Pretty much the same as he was this morning. Worse than yesterday, but not catatonic. Yet, anyway."

Archer leaned on the table, staring down at the post-mortem reports. "Did Hollis say anything before they went out about . . . what might happen today?"

"No. She said the whole town's on edge, and that's all she was feeling. Sort of a flood of emotion, I take it. She said she'd get to a landline and call in if she feels or senses anyone struggling the way Jim did. Anyone in trouble."

"And until then, we wait."

"I'm afraid so, Jack."

HOLLIS HAD THOUGHT about it and talked it over with Reese, and had decided that her team needed to be as protected as possible, especially after the brief but chilling attempt to get inside her own mind. But since only three of her team possessed shields she felt would be strong enough—Reese, Victoria, and Galen—it was impossible to send everybody out in pairs.

And she wasn't at all sure about Galen, whether he would even accept—

"I'll go with Olivia," he told her.

Hollis fought to keep from betraying surprise. Now, how had Bishop *known*? She was also aware of a surge of rather panicked uncertainty from Olivia, and smiled at the seemingly most fragile psychic on her team. "I think that's a good idea. Reno can make up the third place. Sully, you go with Victoria and Logan. And Dalton comes with Reese and me."

Dalton, not so angry today but very closed in on himself for someone without a shield, merely nodded without comment.

He really was not what Hollis had expected. At all.

It was Victoria who said somewhat uneasily, "I can't extend my shield to cover anyone else, Hollis."

"Yeah, I know. We can't cover everybody with a borrowed shield, which is why I want one strong shielded mind with each group. Part of your job is to keep an eye on the others in your group."

"Looking for?"

"Anything that bugs you. Distraction. Any actions or words that seem out of character. Just . . . anything you don't like. All of you know each other better than Galen, Reese, and I know you; you're more likely to notice something strange."

Victoria said, "Damn. You mean something like an attempt to control somebody."

"Yeah. It's possible, Victoria. So we have to be prepared for the possibility."

"Okay, but what happens if any of us notice something weird?"

"As soon as he found out about the energy, and especially about how screwed up communications are in the valley, Bishop had the technicians at the house work on a warning and tracking system for us. They're installed in each vehicle as part of the radios."

"Ah," Sully said. "That's what was in the bag Bishop sent with me to give Galen."

"Yeah. Galen installed the enhanced radios in the three vehicles we brought to Prosperity yesterday and last night."

"So we're all on the same channel, so to speak."

"Right. You'll see tracking dots on the screens for each vehicle; that's one reason we're going to spread out in a line and basically work our way across the valley like that. We're far enough apart to cover the valley, but close enough to each other to be able to make contact as quickly as possible.

"You notice anything wrong, get back to your vehicle and hit the red button on the radio—basically a panic button. Alerts will sound in the other vehicles, which is why nobody gets more than a hundred yards away from them. And the tracking dot for the group sounding the alert begins to flash, so we all know who needs help and where they are in relation to the rest of us."

"And then?" Dalton asked dryly. "When everybody rushes to help?"

"Then we help." Hollis looked him in the eye, daring him to question.

He smiled faintly, but didn't push it. Hollis didn't know whether to hope he trusted her and his other team members, or to be worried by his lack of concern for them.

She looked around at her team. "Everybody clear? We're looking for disturbed ground. Old wells, caves, even a plowed field or a gully that looks odd. Trust your instincts. And alert the rest of us if you find anything you consider especially suspicious."

"You mean if it feels wrong?" Olivia asked.

"Yes. If it feels wrong, if your instincts are in any way telling you to stay away, then do that. And call the rest of us.

"You have your maps with your search grids marked. When we're all in position, I want to do a radio check. We *should* have voice communication now. I hope. But even if we don't, the warning and tracking system is designed to work even in the middle of a much stronger energy field than we have here."

In less than fifteen minutes, the team moved out from their hotel and headed to their positions beginning about two miles outside town and a mile from the site of the first death.

Then they went to work.

Hollis was surprised but pleased to find that Dalton was very familiar with maps and with the rougher terrain she had assigned them along one of the outer edge of the valley, though when she thought about it she wondered if she should have been surprised. He had, after all, ended up in Kodiak, Alaska. And given his nature, he probably hiked into the wilderness regularly in order to get as far as he could from other people.

Their radios worked, and rather well, which was another pleasant surprise. "But if we don't find the source soon," she said to Reese and Dalton, "I doubt that'll be the case."

"Is the energy still intensifying?" Reese asked her.

"I think it's stronger than it was yesterday," she told him. "Not so sure it's stronger than it was this morning." She hesitated, frowning slightly.

"Something?" Reese asked.

"I don't know. Pretty much everybody in this valley is worried and horrified, so I'm getting a lot of that. A sort of . . . uncomfortable feeling of people watching each other. But for just a minute there, I thought I got a flash of something else. Something . . . driven."

"A consciousness trying to control another mind?"

"Maybe. I'm not sure." Her frown deepened, and she added slowly, "You know, that attempt this morning, as eerie as it was, wasn't nearly as powerful as I'd expect. Unless . . ."

"Unless," Dalton supplied, "everything that happened yesterday took more energy than whatever this consciousness expected. From the timeline you gave us, it looks like the worst murders took place early in the day. By the time Deputy Lonnagan managed not to kill his wife, it was late in the day. What if that was less about his ability to resist and more about how much energy had been expended in that . . . mad rush to kill as many people as possible while scaring the shit out of everybody else?"

Hollis blinked, surprised. She was sitting turned in her seat so she could see both her team members, and caught a glint of amusement from Reese.

"That could be it, couldn't it?" Dalton asked absently as he studied the map.

"Yes," Hollis told him. "That could definitely be it."

"Makes sense," Reese murmured.

"None of this makes sense," Dalton said, and then added, "I think there's a ravine up ahead we should probably check out."

"FOR ALL THE world," Hollis told Bishop much later when she reported in that night, "as if he'd said nothing remarkable. Did no one ever tell Dalton he's a born cop?"

"Apparently not," Bishop said.

"I think he's right about the energy field. And I'm beginning to understand why we got the summons when we did. I'll bet nobody noticed anything out of the ordinary on Monday. Either the energy field didn't exist then, or else it was . . . contained . . . much lower to the ground and in a much smaller area around the source."

"Do you believe it hadn't begun affecting anyone yet?"

"The opposite," Hollis told him. "Reese and I stopped by the station before we came back to the hotel, and Katie filled us in on the results on all the deputies interviewing family and friends of those affected. It seems that both Leslie Gardner and Sam Bowers were class parents last weekend when their kids' class took a little prospecting trip out into the valley."

"You believe they found the source."

"I think there's a good chance they did. And probably never felt anything other than a twinge in their heads or a faint pressure they believed was the start of a sinus headache. Family reported that both of them suffered from allergies."

"Very thorough deputies," Bishop noted.

"Yeah, Archer has them well trained. They got a specific location for that class trip, and according to our maps it's in a grid section we would have searched tomorrow. An area up against the raw cliff face that looks so weird all around the base of the valley. Which would have been a perfect place for kids to dig up pretty rocks."

"What's the plan?"

"We'll all head to that area first thing in the morning. If we find the source—and I hope to hell we do given that it's probably building up to attack mode again—then we'll try to seal up the portal. Any ideas, by the way, on how we can do that?"

"Call me in the morning," Bishop said, "before you head out there. We're still working on possible solutions."

"Good, because I haven't given it much thought," she said ruefully.

Unsurprised, he said, "We'll try to have some

options for you. And one, I'm sorry to say, may be the weather."

"What?"

"Afraid so. The latest forecasts show a storm system moving over the mountains sometime tomorrow."

"Anything more specific?" Hollis wasn't happy for several reasons. Because storms still bothered her, because they still interfered with her abilities, and because she was uneasily aware that the electrical and magnetic energy of a storm could very well intensify, even feed, the energy field in the valley.

Hell, it could detonate the energy, for all they knew. And, poof—no valley. At all.

"Any unusual danger from this storm?" Hollis heard herself ask.

"No, nothing out of the ordinary, not for Prosperity and the valley. According to the weather service, that area of the mountains is well known to play host to highly unpredictable weather, going back hundreds of years."

Hollis felt an odd sensation she couldn't immediately identify, and when she could identify it, all she knew was that it was a deeply unsettling sense of familiarity.

"Hollis?"

"Yeah, I'm still here," she said slowly.

"Are you all right?"

"Yeah. Just . . . déjà vu, or something."

"Or something?"

She concentrated, trying to grasp an illusive feeling

even as it vanished like smoke through her fingers. "Whatever it was is gone now, Bishop. Probably not important."

"You know better, Hollis."

She drew a deep breath and let it out slowly, her gaze meeting DeMarco's slightly anxious one. "Well, if I'm aware of it later on I'll try to hold on to it longer. I don't know what else to tell you, Bishop. Look, I'll call you in the morning before we head out."

"All right. I'll have whatever information and suggestions we settle on ready for you."

"Thanks. Talk to you tomorrow." She hung up the phone, then looked with faint surprise at the handkerchief DeMarco held out to her. A slight tickling beneath her nose prodded her before he could, and she held the cloth to nostrils pinched shut, continuing to breathe through her mouth.

Neither one of them said anything for several long minutes until Hollis dabbed at her no-longer-bleeding nose.

"How weird is that?" she murmured.

"Hollis?"

"I wasn't trying to *do* anything, Reese. Except . . . to figure out what suddenly felt familiar. Bishop said something about the weather here being unstable going back hundreds of years, and I felt like . . . like I should have *known* that."

"How? Why?"

"I have no idea. It was just a flash, a feeling of familiarity. Then it was gone."

"You said déjà vu."

"It was the first thing that came to mind. Just that the information about the weather didn't surprise me. As if I . . . Hell, I don't know."

"You're scaring me a little bit."

"I'm scaring myself." She shook off the sensation as best she could, even though it left a lingering chill. "Very weird feeling."

"Are you expecting a spirit?"

She blinked at him. "What? No. Why?"

He reached over to touch her arm, his thumb gliding over gooseflesh. "You're cold."

She stared at her own arm, then frowned at him. "Yeah, I am. I must be more tired than I thought."

After a moment, he said, "I think tonight the hot shower should come before the hot meal."

"I think you're right."

FOURTEEN

Even though it was still very early when they set out the next morning, heavy clouds were already beginning to tease the mountain-made horizons, and now and then a faint rumble could be heard in the distance.

"I hate storms," Hollis muttered. "Especially the ones that rumble around and around as if they have no idea where they want to *be*."

They were still at the hotel and about to climb into their vehicles, none of them happy about the storm.

"Maybe it'll miss us," Dalton offered.

"Are you a betting man?"

"Not really."

"Good," Reese told him. "She always wins."

"It's not my fault you don't know how to bluff," his partner told him virtuously. "Stone face or no stone face."

Dalton lifted an eyebrow at the larger man. "Way I heard it, you don't have any tells. At all."

"I don't. Except with Hollis." He made the admission calmly and without any sign of embarrassment whatsoever.

Dalton wanted to say something about that, but whatever it was vanished from his mind. He found himself swinging around abruptly, from the open door of the SUV, staring toward the end of the town that was not their destination. He was barely aware that Hollis and Reese were also facing the same direction, their faces grim.

"Oh, shit," Hollis muttered. She lifted both hands, her fingers massaging her temples. Hard.

"I'm only picking up intention," Reese said, his voice unusually tense. "Scattered thoughts."

"I'm getting more. A teacher. Young. Loves her work. But . . . she's been getting more and more irritable lately. It's not her nature, not at all. But her head won't stop hurting. She needs to . . . fix her life. And she— Oh, Christ, she has guns. More than one. And she knows how to use them."

Galen, Reno, and Olivia approached them from one direction, while from the other came Sully, Victoria, and Logan.

Galen said, " I studied that school when I drove all through Prosperity. Place is close to being a fortress. It's a newer school, and with all that's happened in recent years, they're all about security."

"Maybe a fire drill?" Olivia suggested.

Victoria said, "I'm pretty sure they warn the teachers in advance now. So if there's anything unexpected, they know to get the kids somewhere safe."

Sully said, "I can't pick up anything until I'm a lot closer. But get me close enough and I'll tell you every single thing she's feeling."

Hollis was trying hard to sort through impressions, the panic and anxiety of the townspeople, the wordless terror of children. That angry, painful determination to fix a life that hadn't been broken . . .

"Hollis, you have to stop." Reese was there, holding his handkerchief to her bleeding nose.

"I can't," she said thickly. "You know I can't. How many kids will she kill? How many other teachers? That thing in her head's controlling her, and it wants a bloodbath—"

"You're feeling that?" Reno asked sharply. "The consciousness behind the energy?"

"Yeah. Yeah, I think so. And it *is* familiar, dammit, I know it is."

Reese didn't waste any more time getting both arms around her. "Hollis."

"That's better," she murmured. "Don't let go."

"I'm not about to," he said, grim. He was standing behind her, one arm around her, holding her hard against his own body, while his free hand held the handkerchief to her nose.

Softly, Dalton said, "Reese, her ears."

They were bleeding too.

"Enough of this," Reese said in a voice few had probably heard since his military days.

"No." Hollis's voice was quiet, but no less fierce. "She's planning it now. I can't get her thoughts, just those awful feelings. Her mind's full of blood, just blood. We have to get closer to the school." Her eyes were . . . odd. Almost glowing.

"Except for vehicles there's no cover," Galen said in a calm voice that would have deceived anyone who didn't know him.

"Then vehicles will have to do," Reese said.

"Archer—" Sully began.

But Hollis was shaking her head. "Not yet. We have to get close enough to know for certain what's going on there before we call in the troops. If we call them in. Trained negotiators are too far away, and you know that's what he'll want. Never mind that it won't work. Never mind that you can't negotiate with evil. Kids are going to die unless we stop this. And we have to be quiet. He wants a big show. He *wants* a lot of cops. Media. Panic. He wants his bloodbath."

"Who?" Reno asked. "Who's controlling her?"

"I think it was . . . what started as a . . . mindless evil. It just wanted to kill, to torture. To destroy."

"But you said he seemed familiar—"

Dalton said to Reno, "Explanations later. I say we pile into two of the vehicles we have here and haul ass to that school."

She stared at him. "You're picking up thoughts."

"Well, of course I am," he said irritably, grabbing her arm to hustle her into the light-colored BMW that was closest.

Getting to the school was quick and easy, in part because Galen, leading the way in the black SUV with Hollis, Reese, and Olivia, tended to imprint maps in his head after exploring, and so took secondary roads where no traffic or traffic light slowed them down.

And the school itself was as Galen had described, a modern building designed to keep children safe inside. There were numerous exits, of course, but every single member of Hollis's team knew that their best chance of getting all the children out alive would be to instantly incapacitate the female teacher even now being urged by a powerful force to slaughter as many of them as she could.

They gathered initially behind the hulking cover of the black SUV, and one glance was enough to show that both Sully and Dalton were being all but overwhelmed by the thoughts and emotions battering them.

"Kids," Sully muttered. "Somebody for God's sake teach me how to tune out kids. It's utter chaos."

Dalton nodded agreement, but his eyes were clearer and he was frowning.

"Stay mad," Hollis told him softly. "It's working."

He sent her a quick glance. "Figured out my secret, huh?"

Hollis was still being all but held upright by her partner, but it appeared both her nose and ears had stopped bleeding. "Enough," she told Dalton. Then she added to him and Sully, "You two need to circle the building. Slowly. Do your damnedest not to be seen. We need to know *exactly* where she is. We can't afford to make a mistake."

"Copy." Both Sully and Dalton moved out, cautiously.

Reese was looking at his partner. "She has guns."

"We're going to make sure she never fires one of those guns."

"How are we going to do that?" Reese asked politely.

"We're going to depend on our rookies."

"Hollis—"

"You said it yourself. Bishop said it. They were summoned, just like we were. They were meant to be here, meant to have parts to play in all this. *We* can't stop this without them. Every one of them has a gift we can use. Every one of them."

After a moment, Reese said, "Archer's going to shoot all of us."

"It all happened so fast," she said in an innocent tone. "We just had to act."

"Right." Then Reese frowned. "I think Dalton's getting close."

"Good. Judging by the way she's feeling, we're running out of time."

"If you start bleeding again—"

"I won't. You're sharing energy with me. Thank you, by the way."

"You're welcome. And stop scaring me like that, will you?"

"I'll do my best." She turned her head to watch as Sully and Dalton slipped back through the cars in the lot until they reached the SUV.

"We maybe caught a break," Dalton said. "She's in a fairly small classroom at the very end of a hallway. But it's packed with kids, little kids. I managed to catch a glimpse of a heavy-looking duffel bag half hidden behind her desk. She looks . . . I don't think it's going to be much longer."

"Not much longer at all," Sully added. "There isn't just one voice in her head; there are dozens, hundreds, all whispering the same insane shit. I doubt we've got more than a couple of minutes before she digs into that bag and starts shooting."

"Okay, then we move." Hollis gestured for Galen, Olivia, Logan, Reno, and Victoria to draw closer. "And this is what we're going to do."

WHITNEY NEELE KNEW, deep, deep down inside of her, that what she was thinking, what she was going to do, was insane. She knew that. Somewhere deep inside. But wherever that place was, she couldn't seem to reach inside and grab hold of anything that would allow her to grip her own sanity. It seemed to have gone spinning off into some dark, noisy place.

So there was just here.

Just her usual classroom with her usual, really very noisy students all talking and laughing at once. Even though they were supposed to be paying attention to her. Even though she had already told them more than once to take their seats and listen to her.

She had told them.

She had.

The voices in her head were adding to the cacophony until she could barely hear herself think. Until she couldn't think, couldn't do anything but, finally, give in and just stop fighting the voices. What was the use, after all? The voices would win. They would always win.

Always.

HOLLIS AND VICTORIA made it all the way down the interior hall to Miss Neele's classroom without being seen. Both knew they were on borrowed time, not only because Whitney Neele's face looked curiously plastic, curiously without expression, but also because Reno and Logan were in the school office hopefully buying at least a little time with some unbelievable explanations that surely wouldn't hold the principal long.

Sully waited just outside the windows, ready in an instant to burst through them, and Reese had found his way into a supply closet that opened right into the classroom near the teacher's desk.

"I can't," Victoria whispered for at least the tenth time. "I've never been able to—"

"All you have to do is keep her still," Hollis whispered back. "Just for a few seconds, just long enough for me to get my hands on that bag. Once the guns are out of her reach, either one of us can take her."

"Hollis—"

"Just concentrate, Victoria. I promise you, you can *do* this."

Victoria was pretty sure nobody had ever bet their life on her before, and she was damned sure nobody had bet the lives of dozens of kids on her, so she drew a deep breath, concentrated as hard as she could, and stopped Whitney Neele from ever touching one of the guns in her bag.

HOLLIS THOUGHT ARCHER was honestly too stunned by what had so nearly happened at the school to have thought of most of the questions he should have asked. And Katie helped along with that, encouraging the kids to tell their self-important stories at the top of their lungs even though not a single one of them had any clue as to what had so nearly happened.

And Hollis, having picked up a few slippery tricks from Bishop over the years, managed to get herself and her people off school grounds and back to the even more necessary task of searching the valley for a doorway or portal for evil. And without explaining a single word more than she had to.

"You're dangerous," Dalton told her.

"Only on odd Thursdays. Besides, it worked, didn't it?"

"You're a brave man," Dalton told DeMarco.

"You have no idea," DeMarco replied.

"Very funny," his partner told him, then bent her

attention to the map. "Okay. I think a few more yards should do it. From there, we should move on foot."

Dalton looked at her. "Are you sure you're all right? I mean, you look chipper as hell, but for a while there I thought we might have to call EMS."

"I'm tougher than I look," she told him.

"And too stubborn to argue with usually," DeMarco added.

"I'll get you for that," Hollis told her partner, but didn't follow it up with any details, rather to Dalton's disappointment.

They had driven their vehicles to within fifty yards of the location marked on Hollis's map, and were now approaching the area cautiously. Hollis, DeMarco, and Galen were all armed now, even though Hollis was certain nothing living awaited them. Nor did she expect spiritual energy, since the pressure and faint but pounding headache she was always conscious of whenever she was in this valley and outside DeMarco's shields had never once reminded her of a spirit's visit.

But it hadn't gone away, either.

Mediums. I'm here. Logan's here.

Why would we need mediums?

"Hey, look." Dalton, several yards to the left of Hollis and DeMarco, was pointing at the oddly sheer cliff face they were approaching.

For a moment, Hollis didn't see whatever he was pointing at, but then a shaft of sunlight fought its way through the clouds and touched the cliff face. There was a brief glitter as the light touched bits of mica embedded in the raw earth, and that was when Hollis saw the opening.

It seemed to dance before her eyes for a moment or two, a gash in the earth and hard rock that was less than a cave and more than a simple crevice. About twice the height of a tall man, the opening was clearly no more than a couple of feet wide.

And the tumble of granite boulders piling at the base of the shadowy opening was mute evidence that it was either recently created—or recently opened.

Sully said, "Didn't Bishop say something about tremors being recorded here?"

Hollis nodded slowly, her gaze on that oddly inviting doorway. "Yeah. Very faint tremors over the last month or so. Not bad enough to damage anything man-made, but still worrying in a moderate earthquake zone."

Victoria said, "Shield or not, I can feel something coming out of there. Almost like hot air."

Ha! I knew she was sensitive to energy, Hollis thought.

While she was busy coping with a return of that odd sense of familiarity, it took Hollis a moment or two and a surprising amount of willpower to tear her gaze away to look at the younger woman, and then before she could say anything to Victoria, she saw just beyond her Galen, who was standing utterly still and staring at the opening with a completely unfamiliar, almost mesmerized expression.

Hollis felt a sudden stab of anxiety she couldn't have explained. "Galen—"

"It's familiar," he said slowly. "I . . . want to go inside."

"Nobody's going in there," DeMarco said.

Hollis was trying to juggle about a dozen different thoughts, one of them an echo of Galen's desire to enter the portal.

That's what it is. A portal. A doorway. Why shouldn't we go inside? How could that be wrong?

"Hollis?"

We don't have much in common, Galen and me. But there is one really big thing. Except that it can't possibly be connected to this, can it? It was—what was it? A year and a half ago? And far away. Well, relatively.

"Hollis."

She suddenly became aware of Reese's hand gripping her arm, and stared down at that touch for an instant before looking up at him. And feeling the almost tactile sense of a cool breeze blowing past her, maybe even through her.

"Back with us?" he asked politely.

Hollis blinked at him. Then she drew a deep breath and let it out slowly. "Wow. Whatever you've got packs quite a wallop."

"Hollis."

"Well, it does." She heard quiet laughter, and realized it was Victoria and, rather surprisingly, Dalton, who were laughing at her. Or with her. Whatever.

She straightened slightly, wondering if the urge to lean against him had blown in with the breeze. Reese didn't let go of her arm, which she was glad about because that cool breeze was dissipating the last wisps of whatever had drifted into her mind.

And that was a sobering realization.

Very sobering.

"We need to close that up," she said quickly. "Now, before the storm gets here."

"Shouldn't we—" Logan began in an unconsciously fascinated voice.

"No, we shouldn't. Reese was right. Nobody's going in there." Hollis forced herself to remember every suggestion Bishop and his team had made about how to close and seal this portal.

Her instincts were peculiarly quiet about it.

"I can do it," Olivia said suddenly. She was standing only a few feet away from Galen, her anxious gaze leaving him to fix on the portal still yards away from them.

Reno said, "Those rocks look damned heavy."

Olivia sent her a quick smile. "I used to think that mattered. Studied all sorts of formulas about mass and density. Until I realized all I really had to do was *want* to move something."

It had been one of the possibilities Bishop had suggested, Hollis remembered. Depending on what kind of portal they found, and whether there was enough relatively loose rock around it. It was, he'd said, one possible reason why Olivia had been summoned.

And it looked like enough rock to Hollis. "If you're sure," she began.

"It's what I do," Olivia said.

Then things began to happen so quickly it was

almost a blur of motion and sounds and cold darts of fear.

Olivia began to lift both hands, rather like a small but very determined magician about to conjure, and when there was sudden movement from the portal, most of those watching realized on some level it was happening too fast, that Olivia had not had time to do this.

A huge boulder none of them had paid attention to several yards to one side of the portal rocked suddenly, then lifted and hurtled toward Olivia as though flung by some careless giant.

A threat, Hollis realized in those frozen seconds. *I should have known only rage would have been the result when we stopped his bloody school massacre. He's beyond angry. He wants to kill us all.*

And energy, once freed, was not easily contained again. Except by a fury even greater and more powerful than disembodied energy could ever be.

"Olivia!"

Hollis wondered, later, when there was time to wonder, whether Galen's instincts had kicked in. So many years spent watching over various SCU agents, guarding their backs, protecting them and what they were doing.

Maybe that was it.

Or maybe it was something else.

He moved with blinding speed, grabbing Olivia and both pulling her out of the way and pushing her to safety, out of the path of the boulder.

It slammed into him with an audible sound Hollis

had never gotten used to, over half a ton of granite meeting flesh and bone, crushing and mangling.

"No!"

Wrenching herself away from Sully and Logan, who had practically caught her in midair, Olivia darted around the boulder toward the portal, and lifted both arms as she had before. But this time there was a roar like a tornado passing, and the rocks and boulders piled around the portal and for yards in every direction were swept up as if in that tornado, lifting and swirling, and then slamming into the portal with terrific force.

As if they knew, the smaller rocks and boulders wedged themselves into the cracks and crevices while the larger ones found larger openings, granite scraping across granite as they forced themselves in tightly, blocking the portal until there wasn't a single chink where anything could have gotten in. Or out.

In the sudden silence, Hollis felt her ears pop, and yawned widely to ease a different kind of pressure. "Wow," she muttered. "Cool ability."

Dalton, surveying the closed portal with calm satisfaction, said, "I'd forgotten how impressive that was."

Hollis looked at Olivia as she slumped slightly, then looked up at her partner. "Looking fragile does not mean being fragile," she said in a tone of realization.

"I figured that out a while back," DeMarco said.

"Yeah?"

"Yeah."

Before Hollis could comment further, there was a

groan and a curse from beneath the rock, followed by Galen's voice. "Little help here?"

Olivia whirled with a gasp, her hands lifted again, and the boulder rose off Galen's fallen self and rolled away.

"Damn, that hurt." He didn't sit up immediately but did lift a hand to rather gingerly work his jaw. There was blood on his face, on as much of him as was visible, and under the fascinated eyes of the observers, it seemed to soak back into his skin, disappearing within moments.

Olivia dropped to her knees beside him. "I thought you were dead," she said unsteadily.

"That was why," Hollis realized suddenly. "Why you had to be here."

"That was why." He moved a bit gingerly, telling Olivia, "It's not so easy to kill me." He sat up finally with no more than a wince. "People are always trying to kill him," Hollis told Olivia. "Even Reese did once."

Olivia stared up rather uncertainly at the tall blond man standing beside Hollis.

"It's a long story," DeMarco told her.

"No, it isn't," Galen said. "You shot me. Twice."

"There were extenuating circumstances," DeMarco said, then added almost immediately, "Let's not get into war stories, all right, Galen? We're not quite finished here."

"I didn't think so." Galen got to his feet and stretched briefly, then extended a hand to help Olivia up.

"You're going to give them all the wrong idea,"

Hollis told him severely. "Not everybody can come back from death."

Galen eyed her. "No?"

"There were extenuating circumstances," she said after a brief pause.

"Uh-huh. I think I heard somebody say this portal needed to be sealed?"

"Right. Yes. The portal may be sealed with rocks, but it needs energy to seal it for good. And then there's all the energy contained in this valley. Until that's transformed or allowed to disperse harmlessly, some other citizen could pick up a few guns and decide to hold a turkey shoot."

A sudden rumble of thunder made Hollis wince. "Damn. I don't know if that's going to help, or just get in the way."

Dalton, frowning at her, said, "You don't need to channel the lightning?"

"God, I hope not. That's—very disconcerting. And unpleasant. No, I think there's enough energy left here in the valley."

"Energy that came through the portal? Sure you want to do that?"

"I think it's the only thing that will truly seal the portal," she told him. "At least, that's what my instincts are finally telling me. The energy was created there. It's where it belongs. And now's the time; the energy is still tied in a way to the portal, but the longer we wait to put it back where it belongs, the harder it's going to be. This is where it needs to go."

"What about the consciousness?"

"It's still in there," Hollis said, nodding toward the blocked doorway. "Underground, where it came from. I think. I still have that sense of familiarity, but it's . . . tenuous. I'm not sure I'll ever figure out what that was about. Not sure I can, either, as long as it stays buried the way it belongs. Anyway, if we ever figure it out, I'll bet we find some human-shaped monster behind it." She frowned at her partner. "We'll need to check all the old wells and any other openings we can find in the valley for energy. I think once this main energy field has been redirected to seal the portal, any other opening should be easy to block. May take some time, though."

"It's still early," DeMarco noted. "And we can easily stay another day or two."

"That sounds good," his partner told him. She opened her mouth to say something else, then stared past DeMarco, her eyes widening.

They all turned, instinctively to see what Hollis was staring at with such pleasure, and Hollis was heard to say much later that it was the sort of thing that made psychic rookies either sign on for life—or take to their heels.

Nobody ran.

"Ruby," she said with more than a little awe. "I thought I'd never see you again."

She had been young in life—her most recent life, at any rate—but there was something very wise and very ancient in her eyes. She touched down lightly only a few feet from Hollis, smiling, her wings folding neatly so they were very nearly invisible.

"I had to visit you here," she said, her voice sweet without being at all childlike. "This was where Samuel began, you know."

"What? The Reverend Adam Deacon Samuel? How many times do we have to kill that son of a bitch before he stays dead?"

"Who is—or was—Samuel?" Reno asked, her fascinated gaze on the angel.

"I think he was Satan," Hollis told her. "Some might disagree. He didn't have any charm at all."

Ruby was smiling. "His flesh died long ago, you know that. Even the vessels he borrowed. But even evil has its beginning somewhere, sometime. This place was the nexus of his beginning. You've known for a long time, Hollis. That there hadn't yet been an end to him—and that there had to be. Which is why you—all of you—were summoned here. To finish it."

Logan spoke slowly. "Are you a spirit?"

"That depends," she replied gravely. "Are you glad you can see me?"

He drew a breath and let it out slowly. "I really think I am."

"Then I'm a spirit. And we'll see each other again, Logan. But first a few of us are going to help you and Hollis and Victoria make a few doorways in that energy dome. And then they, with Reese's help, will bring the energy needed here to seal this portal once and for all."

Suddenly finding her voice, Victoria said, "Me? That's impossible. I don't . . . I'm not . . . Energy isn't my thing."

Hollis laughed suddenly. "I think you're all going to find that *impossible* is a word we don't use in the SCU. There really isn't a place for it there."

"But—"

"Come on, Victoria. Why don't you help us?"

Victoria shook her head. "What? I can't do that."

"Of course you can," Hollis told her.

"I don't know *how*."

"Of course you do."

"Hollis—"

"Come on, we'll show you."

"Oh, damn." Victoria glared halfheartedly around at her team members, then moved toward Hollis. "Everybody better stand back. Angels can't be killed, can't they? Ruby—"

"I'll be fine, Victoria. And so will you."

"But *I don't know what I'm doing*."

But in the end, of course, Hollis and the others were right.

Victoria did know what she was doing.

THE REALLY PECULIAR thing, Archer told them later, was that he had managed to trace the nearly ancient belt and gloves they'd found not far from the sealed portal. The items had belonged to a man who, though unnoticed by the history books, had quite likely been one of the first serial killers to ever visit evil on the young colonies of America.

Hunted by a group of men from an eastern territory, accused of murdering at least three young women, Adam Deacon had been run to ground in the valley near what had been a small mining camp where Prosperity now stood. Caught with blood literally on his hands and the body of the favorite daughter of a wealthy family at his feet, he had been chased up into the mountains by a mob howling for his blood.

There hadn't been much law and order in those days, and when miners had thrown his mostly dead body into an abandoned shaft and collapsed it behind him, no one had thought it anything other than justice.

Archer hadn't been able to find out much more about Deacon, but Bishop had more resources, and he soon found out all they were ever likely to about Adam Deacon. He'd been accused of at least another dozen murders, all of them bloody.

But the most peculiar thing was that, as a young man before his rampage began, Deacon had been struck by lightning.

Twice.

CHARACTER BIOS

(In Order of Appearance)

OLIVIA CASTLE

Born telekinetic—Vermont (28; five feet and petite; straight copper hair in a shoulder-length cut framing a heart-shaped face; huge blue eyes that always appear startled; childlike voice) One of the more physically fragile psychics of the group, her abilities are nevertheless impressively powerful—and normally under at least nominal control. But not on the Tuesday morning in October when it all begins. Suffers from horrible headaches. Has a cat named **Rex**, who is a brindle-tortie with Siamese blue eyes and an impressive vocabulary. Rex goes everywhere with her.

LOGAN ALEXANDER

Born medium—San Francisco (30; six-one; shaggy black hair; oddly light blue eyes) Always surrounded by the dead, and they always want to talk to him. Whether he wants them to or not. He is absolutely incapable of keeping them out, and because of the fallout from that (reacting to and talking to spirits other people can't see) he's led something of a nomad's life, never living in one place more than a few months. But it's a spirit who first tells him something strange is going on, and that he needs to go to Prosperity. One spirit named Oscar. And then many more.

RENO BELLMAN

Born seer and clairvoyant—Chicago (29; five-eight; willowy; shoulder-length black hair; exotic green eyes) Experiences visions both asleep and awake. One of the unique qualities about Reno as a seer is that if she touches someone else while experiencing a vision, that person experiences it as well. Even nonpsychic people. Another trait unique to her is that the strongest visions remain with her for some time—and she can "revisit" them at will. She is what's known as "wholly receptive" in her abilities; because she never needed a shield, she never built one and so is more than usually threatened by external energies.

TONY HARTE—FBI SPECIAL CRIMES UNIT

(Thirties; tall; slim but athletic; brown hair; brown eyes) A clairvoyant but not especially strong, though often able to get a sense of how the people around him are feeling, Tony has a number of other skills that make him valuable to the Special Crimes Unit, not the least of which is a cockeyed sense of humor that often serves to keep their rather intense unit chief grounded in the here and now. Has been with the SCU longest of any psychic on Bishop's team.

NOAH BISHOP—FBI SPECIAL CRIMES UNIT CHIEF

(Thirties; tall; wide-shouldered; black hair; silver-gray eyes) Profiler, pilot, sharpshooter, and highly trained and skilled in several martial arts. Plus has mastered a number of esoteric skills often useful in his work such as lock picking.

An exceptionally powerful touch-telepath, he also shares with his wife, Miranda, a strong precognitive ability, the deep emotional link between them making them, together, far exceed the limits of the scale developed by the FBI to measure psychic talents. Also possesses an "ancillary" ability of enhanced senses (hearing, sight, scent), which he has trained other agents to use as well, something they informally refer to as "spider senses." Whether present in the flesh or not, Bishop virtually always knows what's going on with his agents in the field, somehow maintaining what seem to be psychic links with almost all of his agents without in any way being intrusive.

Appearances: *Stealing Shadows, Hiding in the Shadows, Out of the Shadows, Touching Evil, Whisper of Evil, Sense of Evil, Hunting Fear, Chill of Fear, Sleeping with Fear,*

Blood Dreams, Blood Sins, Blood Ties, Haven, Hostage, Haunted, Fear the Dark, Wait for Dark, Hold Back the Dark

MIRANDA BISHOP—FBI SPECIAL CRIMES UNIT

(Thirties; tall; athletic; voluptuous body; black hair; electric blue eyes) Profiler, black belt in karate, sharp-shooter. Miranda is a touch-telepath and a seer, remarkably powerful, and possesses unusual control, particularly in a highly developed shield capable of protecting herself psychically, a shield she's able to extend beyond herself to protect others. Shares abilities with her husband, due to their intense emotional connection, and together they far exceed the scale developed by the SCU to measure psychic abilities.

Appearances: *Out of the Shadows, Touching Evil, Whisper of Evil, Sense of Evil, Hunting Fear, Chill of Fear, Blood Dreams, Blood Sins, Blood Ties, Hostage, Haunted, Fear the Dark, Wait for Dark, Hold Back the Dark*

CHIEF DEPUTY KATIE COLE—PROSPERITY SHERIFF'S DEPARTMENT

(32; medium height; dark blond hair; sharp hazel eyes; easy manner) Has been drawn to this area, this town, inexplicably. Has been at some pains to hide her psychic ability, which is unusual and not a little unsettling. She has the ability to paralyze people, to freeze them in their tracks. It only lasts a few seconds, and she uses it only as a last resort. She also, rarely, "hears" a voice in her mind, a voice that always warns her of something dangerous. She has learned to listen to that voice.

GALEN—FBI SPECIAL CRIMES UNIT

(Thirties; very large and powerful; impassive face and unreadable dark eyes) Guardian, watchdog. Galen was not born precisely psychic, though his primary ability is paranormal, unique, and extraordinary. To date, he has been "killed" several times (including by DeMarco) but possesses the ability to not so much heal himself as . . . resurrect himself. Regenerate. So far, he has sustained a number of injuries that should have killed him—and has come back from each one, within minutes. He has also, fairly recently, been exposed both to an extremely negative blast of energy and the traumatic knowledge that enemies of the SCU with whom he shared an unknown connection used him, without his awareness, to "spy" on the SCU. The blast of energy and the events that led to it have awakened latent abilities Galen did not know he had, is not certain he wants, and has successfully hidden from most of the other SCU agents. Most of them.

HOLLIS TEMPLETON—FBI SPECIAL CRIMES UNIT

(Thirties; medium height; slender; large and unusual blue eyes; short brown hair) Profiler. Her primary ability is as a medium and she's the most powerful medium in the unit, but Hollis is unique in several ways, not the least because she has, from case to case, awakened or even created numerous other psychic abilities, more than any psychic in the SCU or Haven, more than any psychic Bishop has ever known. And those abilities tend to be full-blown almost immediately, though never perfectly under her control.

One theory that could explain Hollis's numerous abilities could be the extreme trauma of her psychic awakening (see *Touching Evil*), which was the most horrific and brutal on record. But other agents in the SCU and operatives in Haven have suffered extremely traumatic psychic awakenings without continually gaining new abilities as Hollis has.

She is unique within an extraordinary group of unique people.

In addition to being a medium, she is able to see auras; heal herself and others; recognize true evil no matter how it attempts to hide itself; and sense, define, channel, and use sheer energy, even dark energy, without being harmed by it. Most recently she has awakened or created an extraordinarily strong ability as an empath. She also consistently tests at the higher, more powerful end of the scale the SCU has developed to measure psychic abilities—with every new ability gained.

Hollis, more than any other member of the unit, is proving there well may be no limits to what the human mind can achieve.

Appearances: *Touching Evil, Sense of Evil, Blood Dreams, Blood Sins, Blood Ties, Haven, Hostage, Haunted, Wait for Dark, Hold Back the Dark*

REESE DEMARCO—FBI SPECIAL CRIMES UNIT

(Thirties; tall; powerful; blond hair; light blue eyes) Originally one of the former military "civilian" operatives for Bishop, Reese has specialized in the past in deep-cover assignments, some long-term. Until he was partnered with Hollis. Pilot, military-trained sniper, profiler.

An "open" born telepath, he is able to read a wide range of people. He has a unique double shield, which sometimes contains the unusually high amount of sheer energy he naturally produces. He also possesses something Bishop has dubbed a "primal ability": He always knows when a gun is pointed at or near him, or if other imminent danger threatens. At least twice, that primal ability has saved the life of his partner.

Appearances: *Blood Sins, Blood Ties, Haven, Hostage, Haunted, Wait for Dark, Hold Back the Dark*

DALTON DAVENPORT

Born telepath—Alaska (33; just under six feet; wide shoulders and strong bones, but too thin; brown hair; hazel eyes that change color according to his mood and his abilities) Was one of those unlucky souls like Diana

Brisco Hayes who was medically diagnosed with mental issues and spent much of his life on medication, institutionalized. He is not at all eager to call attention to himself by using his abilities and most definitely does not want to be part of a team. Any team. In *Hold Back the Dark* he does not have a choice.

SHERIFF JACKSON ARCHER

Foxx County Sheriff's Department, based in Prosperity (38; six feet; dark brown hair; level gray eyes) A highly intelligent man and a very good cop, he has been uneasily aware of something unnatural happening in his town. It's neither definable nor definitive enough for him to call in specialized help, at least in the beginning. And then people begin to die in ways and for reasons that make no sense to him.

VICTORIA STARK

New Orleans (26; medium height; thin but much, much stronger than she looks; silvery hair cut short; very large green eyes) Psychic abilities triggered in childhood; no specific definition for them, but possesses very strong shields. Has not found her "gift" of being able to put people to sleep for "naps" to be of much use in life. *("Great for bad dates and noisy roommates. Otherwise not so much.")* But she has another ability, one Bishop and the SCU had believed was virtually impossible: To a certain extent, and depending on who it is, she can control the thoughts and actions of others. It is an ability she herself considers dangerous in the extreme, and therefore to be used only as a last resort. Both abilities have been growing more powerful since her childhood.

SULLY MAITLAND

Born empath—Montana (32; six-two and powerful; dark hair graying at the temples; intense golden eyes) One of many psychics cursed with headaches and blackouts; for Sully the blackouts are sometimes a blessing. It's the only real peace he has, since the feelings of every soul within a hundred yards of him wash over him like an extremely painful tide. One oddity is that he also senses the emotions of animals. Not thoughts, he has no ability to communicate with them as such, but he knows what they feel. Not all animals, but most. Including birds, especially crows.

DR. JILL EASTON

Part of the network of doctors in North Carolina trained to act as medical examiners, and familiar to readers of *Wait for Dark*, she has a new partner, **Austin Messina**, and both are non-SCU psychics, among the group Bishop is able to call on for help.

PSYCHIC TERMS AND ABILITIES

*(As Classified/Defined
by Bishop's Special Crimes
Unit and by Haven)*

Adept: The general term used to label any functional psychic; the specific ability is much more specialized.

Latent: The term used to describe a person with inactive psychic abilities; these people rarely even know about those dormant extra senses.

Clairvoyance: The ability to know things, to pick up bits of information, seemingly out of thin air. Often requires touching an object, but stronger clairvoyants often simply have the knowledge or information come to them unbidden.

Telepathy (touch and non-touch or open): The ability to pick up thoughts from others. Some telepaths only receive, while others have the ability to send thoughts. A few are capable of both, usually due to an emotional connection with the other person.

Empathy: An empath experiences the emotions of others, with varying degrees of intensity unique to the individual psychic.

Empathic Healer: For some empaths, their emotional connections to others is so powerful that they are able to share physical pain and injuries, and to heal those injuries. Depending on the seriousness of the injury, an empath-healer can endanger his or her own life in healing someone else. A rare empath can feel and share injuries to the mind and soul as well as the body, and is able to heal devastating emotional and psychological trauma so that a victim of violence can move past that.

Absolute Empath: The rarest of all abilities. An absolute empath can literally absorb the pain of another, to the point that the empath physically takes on the same injuries, healing the injured person and then healing themselves. If they have the strength.

Mediumistic: Having the ability to communicate with the dead; some see the dead and some hear the dead. Most mediums in the unit are able to do both, though there are of course differences unique to each psychic.

Medium-Healer: The ability to heal injuries to self or others, often but not always connected to mediumistic or empathic abilities. For medium-healers, the theory is that since they are sensitive to the electromagnetic energy of death, they are also often able to "tune in" the energy of life as well, and manipulate those energies in order to heal themselves and others. It can be extremely dangerous for the healer, depending on the individual's strength and how serious the pain or injury they attempt to heal, since it always depletes their own life energy.

Precognition: The ability to correctly predict future events. The SCU definitions differentiate between predictions and prophesies: A prediction can sometimes be changed, even avoided, but a prophesy will happen no matter what anyone does to try and change the outcome.

Psychometric: Having the ability to pick up impressions or information from touching objects.

Regenerative: Having the ability to heal one's own injuries/illnesses, even those considered by medical experts to be lethal or fatal. (A classification unique to one SCU operative and considered separate from an empathic or mediumistic healer's abilities.)

Telekinesis: The ability to move objects with the mind. A very rare ability.

Telepathic mind control: The ability to influence/control others through mental focus and effort; an *extremely* rare ability. Though some psychics the SCU has encountered have displayed this ability to some degree, and they've seen it between blood siblings, Bishop believes it to be a negative ability (taking away control from others), and highly dangerous because of that.

Dream-projecting: The ability to enter another's dreams.

Dream-walking: The ability to invite/draw others into one's own dreams.

Spider sense: The ability to enhance one's normal senses (sight, hearing, smell, etc.) through concentration and the focusing of one's own mental and physical energy.

UNNAMED ABILITIES:

The ability to see into time, to view events in the past, present, and future without being or having been there physically while the events transpired. Another rare ability, it seems to be a combination of clairvoyance, precognition, and sometimes mediumistic traits, though the ability is so rare it hasn't been studied in depth.

The rare ability to cause another person, even another psychic, to sleep.

The rare ability to even momentarily freeze another person so they are unable to move.

The ability to see the aura or another person's energy field, and to interpret those colors and energies.

White = healing
Blue/lavender = calm

Red/rich yellow = energy/power
Red alone = almost always reflecting rage
Green = unusual, tends to mix with other colors,
    peaceful
Metallic along the outside edge of an aura =
    repelling energy from another source or
    projecting a protective shield
Metallic within an aura, close to the body = holding
    in a dangerous amount of sheer power
Black = extremely negative, even evil, especially if
    it has red streaks of energy and power

More than one color in an aura is common, reflecting
the outward sign of human complexities of emotion.

The ability to absorb and/or channel energy usefully as
a defensive or offensive tool or weapon. *Extremely* rare
due to the level of power and control needed, and *highly*
dangerous, especially if the energy being channeled is
dark or negative energy.

AUTHOR'S NOTE

The first books in the Bishop/SCU series were published back in 2000, and readers have asked me whether these stories are taking place in "real" time and if, at this point, more than seventeen years have passed in the series. The answer is no. Once it became clear the series would be a long-running one, I chose to use "story time" in order to avoid having my characters age too quickly. Roughly speaking, each trilogy takes place within a year or a bit less.

So, from an arbitrary start date, and counting the third book in the series, *Out of the Shadows*, as the first book in which the Special Crimes Unit is officially introduced, the timeline looks something like this:

Stealing Shadows—**February**

Hiding in the Shadows—**October/November**

YEAR ONE:

Out of the Shadows—January (SCU formally introduced)

Touching Evil—November

YEAR TWO:

Whisper of Evil—March

Sense of Evil—June

Hunting Fear—September

YEAR THREE:

Chill of Fear—April

Sleeping with Fear—July

Blood Dreams—October

YEAR FOUR:

Blood Sins—January

Blood Ties—April

Haven—July

Hostage—October

YEAR FIVE:

Haunted—February

Fear the Dark—May

Wait for Dark—August

Hold Back the Dark—October

So, with the publication of *Hold Back the Dark*, the Special Crimes Unit has been a functional (and growing) unit of agents for about five years: time to have grown from being known within the FBI as the "Spooky Crimes Unit" to becoming a well-respected unit with an excellent record of solved cases—a unit that has, moreover, earned respect in various law enforcement agencies, with word quietly passed from this sheriff to that chief of police that they excel at solving crimes that are anything but normal using methods and abilities that are unique to each agent, and that they neither seek nor want media attention.

An asset to any level of law enforcement, they do their jobs with little fanfare and never ride roughshod over locals, both traits very much appreciated, especially by small-town cops and citizens wary of outsiders. They regard both skepticism and interest with equal calm, treating their abilities as merely tools with which to do their jobs, and their very matter-of-factness helps normally hard-nosed cops accept, if not understand, at least something of the paranormal.

Wake up.

You need to wake up.

Henry, you have to wake up.

They're going to kill you.

Henry McCord had a lifetime of practice in hiding the fact that he saw dead people. A medium, that's what it was called. He'd been a medium for thirty-six years, more or less. He could actually remember the first time he had seen the dead and understood just what he was seeing. At his grandfather's funeral. The old man had stood on the other side of the casket and winked at him.

Henry had been six.

So, thirty years, really, of learning to cope in whatever way he could. Realizing early on that grown-ups didn't want him to talk about the dead people, that it made them really uncomfortable. Which had puzzled a childish

Henry, since it seemed to him they would have liked to know that they didn't just go into the ground in a box and get covered with dirt, that there was something more than that. It had reassured Henry, at least then.

Now . . . he didn't even know if he still believed that. And despite his several conversations with Bishop, he was still unconvinced that he could ever learn to control his abilities well enough to make some kind of better use of them.

He still didn't get how seeing dead people could be put to any real use at all, far less some larger, more important use. Not even in investigating crime, since Bishop had told him somewhat ruefully that the dead, especially the murdered dead, seldom showed up to help in any way at all, far less to tell those investigating the crime who had killed them.

So what was the use in that?

What made that a larger, more important use of his abilities?

Having some sort of control over what he could do had appealed to him, if only when he'd thought he might be able to control it. He had tried. When he was alone. When he could try without fearing somebody would come along with a giant butterfly net and scoop him up and take him away to a mental hospital where his "gift" would be medicated away . . .

They took you. Not doctors. The others.

Others. The others. The others?

What the hell?

Henry had thought he was asleep and dreaming,

but . . . it didn't feel like it was a dream, that voice in his head. It didn't feel like his soft bed beneath him. It felt like something cold and hard, something not a mattress. Something that was maybe metal.

And . . . he was almost sure he couldn't move. Almost sure his wrists were tied down. His ankles. Something tight around his head holding it still.

They've got you, Henry.

Who's got me? He wanted to ask it out loud, but something told him he should remain silent. And he wasn't sure he could have said anything out loud anyway. His mouth felt like it was full of cotton and his entire face felt like he'd been shot up with Novocaine.

Them.

It meant nothing to him, and yet . . . and yet it did. It frightened him on a level so deep it was primal. It meant coldness and darkness and . . . and shadows. It meant shadows moving all around him, implacable and remorseless, bent on doing . . . whatever it was they meant to do to him. It meant something cold and slimy had slithered into his life, into his mind.

Maybe into his soul.

Not spirits? Not the dead? He asked not knowing if there would be someone, anyone, to answer him. Not knowing if the voice inside his head might not be his own.

No, Henry. The dead aren't curious to know how you're able to see them. The dead don't want to turn you inside out to learn what makes your ability work.

Henry felt an even deeper, icy jolt of terror.

Unlike what he'd seen in various movies and TV shows about ghosts and hauntings, Henry had never had to face a negative experience because of his ability. No angry or malevolent spirits, no spirits that looked disfigured or deformed or even showed the causes of their deaths. None who had made any attempt at all to frighten him.

Just helpful spirits dressed in period costume who led the way through basements and attics and storage buildings to things that belonged in whatever building he was restoring. That was all.

Henry had never been afraid of them.

He was afraid now.

They'll use your fear. You have to—

Who are you?

Henry—

Who are you? How do I know you're even on my side?

What is your side, Henry?

It's— I want to live. I want to go back to that house I was restoring near Charleston. I want to go back to my life.

Then you need to listen to me.

Why?

Because I survived what you're about to go through. Because I didn't let them break me. And you can't let them break you.

But—

Listen to me. You have to answer them when they ask you questions. You have to be helpful. Because if they can't get any answers from asking, then they'll start cutting. And burning. And . . . putting things inside you.

Things?

Things to . . . examine you. Things to help them get answers. So you have to answer them. You have to try as hard as you can to keep them talking.

But I don't know much. About how it works, what I can do.

Don't tell them that, Henry. Not until you have no other choice. Because when you tell them that, they'll want to find out if you're lying. They'll hurt you. They'll try to break you.

How?

Just . . . don't let them do that. Do you hear me, Henry? Cooperate. Answer their questions. Don't make them hurt you.

Who are you? he demanded insistently.

A friend. Please, Henry, just . . . hang on.

JUNO HICKS LEANED against the hard wall, trying not to pant out loud because she'd been tired to begin with and the effort had been so great. To reach through walls, over an unknown distance, and touch another mind, a mind not hardwired as hers was to communicate like this.

Not another telepath.

Still leaning back against the wall, she looked around at the tiny cell that had become her world. Eight feet by twelve feet.

She had paced it off.

That was her world, and had been for God only

knew how long. A narrow cot. The kind of stainless steel toilet-with-sink arrangement found in prison cells, right out in the open with no privacy. One chair, bolted to the floor.

One chair.

She had never sat in it, avoided it instinctively for some reason she didn't question. And none of *them* had ever sat in it. None of *them* ever came into this room, except to drag her out of it.

She knew they watched her, even though there was no observation window or port or camera she could see. But they watched her.

She knew they watched.

And maybe she'd taken a chance reaching out to Henry, talking to him, when all she'd intended was yet another desperate telepathic exploration of whatever lay beyond these walls, beyond the short hallway and the other . . . The Room . . . that was all she knew of this place, all they'd allowed her to see, at least with her eyes.

So she reached out, hoping to sense something that might help her. If she got the chance. If she could run. Silent, hoping none of the psychics who had sold their souls to *them* were nearby, or if they were that they were unable to detect her efforts.

She was very careful.

But today she had touched Henry's mind. And recognized him as another prisoner, another . . . subject. New, frightened, bewildered. In no shape to answer the questions she had wanted so desperately to ask him.

Do they know about us?

Will anyone come for us?

Does anyone care what's happening to us?

No, Henry could not have answered those questions, not today. Maybe . . . maybe later. She hoped. She hoped so bad. For some kind of news.

For some kind of hope.

But for now he was another victim. Someone she had to try to help, to try to warn. So maybe he would know just enough to escape their punishments.

She held up one hand and stared at it, at the bandage that made her hand a fist because it covered the stumps of what had been her fingers.

"Hold on, Henry," she whispered. "Hold on as long as you can."